THE IRISH MIDWIFE

STACEY REYNOLDS

Storm

Ebook ISBN: 978-1-83700-414-0
Paperback ISBN: 978-1-83700-415-7

Cover design: Debbie Clement
Cover images: Alamy, Shutterstock

Published by Storm Publishing.
For further information, visit:
www.stormpublishing.co

This book is dedicated to my readers. It's been a beautiful journey so far.

PROLOGUE

Garda Officer Sean O'Brien walked through College Park on the Trinity campus, smiling to himself. These college kids were something else. He got suspicious looks from many of them—a throwback notion from that feckin' hippie uprising the world had to deal with a decade ago. He'd been a young lad, but he remembered it well enough. Mostly from the TV and his father's cursing. Now it was bad music, bad hair, and worse clothes. Christ, he would be glad to see disco dead and buried. Give him a good trad session any day of the week over the bloody Bee Gees. Those brothers sounded like they had their bollocks in a vice. At least the hippies had played better music. Creedence Clearwater Revival, for one. Ugly bastards, but a good tune now and again. And that Janice Joplin had the sort of wild sensuality which you could admire. She'd played by her own rules. It was too bad about the drugs, which brought him back to the current state of the university eejits. Acid, PCP, and cocaine trickled into Ireland on the heels of an American epidemic. Even heroin kept showing up like a bad penny.

He was headed to the western edge of the university, where a patrol car would pick him up and drop him just east of the housing complex located in the dodgy part of Dublin 10. It wasn't a bad neighborhood so much as a rough one. They took care of their own, but they didn't like outsiders. They'd undoubtedly be closed-lipped with the guards. The Garda were raiding a home in a derelict building, and they were letting Sean in on the action. He'd taken three overdose reports from the university area, and the supplier was getting ready to get the proverbial boot up the ass. The older uniformed officer was waiting on the corner for him, shaking his head.

"Ye don't have to look so damn pleased with yourself, lad. Best to get your head straight. This isn't a game."

Sean slid into the passenger side. "I'm not pleased with myself. I'm glad to be doing some good for this city. It's rough work, seeing those kids lying on a slab in the morgue. They're poisoning our city. You should take it personally!"

"I do take it personally. I'm just too old for door kicking. I'll leave that up to you and your thick-headed brother." His smile was affectionate. Sean liked Sam O'Leary. He was an old timer, well past retirement eligibility. He just couldn't imagine doing anything else. His wife was dead five years, his kids grown and living in England and America. He had bushy eyebrows and sideburns just outside of regulations, but no one dared to tell him to shave them. Sam O'Leary had paid his dues. He was a legend, despite his words.

He'd been demoted back to Garda officer from sergeant eleven years ago for excessive force. He'd come across a grown man in his back garden beating his own child half to death. The child had picked a turnip without asking because he hadn't eaten in two days. So Sam called an ambulance for the child and proceeded to give the man twice the beating the boy had received. In Sean's eyes, that made him a hero. But the man had been a councilman's ne'er-do-well nephew, and the bastard of a chief superintendent had hung Sam out to dry. He'd refused to quit and refused, after a regime change, to ever accept another promotion. He would leave the Garda as he'd come. A regular officer patrolling his city.

They arrived at the drop-off site and Sean entered the satellite Garda station, a little surprised to see his brother standing in the circle of men. "Christ, man, you're too much. Isn't this supposed to be your day off?"

William smiled, and Sean understood why he had the girls after him. He looked like an overgrown boy, determined not to be left out of the fun. "Aye, brother. I switched shifts with Burke. He's got a wedding this weekend, and his wife was fit to be tied. He was more than happy to trade. You didn't mean to be carrying on without me, did ye?"

Hours later in the dim light of the pub, the lads who had accompanied them on the raid were well in their cups. William took a sip, eyeing his brother. Sean said, "Nothing like a bit of door-booting and ass-kicking to make the boys want to go on the piss."

William raised his brows, wiping the foamy lager from his lips. "It was a bit of good fun, wasn't it?"

"It was. High marks all around. The rotten bastards are behind bars and a substantial amount of cocaine seized. Not to mention the boatload of acid tabs they found. Well done on that door, by the way. Ye know, they've got battering rams for that. When you're an old man with bad hips and knees, you're going to regret showing off."

"Aye, but we'll have good stories, you and I." He nudged his brother affectionately. "The lads will be begging. *Grandda, tell me about the bad men you arrested. Tell me about that high-speed chase again,*" William said in a high, childish voice. "Someday, when we're limping out of bed and our cocks don't work, we'll only have our stories and our elderly brides to make us happy."

Sean looked affronted. "Speak for yourself. The day my cock quits working, I'll head right off the cliffs."

William looked thoughtful. "It'll be nice, someday, to be able to go home. Don't you think?" They both knew it to be true. Where one went, the other followed. They'd signed up together. When William had been assigned to Dublin, Sean had gone with him. There was no way he was letting his brother work the streets of

Dublin while he went to a safer city. When they went home, they'd do it together as well. William continued, "We'll find our mates and be quit of this damn city. No drug overdoses or bodies in dumpsters. We'll sing in the pubs, work easy days, and have lots of children. That is, if your cock works as good as you remember. How long has it been, brother? You're like a monk these days."

Sean shrugged, not irked by the jibe. "Since Sarah Jennings."

William choked. "Christ, Sean, that was over a year ago! I thought you were just being discreet!"

"Aye, well, I don't go through 'em like you do. How many this month?"

"I'll have you know it's been two since last January. I'm not far behind you, Friar Sean." William motioned for a refill. "It starts to chafe a bit, doesn't it? Fast girls are a bit of fun for a time. Christ, they're eager enough. And more power to them. Women certainly have a different mindset in the city. They're as bad as us, with the sexual revolution and all that."

Sean agreed. "Yes, it does chafe, but it isn't them. It'd be hypocritical to blame the lasses. It's the whole thing. It just seems like there should be more to it than the pleasure. I need more. I had a couple of years when I was figuring it all out, having fun with it. And, like ye said, they offered it up easily enough. I just don't want that anymore. I'd rather do without. Sarah Jennings left my apartment after a night of shagging with a quick kiss and said, *thanks for a great time, Seamus*."

William burst out laughing. "She never did? She called ye the wrong feckin' name?"

Sean laughed as well. "Well, she did leave a message on my door a few days later. *Seamus, I'm dying to see you again. Call me.*" He spoke with a dramatic, breathy, feminine voice. William was crying now, he was laughing so hard. "As if I'd call the trollop after she couldn't remember my name. She made me feel cheap!" Sean said, dramatically putting his hand to his heart.

"Yes, well, we've all known a Sarah Jenkins or two. So, given the schoolhouse sweetheart, Peggy Ryan, and that radio dispatcher after her, then it's only been three altogether? Are ye sure you're done playing the field?"

"Oh, I'm sure. The next woman I bed is going to be worth the trouble. She's going to say my name and mean it. The right name for all that."

"It's a good dream," William said softly. "All right then, it's a deal."

"What do you mean, *it's a deal*?" Sean cocked a brow.

"I mean, if you're all in, then so am I. You don't think I'm going to let my brother be the better man, do you? I'll swear off women until I find her." It went without saying who *her* was. William was speaking of his mate. The O'Brien family had a centuries-old legend. Stories of the O'Brien men having one true mate; of love that lasted a lifetime; a true, passionate, all-consuming love. They loved deeply and forever. They'd been weaned on such stories. "It'd be nice to have what Mam and Da have. All these years and they're still so in love. It's rather sickening, actually, but it's inspiring, too. Do ye think we'll ever have that? Like them and our grandparents?"

"I don't know, William. We're young, I suppose, so it's not too late. I just doubt I'm going to find her in Dublin."

"Amen to that, brother," he answered, and they both took another sip.

ONE

Two Months Later

Springfield Road, Belfast, Northern Ireland

Sorcha Mullen shouted through the bathroom door for the third time: "I can't wait any longer, ye thick-headed lout. I'm going to miss the city bus!"

"Sorcha Mullen, ye'll wait, or I'll call Mam as soon as you're out that door." John Mullen's voice was calm but purposeful. "We've got until half seven to get you to the bus. Hold yer water, for the love of Christ."

"That's it, I'm gone! Whoever the lass is that you're shaving for, I hope she's worth it!" Sorcha Mullen didn't make idle threats. She slid on her corduroy coat with the faux shearling trim, palmed the handle of her student satchel, took her medical bag in the other hand, and exited the flat without a backward glance. This whole business of her brother walking her everywhere was a load of shite anyway. It had been several years since she'd been accosted in the street. The van that pulled up during her dark walk home from a night course had changed her life forever. The night she'd fought for her life. The night that her brother, not even out of school, had saved her. The Shankill Butchers were in jail, however, and if she waited for a day in Belfast when there was no trouble, she'd never leave the bloody flat.

Her brother caught up to her, shaving soap sticking to his right ear. "Sorcha, one of these days you're going to have a husband, and he'll likely turn you over his knee."

"I'd like to meet the man who'd try that. I'd stake him through the heart," she said lightly. Almost giddy. *The sign of a true psychopath*, her brother thought. The truth was, he admired his sister's spirit. She was certainly a handful, but the man who won his sister's heart would need to be the thing of legends just to stand up to that harridan tongue of hers.

"What time are you done, sister dear? I'll come by the Mater to pick you up." She smiled up at him. He was certainly a handsome devil. And he worried about her. He remembered with perfect clarity the night she'd almost been forced into that van. He'd saved her—he'd been little more than a boy, but he'd saved her. Then he had calmly wrapped her wounds while they waited in a nearby church for the police.

She pressed her hand to his cheek. "There's no need, John. I'll be late, so I'll have to grab the last bus. I've got a meeting at the school at four, and then I'm back to work, with a schedule of late home visits afterward. They've got me running all around town today. Just have something warm and edible waiting for me when I get home. And no bleeding takeaway! Make some chops or jacket potatoes or something." Sorcha knew her brother could cook. After a ten-hour shift at the mill, however, he rarely did. She turned, giving him an indulgent look. "Thanks for walking me, little brother. I love you. Be safe and don't go lipping off to the guards if they stop you."

He grinned. "Some of them look younger than I am. It's fun to give them a time of it."

She tugged his shaggy hair. "You heard me—and stay away from those O'Rourke brothers. Promise me, John."

The O'Rourke brothers were deep in the politics of the IRA.

Foot soldiers, yes, but also zealous recruiters. They'd been working on her brother since he was fifteen.

"Don't worry about Connell O'Rourke or that mouth-breather of a brother, Den. They haven't bothered me for months." He kissed the top of her head. "Take care, love. If you need me, call the mill."

Sorcha mounted the city bus, cringing at the crowded conditions. She hated it when it was this packed. At night, when the city was dark and most people had gone home, she liked the long, peaceful ride. Today, it was like a sardine tin. She'd taken her first nursing courses at St. Mary's Training College, and it had been a steady, predictable routine. Now that she was putting her skills to practical use, she had to go through the city at all hours, transferring buses and traveling on foot. She'd had a bike, a while back, but it'd been stolen last year, and so here she was. It wasn't that she couldn't afford to replace the bike. It was more a matter of understanding the city she lived in. Why bother replacing it if it was going to get nicked by some junkie or delinquent?

She'd been exclusively studying midwifery for a year, and the nuns who ran the midwifery school had kept her busy. She apprenticed under a senior midwife on the maternity ward of the Mater Infirmorum Hospital. It was an old hospital, but the maternity ward had an excellent department head. The bus headed down Crumlin Road, and Sorcha's mood grew somber as she took in the armored trucks, the barricades, and the police stations that had RPG-proof barriers. And the walls. Always the walls and the gates separating the city: a symbol of the occupation. There were prisoners, even now, rotting in the Crumlin Road Gaol. She thought about her brother, so young, but no younger than some of the lads who had been gunned down in the street during clashes with the British military.

He was such a good lad. Smart enough to go to university, but breaking his back in the linen mill. She pushed aside the dark thoughts, knowing that no amount of tears would fix this city. She'd endure the sights because she must. She wouldn't let politics or military or men and their power struggles keep her from finishing school. She was so close, and her work was valuable. Belfast needed good nurses. Someone had to stay. That thought led her in another direction. Why had Mother Superior, who was the person overseeing her training program, asked to see her, along with the headmaster of the midwifery school? She had high marks, she was competent, and she was never late. She didn't think it could be anything negative.

When they arrived at the hospital, she reported to the maternity ward, looking out for her fellow students and her overseeing midwife and physician. The midwife was a wonderful woman named Betty McMillen. The overseeing O&G doctor, like any great man, was extremely arrogant. He also took perverse pleasure in seeing her temper rise. Dr. Nigel Childs was an excellent physician, however. Despite their differences—the main issue being that he was a Protestant and had an English father—he never treated her as any less. In his view of the world, medicine and politics didn't mix. She'd learned a lot from both him and the sisters who had directly overseen her education.

She hurried from the nurses' locker room, making sure her hair was tamed and her cap was straight. She smoothed down the white apron that covered her blue uniform. Clean and starched, as it should be. White shoes gleamed against her nude pantyhose. She went to the classroom where the final-year students met, greeting their tired faces. This semester was going to be the death of all of them.

Sorcha warmed at the sight of the young woman in front of her. She'd never tire of this work. Of the rush and the excitement. Of watching a new life wriggle its way into the world. Of the strength inside a woman when the spirit and the body joined forces. Like a dramatic tragedy unfolding, but then soaring upward out of the horror and delivering the miraculous. The blood, guts, tears, and joy of childbirth.

"That's it, Deidre. Breathe and rest a moment. You're doing grand, darlin'. You'll have this lad out in no time."

The woman's eyes misted. "Do you really think it's a boy? Truly?"

The doctor came in behind Sorcha. "She's practically psychic, this one. I've never had a nurse with such an accuracy record. She's only been wrong once."

Sorcha stiffened. "I was not wrong. It was a case of misdiagnosed twins." She nodded at the girl. "She hadn't had any pre-term care other than some quack in her neighborhood clinic. He told her there was only one, but she was carrying twins. I said it was a girl and it was," she said simply. "She just brought a brother with her as a bonus." The woman's eyes bugged out. "No, no, lass. There's only one. We've checked you thoroughly."

The relief on the woman's face was amusing. "It's not that I wouldn't love them both, but it's an awful lot at once, don't you think?"

Sorcha smiled. "Oh, aye. Ye can take me out back and shoot me if I end up pregnant with twins. Better yet, shoot the da." It made the woman laugh, as she'd meant it to. Then another contraction seized her. The woman squeezed through it and fell back, exhausted.

"Do you have a husband?"

"Heavens, no. Who's got time for all that? He'd be pestering me for his supper and then where would you be?"

The doctor came next to her and feigned insult. "You know, Nurse Mullen, I have done this sort of thing before. Very well and for many years, I might add. We'd muddle along without you."

"Yes, Dr. Childs," Sorcha said like an unrepentant child, winking at her patient. "Now, could you help me get that other knee up? Yes, that'll do. I think this is going to take one or two more pushes and we're done. Do you feel it, sweet girl? Yes, here it comes. Both barrels, Deidre. Don't be shy, love. Scream yer wee head off if you like." The result of this little pep talk shot through the hospital. Two minutes later there was another straining scream and then the musical shrieking of a newborn's cry.

They cleaned themselves up as the woman was taken to her room, and her son was placed in the nursery.

"Well done, Nurse Mullen. But let me ask you something. Why do you tell them to scream? Isn't there some benefit to keeping them calm? I think they heard her in the Parliament building."

Sorcha shrugged. "I don't tell them to scream. I merely tell them it's okay to scream. And it is useful, I think. Especially near the end when they think they can't go on for another minute. It's a war cry, Dr. Childs. She's in battle, isn't she?" She said this like there was no arguing the point. "It's a fight as old as time. A hundred years ago, we'd be losing them in childbirth. The body doesn't forget. We have these tidy hospital wards and shiny instruments, but her body is in the throes of combat, being split in two, and sometimes a woman needs to have a good shout."

Sorcha sat in the chair outside the headmaster's office feeling much like a girl in primary school. She remembered with perfect clarity being sent to her headmaster's office three times in her first month at the integrated school. It had only lasted a month before both her parents and the school authorities had declared it for the greater good of all parties concerned that Sorcha Mullen be permitted to return to her Catholic primary school. She'd been teased for her red hair, her religion, her clothes, her flushed skin, and her accent, which was always coarser and thicker in a temper. When she'd finally snapped, resulting in a string of Gaelic expletives that she'd learned from her grandda, she'd been swatted. Both for speaking Irish and for the display of temper. And... she may have taken her lunch pail to the side of Ricky Kensington's useless head.

Now here she was, and this time having no clue what was in front of her. She'd neither assaulted nor insulted anyone, so she was hoping for some good news. As the door opened, she saw

Mother Superior as well as Dr. Childs and Nurse McMillen, or Nurse Betty as everyone called her. "Come in, Nurse Mullen. Please have a seat." She took a seat next to Betty, suddenly very nervous.

The headmaster was an elderly man, but no less diminished by age. "You're no doubt wondering why we've gathered all your mentors in one room. I will put you out of your misery by telling you that you've done nothing wrong." Sorcha relaxed a bit. "In fact, you are the most promising student in your class. Your high marks aside, you have won the respect of everyone in this room. You are, by all accounts, going to make an excellent midwife."

Sorcha blushed. "Thank you, headmaster. Truly, I'm humbled. Their respect isn't easily won, and I thank them as well, for their faith in my skills."

"Too right. But we haven't come here today merely to boost your ego, Nurse Mullen. A rare opportunity has opened up that we feel is a perfect fit for a student of your caliber. We'd like you to intern at the Royal Jubilee Hospital under their new chief. He's brought in an American colleague who has been using spinal blocks in Caesarean cases."

Sorcha wasn't sure she'd heard them correctly. "I'm sorry. Perhaps I'm a bit slow. Midwives don't have surgical privileges. What exactly would I be doing?"

The headmaster answered, "Excellent question, although from what I hear of your temper, you'd be good with a blade."

Sorcha blushed, shooting Dr. Childs a look. "Aye, well. My mother says it's from the Mullen side of the family. I come by the reputation honestly. Now, that aside, it's certainly intriguing, I'm just not sure..."

"If you'll indulge me, I think Nurse Betty can answer some of your questions, and Dr. Childs can answer the rest."

Betty cleared her throat. "As you know, we're a small maternity ward. Twenty-some odd beds and no more than two dozen patients at a time. With this large class of final year students, there's not much chance for a student to get their own caseload. Royal Jubilee is a maternity hospital. Top notch and attached to Queen's University. I think you could learn a lot there. Maybe even come back here and share your knowledge with the next class."

"You mean for me to teach? I'm sorry, Nurse Betty. I love the school and all of my mentors, I truly do, but I don't want to teach. I want to be with my patients. I want to catch babies. It's all I've ever wanted to do."

"And you will. You'd teach on the job, short term. And you won't be alone. Dr. Childs will be attending once a week as well, to see what there is to learn from this American."

That's when Dr. Childs took over. The heavy guns, so to speak. "If we can get a feel for the procedure, we can decide if it's something we want to implement with our own patients. Spinal blocks and epidurals aren't new, but we've seen quite a surge in popularity in the last five years. There are certainly risks and side effects, but general anesthesia carries those as well. You're not a surgeon or an anesthesiologist, but you are on the front lines with these expectant mothers. You have the opportunity to receive feedback from the patients, track side effects, and even participate in a referral process when you are caring for a patient who is suddenly a candidate for a Caesarean. That aside, it's an exceedingly busy hospital. You will have many more opportunities to "catch", as you call it. And you won't be tossing coins for a crack at a new patient. You'll have more than you can handle." Then, as if to sweeten the deal, he added, "And they've got three new ultrasound machines." Sorcha almost groaned. Their maternity ward was impatiently awaiting their first ultrasound machine, and she'd been dying to take one for a spin. He knew just how to get to her.

Sorcha said, "Well, since no one is willing to talk about the elephant in the room, then I must. How is this hospital staff going to feel about the fact that I'm a Catholic? They'll likely put me cleaning bedpans."

"They won't know. The head of the department is the only one who will be aware of your background, and it should remain that way," Dr. Childs said, adding, "It's none of their bloody business what side of the wall you're on. It has no place in a hospital."

Sorcha saw Mother Superior squirm. "And what do you think, Mother Superior? You've been very quiet."

The sister answered, "My concern is that you maintain the integrity of your faith. This is a grand opportunity, aye—as long as you remember who you are, child. There will undoubtedly be times when your conscience will dictate that you step away from certain treatments."

So don't go passing out condoms and diaphragms like the rest of the heathens, Sorcha thought wryly. She loved her faith. She really did. The problem was, the church taught abstinence, which rarely worked in her experience treating the young and fertile. They also taught that it was a sin to prevent the conception of a child. How many girls ended up hidden away with a swollen belly because they couldn't access birth control? She'd always battled with this particular subject. She was very much opposed to pregnancy termination. She was young, but she knew what it was like to sit with a scared young woman who didn't want to be pregnant and talk her out of a back-alley abortion or a ferry trip over to England. She'd seen a few women through their unwanted pregnancies, only to have them give up the child for adoption. Not to mention the tired, overworked mothers who had too many children and not enough space or income to adequately feed them. Households where another child was not considered good news. It was altogether heartbreaking. So the idea of birth control seemed a good compromise, but it was a battle between her brain and her heart. The spiritual versus the scientific. She wouldn't share that little bit of inner turmoil with the Mother Superior, however.

"Okay, I think I'll go for it," Sorcha said, nodding to herself more than anyone. "When do I start?"

"You start on Monday. You'll work on a rotation. Four days on, three days off. During those three days, you'll spend two days continuing your home visits on this side of town with your current patients. At least until they've all delivered. Then your schedule will ease up a bit. One of the other girls will take over your lactation consulting visits. Once you don't have any patients in this part of town, you'll be assigned new home-visit patients near the Jubilee."

Sorcha's face must have registered some surprise. "Yes, in Protestant homes. I must reiterate that you keep your private affairs to yourself." Her religion, she understood. "The overseeing midwife and doctor need to be able to track your work locally. Do you have an issue with this arrangement?"

Sorcha stiffened her back. "Of course not. It's not me you have to worry about, is it? I don't bring politics into my medical care. I'm a nurse and a midwife for anyone who has need of me." She turned to the Mother Superior. "Wasn't it Christ himself who spoke to the Sumerian woman? If someone needs me, I'll do all I can for them. If I can learn from this hospital, then I'll go. The rest, I'll just have to take on faith."

Edith Mullen stared across the table at her two grown children and felt the tears threaten. "You both look tired. You're working too much, to be sure."

John said, "They're threatening a strike again, Mam, so I'm putting in overtime to pad the accounts. Don't worry yourself."

His father leaned over his mother and filled her teacup. "Asking your mother not to worry is like asking a bird not to fly. It's what she does. Do you think they'll strike? If they do, then ye need to stay out of the troubles. It's no doubt the IRA stirring things up. Come home, and we'll find you work around here. Or better yet, go to school with your sister. We aren't destitute, lad. You had high marks in school. You don't need to be working in the factory."

Sorcha sighed. "I've told him that a hundred times. He won't listen."

Edith looked at her daughter, refocusing her attention. "And what about you, pet? When this schooling is done, can't you find a local clinic out of the city? You're top of the class, love. You could go anywhere. Let us sell that old flat, and you can move home until you find a nice husband."

Sorcha gave her brother a dark look as he chuckled into his teacup. "I don't need a husband, Mam. Women do survive without them. I'm not doing all this schooling just to have some overbearing man demand clean shirts and a wife who stays home knitting tea cozies. This is 1978. Da, don't give me that look, I'm not talking about you. You're a rare bird, though, aren't you? You support Mammy no matter what she wants to do. A lot of men aren't like that. They like to control everything. I won't be ordered about like a child and told how much or even if I can work. I can support myself."

Her father, Michael, shook his head. "It's the damn TV she gets these ideas from. Women marching, burning their bras. They're off their nut."

"I don't own a TV, Da, and well you know it. And who do you think raised me to be so bloody-minded?"

To which her mother added, "She's got you there, love."

Her father's lips turned up in the hint of a smile. "Someday, Sorcha, you'll find a man who makes you rethink all of your grand plans. A man you can't live without. I dread it and wish it in equal measure. You're my girl through and through." Then he looked at his wife with such love, it caused Sorcha's heart to seize up.

John said, "Ach, they're getting that look again. Please, people, there are children in the room." His father winked at him and kissed Edith soundly on the mouth. He retreated to the kitchen with the kettle, saying over his shoulder, "You just wait, the both of you. Ye may have gotten your brains from the Kavanaugh side, but you're half Mullen. We're a passionate lot."

Edith said dryly, "Yes, and with tempers that are the thing of legends. Best you learn to control both."

Dare to be honest and fear no labor...

—Robert Burns

Sorcha walked into the expansive maternity hospital, both intimidated and in awe. She approached the information desk, only to be greeted by a fresh-faced nurse with a perfectly coiffed cap of blonde hair that was styled like something out of a movie. She took in Sorcha's appearance with a quick glance, then put her hand out. "I'm Nurse Angelina. We'll get you a new uniform straight away, then I will take you to our direct supervisors. Please follow me."

Twenty minutes later she was sitting in the posh office of the hospital chief, Dr. Peters. He sat at his desk with his American sidekick next to him. The Yank actually had his feet up on a desk that didn't belong to him. He seemed very curious about Sorcha. After she had a brief exchange with the head doctor, he said in a deep southern drawl, "So tell me, Nurse Mullen, what do you think a midwife's purpose is, exactly?"

He was needling her, this arrogant Yank with his feet up. "Well, Dr.— I'm sorry, was it Jesse James or Wyatt Earp? I've forgotten."

He was stunned into a brief stillness. Then he cracked off a laugh. "Some spirit. Well, now. It's Dr. Stirling. And they were cowboys. I am neither a gunslinger nor from the Wild West. I'm a Virginia gentleman."

She gave a pointed look at his feet on his colleague's desk, to dispute the matter, but he wasn't offended. He smiled and slid his feet down. "My mother used to give me that same look, Nurse Mullen. Pardon my manners. Now that you've scored the point, how about answering my question? Do you feel your profession is an outdated notion? Some people would argue, given the advances in obstetrics, there is little need for midwives."

Sorcha didn't narrow her eyes at him like she wanted to box his ears. Nope. She was going to rein in her temper before he sent her packing. "Well, some feel that's the way of it, but I disagree. In

Ireland, you'd have quite a problem on your hands if you didn't have a trained team of midwives at this or any other maternity ward. There aren't enough doctors to treat all the women in this city who are or will be pregnant. I feel a midwife is an important tier in the levels of this particular medical discipline. Ye've got your wee scalpels and your Harvard degree." He raised a brow, but she continued as if she hadn't noticed. "Yes, Dr. Stirling, I did my homework on you. You're very well respected in the field of obstetrics. Your research regarding the practical uses for spinal blocks in Caesarean cases is very impressive."

She leaned in just a bit. "But women like myself have been practicing midwifery since men like you were still scratching pictures on cave walls with little stones and curing hides for winter. My patients are my top priority, not research grants or new equipment. For every woman who goes into your operating room and under the knife, I will deliver dozens of healthy babes into the world. I'll check on their mothers at home for signs of depression or infection. I'll consult on lactation difficulties. I'll soothe her fears and hold her hand while she pushes her child into the world. The truth is, Dr. Stirling, if you didn't have midwives, ye'd have nary a spare minute for your publishing in medical journals or hospital galas. You'd be knee deep in afterbirth seven days a week. Hospitals would raise prices because they'd have to hire three times the number of O&G doctors. I do this because I love it. And you need me to do this because I balance the scales in your hospital. I keep labor costs down, and I keep the mothers of my babes happy. I'll do more with less. Is that a sufficient answer?"

The doctor never took his eyes off her, fascinated but uncowed by her show of spirit. There was a faint grin, the corners of his mouth turning up. He said, "As a matter of fact, it is the perfect answer. I see I've surprised you, Nurse Mullen. Score one for the cowboy." Sorcha's mouth turned up just a bit on one side when he said, "Now, shall we end this little tea party and start doing our rounds?"

. . .

Sorcha walked next to the blonde nurse, who, as it turned out, was very competent and altogether pleasant. "You must have impressed them. There were two other girls who came in yesterday morning, and they sent them back to their host hospitals."

"I wasn't aware it was an interview." Sorcha was a little horrified when she thought about all the things she'd said.

"Yes, well, they were also top of their class and had a little more experience than you. I don't know what you said to them, but they liked you and respected you enough to call the fourth candidate and cancel her interview."

The two doctors had been speaking with the surgical nurses, finalizing their surgical schedule. When they approached, the two men walked into the first patient room and greeted the young woman in the bed. After the introductions were made, Dr. Peters, Sorcha's direct boss, went over the case history. "Mrs. O'Neill is a widow. Her husband died six months ago, and she's apprehensive about doing all of this alone. Nurse Mullen, would you like to take over with her screening and exam?"

Sorcha's face was stricken. The woman was probably twenty-five years old. "Yes, of course. Mrs. O'Neill, I'm truly sorry for your loss." Sorcha approached her bed. "Was it in the conflicts that you lost him?"

The woman's eyes misted. "No. He was too busy working double shifts to be bothering with all that—he died at the mill."

Sorcha's heart sank. "Aye, I remember now. My brother was very upset. He works the day shift. Tell me, madame, where are you staying?"

"Call me Jennet. I'm staying with my mam and da. I couldn't afford our flat without him. He didn't have enough seniority for me to draw any real pension, and my survivor benefit barely pays for food. The government offered me a studio flat in Divis, but I moved back with my parents instead. They've got more room."

"That's good, Jennet. Just what I want to hear. Now, your blood pressure's a bit high, is that normal?"

"Not until the last few weeks. I've just been a bit nervous, is all. I want this baby so badly. It's all I have left of him." Her voice broke with emotion and Sorcha stroked her inner arm. She murmured softly to the woman like she would speak to a frightened child or skittish animal. "That's it. Breathe, love. Be strong. Ye're strong and healthy, and your new daughter will need her mother."

After the screening, the doctors let Sorcha do the exam, observing the spell that fell over the room as Sorcha tended to this wounded soul. Sorcha took off her gloves, helped the woman up, and was surprised when she hugged her. She took her blood pressure one more time, and it had reduced significantly.

When she left to prepare for an ultrasound, the American doctor gave Sorcha his feedback. "Well done, Nurse Mullen."

She didn't like his tone. "But? There's a but in there somewhere. I can see it hangin' o'er yer head." Her accent was pronounced, and the doctor almost took a step back, but he held his ground.

"You need to keep the chitchat to a minimum given the caseload of this ward. Where she lives, how her husband died, you're going to have to leave that sort of care to her friends and family. It's not relevant."

Sorcha snorted, and irritation flickered across the American doctor's face for the first time since she'd met him. She gave Dr. Peters a dry look. Dr. Peters cleared his throat. "Actually, Dr. Stirling, it is relevant. Nurse Mullen, would you care to explain why you asked these questions?"

"The reason I need to know how he died is to determine if she is safe, or if I'm going to be doing her next checkup in the gaol or the emergency room. She's a Catholic, given the necklace she was wearing. This is a divided city, Dr. Stirling, and there are hazards which you best get familiar with if you are going to be of any use to the people here. She's not living in Divis Flats, thank God. If she were, I'd be concerned about rodent feces, asbestos, lead, and other poor living conditions. The people there do what they can to keep their homes safe and clean, but the building is not maintained very well by the government, and there is a lot of trouble in that part of town. It's an IRA stronghold that is often subject to military and police raids. She needs family around her in case she goes into labor, which will be very soon. She's not within walking distance of this hospital or the Mater. Her blood pressure is elevated, which is likely why the clinic sent her here to us. It's not due to preeclampsia, but because in approximately two days, she's going to have this baby without her husband. She's going to raise the girl in a city where her walk to school will be through a war zone. I have a reason for everything I do. I'm not chatting with her for a bit of news. She's my responsibility if I'm standing at her bedside. She has to trust me, and I need to know everything I can to help her through the next six weeks. If that's an issue for you, best call back one of the girls you sent packing yesterday."

Sorcha stood then, daring him to argue with her. Then someone started clapping behind her. She turned and almost groaned. Her face flushed as she stared into the face of Dr. Nigel Childs, her supervisor at the Mater.

"Well, it didn't take you long to lose your temper, now, did it?" He gave her a pointed look and then waltzed up to the two doctors, greeting Dr. Peters and introducing himself to the American. "I just came to see how my star pupil was doing. Don't worry, old boy. She's not as fierce as she seems. And..." He paused, meeting both their eyes. "Don't get any ideas about poaching my best midwife. She'll grow on you, despite the bristling she does, and she'll be returning to my staff as soon as she's learned all there is to know from you and given me the opportunity to steal your ideas. Now, shall we move along to one of these new ultrasound machines you're hoarding? I'm dying to have a go."

Sorcha watched with fascination as the doctor moved the equipment over the patient's belly. Dr. Stirling said, "Dr. Childs tells me that you're quite skilled at guessing the gender of the child without my overpriced contraption. How do you do it?"

She answered, "Well, now, I can't tell you all of my secrets or I'll be out of a job."

He smiled at that. "A few hundred years ago, they'd have burned you as a witch, Nurse Mullen."

"Aye, they would have. More for my shrew tongue than my supernatural skills." She blushed, clearing her throat. "I apologize. I was borderline insubordinate today."

"Borderline? I'd hate to see you at full force." He laughed, and she shrugged as he continued, "You're competent and confident in your abilities, Nurse Mullen. You don't cower when someone questions your motives. If you are going to step into my shoes so that I'm not... *knee deep in afterbirth seven days a week*"—he sounded so much like her, Dr. Childs barked out a laugh for the first time in the history of their acquaintance—"then you will need to possess the strength of your convictions. You'll also need to be thoroughly trained to recognize when you are in over your head. You've got a big ego, Sorcha Mullen. I happen to admire a big ego. But you need to properly assess high-risk patients, recognize abnormalities with this little contraption, and be able to refer the patient out of midwife care if it's needed. That is why you are here. You are also to sway women away from home births. This isn't the Middle Ages."

"I beg your pardon," she said. "Home births are perfectly safe if the conditions are optimal. I would never agree to them otherwise."

He held his hand up, silencing her protests. "I am not as ignorant of this city and its issues as you might think. Barricades, armed military forces boarding the buses, raids, bombings, and debris fires. You can get cut off from your patient because the Army is raiding the neighborhood or you're not able to catch a bus to their flat due to barricades. The security conditions in Belfast turn on a dime. I don't have to tell you this, Nurse Mullen. When you find a husband who can embrace that shrew tongue of yours, you can move to the country. Then you can deliver the shepherd's baby in his little cottage, aid the fishwife with her delivery, or whatever else you Irish get up to out on the moor."

Sorcha couldn't help it. The giggle rose up out of her belly, and she couldn't contain it. The patient was laughing, too. Sorcha looked at her. "It seems your cowboy doctor has been reading Wuthering Heights one too many times."

Sorcha sat across from Angelina in the hospital cafeteria, blowing on a cup of hot tea. "You didn't! Oh my, Sorcha, I admire your spirit. And I think it's one of the reasons he chose you, but you aren't the only one with a large ego. We are talking about male physicians. Tread carefully."

Sorcha let out an unladylike breath. "I know. I know!" She shook her head. "My mam is always getting on to me about my temper. It often gets the better of me. They are both brilliant doctors."

"As is your Dr. Childs. Does he fancy you, do you think?" Angelina asked, trying to play it cool.

Sorcha spat out her first sip of tea. "Heavens, no. He must be almost forty."

"As if that matters. How old are you, Sorcha? I hope that's not too personal."

Sorcha waved a hand. "Twenty-one. I started at the college at seventeen."

"My, you are young. I'm twenty-seven. Practically an old maid." The woman really was so lovely, and Sorcha could hardly imagine her being insecure.

"You're a career woman, not an old maid. And you're gorgeous altogether. I won't believe it's from lack of attention. You're just selective. That's a good thing."

The woman sipped her tea thoughtfully. "I almost married my school friend. We'd been together since we were fourteen. He was my first boyfriend. My first everything. He didn't understand this, though. He thought I should get married at eighteen and be content to wait on him hand and foot. And he's..." She looked around. "He's quite a loyalist. I'm a Protestant, but I don't like what's been going on in this city. I was just out of school when Bloody Sunday happened. It was horrific that such a thing would happen in our country. I mean, I was born here. I understand why they're fighting all the time, but what happened that day was unforgivable. I don't agree with a lot of the IRA's tactics, but for the British soldiers to open fire on an unarmed crowd like that..." She shook her head. "Anyway, I said as much to Richard. His response was appalling. I'm sure you can imagine." She put her cup down. "I don't care who you are or on which side of the wall you live. Wrong is wrong. If they're going to behave in such a fashion, they would do better to just hand the North back to Ireland and be done with it. When I said as much, he slapped me right across the cheek. I walked away and never looked back."

"Why are you telling me this, Angelina?" Sorcha was supposed to keep her religion quiet. She didn't know what to say.

"Because you are a bright, gifted midwife. I think I'll really enjoy working with you, Nurse Mullen. I hope we can be friends, but I won't tolerate bringing politics into this hospital ward. You need to know that no matter who walks in that door, they'll get equal treatment from me. The last girl I reported, and had dismissed, made an off-hand comment about tying the Catholic women's tubes while they were under so they'd stop breeding like rabbits."

Sorcha stiffened. "She's lucky all she got was dismissed. I'd have taken a bedpan to the back of her head."

Angelina smiled at the picture that created in her mind. "Though she be wee, she be mighty. I think you and I are going to get along just fine."

After her shift ended, Sorcha rode the bus back to her side of town. It wasn't a surprise when the soldiers boarded the bus, checking faces and floorboards for anything out of sorts. It was amazing what you could get used to. When she finally got to her stop, she wasn't surprised to see her brother standing there waiting for her. It was, after all, the last bus of the day. If she hadn't been on it, he'd have started combing the main streets for her.

She kissed his cheek, touched at the gesture no matter how many times he did it. "Do you have anything to feed your poor sister?"

"I do. Mam's chicken roast. She stopped by today to see how things were going. She brought homemade biscuits as well. I saved you one."

"One? Out of how many?" Sorcha said indignantly.

"I refuse to answer that question on the grounds that it'll incriminate me." He smiled when she raised a brow at him. "Learned that from an American movie I saw a few years ago. Mam also wants you to call Cousin Ava."

"Da's cousin Ava from County Cork?" She hadn't heard that name in a while.

"Yes, the very one. Apparently, Cousin Maureen is going to Trinity College, and she's been wanting to see you. What's it been, six years? Since Dublin's a two-hour drive, she wanted to know if you'd like to visit on your next weekend off."

Sorcha said, "I haven't been to Dublin since we were kids. I thought Maureen was going to be a nun?"

He gave her a cheeky grin. "So her mother thought. You remember the wee fiend when she was little: we nicknamed her the streaker."

"She was six, John. When I saw her six years ago, she seemed quite different. Unless she had us all fooled, she might be headed for the cloister yet."

TWO

If music be the food of love, play on...

—William Shakespeare

Gus O'Connor's Pub

Doolin, Co. Clare, Ireland

Sean and William walked through the front door of the pub, the smoke hitting them in the face like a hammer. "For fuck's sake, Robby, I thought you were going to ban the smokers to the back section."

"Welcome home, boys. Aye, well, the tourists are agreeable to it, but the damn locals aren't having it."

He said this just as a drunk patron yelled, "To hell with that. The beer is colder on this side."

William walked up to his old friend and plucked the fag out of his mouth, took a puff, and then he put it out in his beer. "Take those filthy things to the back."

Sean laughed. "I thought you quit, brother? Mam would have your hide."

William blanched. "It was just a puff. Don't you go telling her."

His friend, miffed that William had ruined his pint and his cigarette in one go, said, "I'll bloody tell her unless you get me another one of these."

William slapped him on the back. "Get Derry a refill, Robby, and two more. How's the family?"

"They're grand altogether. You might have heard my daughter is expecting her first. She says if it's a lad, they'll name him after me." Pride shone in his eyes.

Sean slapped a hand in his. "A grandda! God bless you all and keep you. That's as good a cause as any to celebrate. Who's playing tonight?"

Robby shrugged, his old eyes crinkling. "Flaherty canceled. I don't suppose..." He let the sentence hang there, giving them a questioning look.

Sean and William grinned at each other. William said, "Give the house a call. Maybe Da will drive over with his guitar. Ye've still got the drum on hand?" Robby went into the back room, bringing out the old goatskin bodhrán and wooden tipper.

Within an hour, the place was alive with music. Robby had even come from behind the bar to drum for a while. Sean was on vocals singing a popular drinking song when he heard his brother fumble with the strings. He looked at him, irritated—William never missed a note. Then he watched his eyes flare and followed his gaze. *Whoa.*

She was lovely, with fair hair and sensual eyes. William growled the words low, just for Sean: "I saw her first. Don't even think about it." Sean looked back at his brother, expecting to see the jesting in his face. What he saw was something different—William was serious.

Sean said, "Well, best come up with a love ballad to woo the lass. She's getting some attention."

William took the mic and said directly to the young woman, "Ladies' choice. Anything you want to hear, love. A ballad? A reel?" The women all turned a steely glare at her. She wasn't a local. "Are you from around here?"

The woman straightened her back, smoothing down her pretty sweater. "I'm from the island."

One of the drunk women from the bar said, "The island? She likely doesn't even have a radio!" A few people chuckled, but the pretty island lass ignored her.

She said, "An Irish ballad would be too easy. If ye want to impress me, how about playing some Bob Dylan?" You couldn't miss the challenge in her tone.

"Bob Dylan? Christ, I don't have to sound like him, do I?" That made the crowd laugh. Then he cocked his head, appraising her. "Bob Dylan it is." He leaned into his brother. "*House Carpenter.* I'll take the lead."

The beautiful woman came in closer, smiling when they started to play. Her friends grabbed a table, and they all sat quietly. *House Carpenter* was a folk song about a ghostly demon lover who seduces a woman away from her husband and children. She mourns the loss of her family but is helpless to resist him as he takes her down to the ocean floor, never to return. There were many versions of the ballad, and Bob Dylan's rendition wasn't the best, but she wanted Dylan, and he'd likely lasso the moon if she asked for it.

Sean smiled as he watched the ladies in the pub get pulled into his brother's spell. He was something to see when he put his mind to a woman. But he only had eyes for the island girl, and she wasn't unaffected. A lovely blush spread over her cheeks under William's intense attention, and it occurred to Sean that something extraordinary was happening. Something tangible in the air. It would be interesting to see if this was the woman that would cause William to break their deal. He doubted his brother was capable of remaining chaste if this woman had a mind to seduce him. Very interesting indeed.

Three songs later, they ended the impromptu trad session. William had nearly jumped off the performing area when he saw

Derry sidle up to the lass, offering a lemonade shandy. Now Derry had been called to heel, and William was seated next to her. His eyes never left her face. She was a beauty, modestly dressed in a soft blue sweater and long denim skirt. She had golden hair, almost blonde but more like honey. The eyes, though, that's what had them all dazzled. Lush brows that curved impishly, and irises like sparkling whiskey. Like pieces of amber.

William was certainly lucky he'd seen her first. He was the envy of every man there, and she was just as smitten. She was clever and playful and not overtly sexual. Less of an intention to seduce, but genuinely enjoying the sport of sparring with his brother. She made William laugh, and that was a beautiful thing. Her name was Katie Donoghue, and she lived on Inis Oirr, the smallest of the Aran Islands. Sean had done introductions immediately, more for William's sake. He was tongue-tied around this woman to start, but now they fell into an easy banter.

She said, "We're here for a hen party. There's not much to do this time of year on the island. And it's no fun runnin' into your da and the parish priest in the pub. They'd likely shoo us back home. So, we came into town. My friend Marjorie is getting married this weekend."

"Yes, well, this is home for us. At least, it was. Sean and I are with the Gardai, and we're assigned in Dublin for now."

Katie smiled at that. "I'm going to Dublin at the start of the month. My mam wants me to take a fashion course at the trade school. My parents tend sheep and sell wool from our small farm. I've been finishing the wool and trying my hand at dying and knitting. It's hard work, but we sell to the shops around here and to tourists."

William touched the edge of her sleeve. "Is this one of your creations? It's beautiful on you."

"Yes, it's one of mine. My da says to stick to the traditional weaves, but the local girls don't want those bulky sweaters. They're fine for the men and the tourists, but the local girls want something a little different, so my mam came up with this idea to let me study." She looked at her watch. "We're going to miss the last boat back. I need to go. Thank you, William. For the song, I mean. You're very good—both of you." She nodded and gave Sean a smile. "Better than Dylan, I think." She nudged her friends. "Drain them, girls. We can't miss the boat."

William was in a full panic. "Katie, we've just... I mean..." He was stammering like a fool, then took her elbow softly. "I'll walk you down to the dock, if you don't mind. Please. It's dark."

Sean walked at a discreet distance with the remainder of the hen party. "She likes him," her friend said simply, "and that's no easy thing to achieve. She's a nice girl. A good girl." Her voice held a warning that Sean admired.

"Don't worry about him. He's an honorable man. And he more than likes her. He's bewitched."

William watched the ferry pull away, and he looked like he was flattened. Like someone in the aftermath of a lightning strike. Was he smoking? He felt like he should have visible smoke pouring from a hole in his chest. "Jaysus, Sean, I'm done in. I'm ruined."

"Well then, I hope you got her number and gave her yours. She'll be in Dublin for six weeks."

Sean watched the tremor go through his brother and couldn't help but think about the legend they'd been told as young lads. He watched the beautiful girl waving at them, against the dimness of the sea and sky, and he wondered if love at first sight was actually a thing.

Sean woke the next morning in his childhood bedroom. He could hear his sister, Maeve, talking with his brother. Or in this case, arguing. He'd come out of the bedroom and was down the hall at the point when his brother had started to beg.

"Maeve, ye said yourself you don't have any plans today. Just come with me. It'll be less awkward, and I'll buy you whatever sweater you want. The women in Dublin are wearing those poncho things. I bet they'll have those in the shop."

Sean smiled at the scene. He reached across the table and stole a rasher off Maeve's plate, settling in like a spectator at a match. His sister liked having the advantage. She twisted her mouth, weighing the matter.

"Anything I want, no matter the cost?"

William ground his jaw. "Ye're a wee mercenary. Yes, no matter the cost."

Their mother interjected. "Maeve, you should be ashamed. Just go with your brothers. They'll likely stay out of trouble that way. He doesn't need to buy you anything."

William spoke over Maeve's protests. "I have to buy something, or else she'll think I've just come to see her."

"But you are going just to see her. Why not speak plainly?" Aoife asked, shaking her head.

"Mam, she works in her da's shop. I've got to play it cool."

Aoife put a plate down in front of him. "The ferry won't be running if the weather's rough. You know the hours are loose at the end of the summer. Why don't you just call the girl?"

William was adamant. "I want to see her—I'm better in person. I might make a cock-up of things on the phone."

Aoife glared at him. "Language, lad. And the only reason you're better in person is because you rely on your pretty face and your broad shoulders to woo a girl. You should try learning how to talk to them. And I don't just mean sweet-talking them. Honeyed words butter no parsnips. Tell her about yourself. Ask her about herself. You've got to practice these things, or I'll never get a grandchild out of either of you."

Maeve curled up her nose. "Ew."

THREE

Sorcha walked down the narrow lane, looking for the blue door with the address of 166 roughly painted with white. This was her last holdout from the Mater Infirmorum Hospital. She'd been waiting for this particular patient to drop for two weeks. It was her first pregnancy, and she had a tense home life. Her husband was a bully, and he'd often fail to bring her to her appointments. She opened the door to the building, going up to the second floor and down the corridor. Sorcha heard a crash as she approached the door, then the husband came barreling out the door and almost knocked her over.

She was stunned at the rough treatment. He'd always been a bit cool toward her, but never so blatantly rude. She smelled the whiskey coming out of every pore, leaving a scent trail as easy to detect as a trail of smoke. Then she saw her. Sinead was lying on the floor, sobbing. She ran to her and noticed her protective curl around her belly.

"Jesus, Mary, and Joseph! Sinead! Are you hurt?" Stupid question altogether. In the four years of schooling and year of midwifery, she'd never seen the like. "Oh, darlin'. Let me have a look." The girl's mouth was split. "Did he hit you anywhere else?"

"I just fell. It's nothing at all." Her whole body was shaking.

"Jaysus, Sinead. I saw him leave. Dispense with the bullshit, please. Did he try to harm the child? I need to know the extent of your injuries."

Her eyes widened. "Oh, no. He'd never hurt the child."

"He knocked you to the ground, Sinead. The child is inside you. Of course he would!" Sorcha knew she was being unprofessional. "Did he hit or kick your abdomen?" The woman shook her head. "Did you fall on your belly?"

"No, I caught myself, but I think my wrist..." She held it up and Sorcha bit back a hiss.

"Okay, Sinead. We've got to see to your injuries. That wrist is broken. Can you walk?" She could see the odd angle of the joint, and the swelling was already starting.

"I can't leave. He'll be back. It'll make it worse." The woman was terrified, but Sorcha ignored her. A neighbor appeared at the door.

"Don't just stand there, lass. Help me. Before he comes back. We can't wait for an ambulance here."

The teenage girl flew into action. "Bring her to my gran's. She can hide there until we get the car around. She's just below, on the first floor."

It went quickly after that. An elderly woman pulled up after they'd taken the injured woman down the fire escape. Sorcha heard the exact moment the bastard came back into their apartment. It made the hair stand up on her arms. She'd no sooner gotten the girl in the car when he came out the back door of the building.

"Get yer fookin' hands off my wife. She's not goin' anywhere." His words were slurred with drink.

"She's injured, sir. She has had a fall, and she is contracting," she added as an afterthought. He obviously didn't understand the lie. "She's in labor, Mr. Fitzpatrick. I need to get her to the hospital."

"I'll drive my own wife to the hospital." He pointed at Sorcha, menace rolling off the ignorant bastard. That's when she snapped.

"You're in your cups, ye thick-headed lout. Ye'll not be driving anywhere! Now go sleep it off before I call the police!" She second-guessed the wisdom of her aggressive tone just as she saw the slap coming toward her. The pain exploded on the side of her face. She fell against the car, and it took a moment for her to come back to herself. When she looked at him, he was white as a ghost. He was apparently as shocked by his assault as she was. She jumped in the front seat of the car and Wonder Granny hit the gas.

Dr. Childs was shaking his head as he took the icepack away and checked the damage. "No broken skin. Just a nasty bruise this side of your ear. You're lucky he didn't fracture that thick skull of yours. It was completely reckless, Sorcha!"

He really was furious. He never called her by her first name. "I know. Jaysus, doctor. Believe me, I'm fully aware of what an idiot I am."

"You should have called the police, stayed hidden and waited for the authorities."

She exhaled, suddenly tired. "She was injured. Do you have any idea what the response time is for this sort of disturbance? Unless something's getting blown up, they can take hours to come around. I just wanted to get her out of there! You didn't see her." Sorcha started tearing up, despite her best efforts. "She's nearly forty-two weeks pregnant, and he beat the poor woman to the ground."

Dr. Childs sighed. "I understand. But you are no good to anyone if you end up maimed or murdered, Nurse Mullen." He'd gained back some of his usual reserve. There was a knock at the door and Nurse Betty, her old supervisor, came in. Sorcha slumped in her arms, suddenly wanting her mother. No one had ever hit her in anger. Well, other than during her attempted abduction. That had been a near miss that would go down in history. But no one who knew her had ever struck her. The men in her family were loving and protective.

"Oh, my sweet girl. There now. You're all right. And Sinead is going to be just fine." She looked toward the doctor. "The police have jailed Mr. Fitzpatrick. His wife won't press charges, but I told them that we would. We can't let this go. If we did, it would be like saying it was okay to assault one of our midwives. It would destroy the home visitation program and put our girls at risk. We must pursue the matter with fervor."

Sorcha wiped her face and shook herself. "I'm fine. What will we do about Mrs. Fitzpatrick?"

Dr. Childs answered, "We're holding her for observation. If she doesn't go into labor in twenty-four hours, I'll induce her. It was the plan all along. She won't be leaving this hospital. They likely won't hold him for long—the gaols are overflowing—but I'm not giving that son of a bitch another opportunity to kill her. Maybe if he's sentenced to some incarceration time, she'll find a better situation." Sorcha could tell how much it was costing him to rein in his temper. He was a good man, likely as horrified as she was.

He hadn't married or had children, and Sorcha suddenly remembered her friend at the maternity hospital. Angelina was very beautiful. She was younger than him by at least a dozen years, but they were both alone. And they were both pretty great. "Did you ever want children, Dr. Childs?"

His smile held a touch of bitterness. "I'm a bit set in my ways for all that. Now stop trying to change the subject. You're done for the day." She started to argue, so he pressed on her bruise with his finger.

"Ouch!"

"Exactly. You can't concentrate with an aching head. And, if you don't do as you're told, I'll have Mother Superior come down here and give you an aching ass with her boot. She's not to be trifled with, I assure you." Sorcha narrowed her eyes at him. "Right, then. Off you go. Nurse Betty will see you into a taxi—you're not walking or taking the bus today. They'll be packed to bursting this time of the day." He nodded at Betty and retreated, a smile niggling his mouth.

"That man is..." Betty cut Sorcha's sentence off.

"Absolutely in the right. You're not working today. I already called the Jubilee. I thought you were headed to Dublin tomorrow anyway?"

"I am, but I can finish my shift. I want to be here when you induce her labor. I'll cancel Dublin."

"I think it's best if you let us handle all that. She is hurting, Sorcha. The father of her child is sitting in a cell at the local gaol, as well he should be. She's likely to focus her resentment in the wrong direction. I know you meant well, and you did a brave thing under frightening circumstances. You did the thinking for a woman who hasn't had the freedom to think for herself in a very long time. She's grateful to you, but she's feeling very conflicted right now. And she's likely feeling guilty and like a failure. She'll stare across the birthing table at you, with a bruise on your face and compassion in your eyes, and it'll likely cut her to ribbons. No, pet. You need to go pack a pretty frock and get out of town for a few days. For both your sakes. I'd imagine your brother will be in a rare temper when he sees your face, as will your parents."

Sorcha's face blanched. "Holy Virgin Mother! I hadn't thought about that. My mam will sell that flat and be packing me off to Glengormley, locked in the boot of her car."

"As a mother myself, I can understand the inclination." Betty's face was kind. "I've got three sons, so you girls are the only daughters I'll ever get. Have a care, Sorcha dear. You're a fighter by nature, as you've had to be." She stroked a finger over Sorcha's scar. Over the gash that had happened the night she'd almost been pulled into a van and murdered by the Shankill Butchers. "This city either makes you stronger, or it breaks you. If you don't slow down, it will do the latter."

"This is my city. I won't abandon it—it's the only place I've ever lived." Sorcha tried to make her understand. "I won't be broken. I'll be back on Tuesday and ready to work again. My shift is at the Jubilee, but please leave me a message at the hospital and let me know how she's doing?"

"That's the spirit. Just don't forget to smell the roses a bit, Nurse Mullen." She'd returned to the more professional relationship they shared with a parting bit of advice. "Dublin is a grand time altogether, but you should take a drive out into the country if you want to see something special. Better yet, take a visit to the coast. People weren't meant to live in cages, and this city can be like a cage when you're standing on the wrong side of those walls."

Dublin 2, Dublin, Ireland

William watched his brother leave for his shift, giving them both a sad smile. Katie was next to him on the sofa, and the energy hummed between them.

"He's lonely, I think." Katie always knew how to cut to the heart of the matter.

"Aye, he is. He'll not settle though. He won't pursue empty comforts."

"And is that what I am?" she asked, but her eyes were strong and vulnerable at the same time.

Katie looked at his beautiful face and couldn't believe she was here with him. After two weeks, the effect he had on her had only strengthened. He had sandy, wavy hair, cut short for the Garda, but soft. So soft. And his eyes were a true and comforting shade of blue. He had a smile that made her weak in the knees. Was this just a fling for him?

"Do you really have to ask me that, Katie, love? Don't you know?" William hadn't said the words. It had only been two weeks, but he felt like he'd go mad from holding it back. He loved her, as crazy as that seemed. Two weeks was a heartbeat, but she was the breath of his body. The pulse in his veins. "Do you not know how I feel, mo chuisle?"

This was not a good time for this conversation. They were alone. Would be for hours. And he was a selfish, randy bastard. She saw his inner turmoil and poked the beast, pulling his face down to her mouth so he could kiss her. "Christ, woman. You'll be the death of me," he murmured against her lips. He dragged her across his lap, hissing as her supple ass grazed his hard cock. She liked the feel of his desire, her breath catching. He took her mouth again, then broke the kiss and took in the sight of her flushed face. She was always stunning, but Katie Donoghue fully aroused was perfection in the flesh. "I want to touch you, Katie. Will you let me touch you? I'll stop on your word, but just let me feel you."

She was breathing hard, her mouth rosy. He ran a thumb over her bottom lip, and that's when she said, "Yes, mo chroí. I want you to touch me. I ache for it."

His eyes flared at the endearment. She was an island girl, and although the Irish had almost lost their native tongue, it was kept alive on the west coast and the island chains. *Mo chroí*, my heart. Words of love, as he'd given to her. He ran a hand through her hair, cupping her neck. His kiss was urgent, but his other hand was featherlight, an exploring finger tracing her collarbone and then slowly to the curve of her breast. She let out a little moan against his mouth as he dipped his two fingertips into her bra and grazed her nipple. Then she was on her back, and his mouth replaced the fingers. She cradled his big body between her hips and arched against his mouth.

"Your skin is so soft. And the taste. You have no idea how beautiful you taste." He pulled down the other cup and gave that side equal attention. That's when she felt his palm running up her leg. He stopped and met her eyes, looking for any sign that she wasn't okay with this. "I'll be gentle, Katie. You'll like it." She had no doubt. The thought of his hands on her sent a ripple of desire through her.

"I don't know what to do, William." He settled between her legs, kissing her as he started to rock his hips. She moved with him as his warm, demanding lips worked their spell. His arousal rubbed into her, pulling her along, then he stopped and gazed down at her, his eyes sparkling with mischief.

"You see? Your body does, Katie. Your body knows exactly what to do. Just let yourself feel it. Right where I'm touching you. Just focus on where our bodies are touching. I'll do the rest." His grin was rakish. Then his hand was under her skirt, and he was thumbing her through her panties. She whimpered, and he caught it with a kiss as he slipped his hand inside.

William cried out like a wounded animal when he finally slid his hand against her naked flesh. She was like silk and honey. He watched her face as he explored her. "Focus, Katie. Feel me right where I am. Rock your hips against me like you did before. Meet my strokes with your own." Her face was frantic, but she started to feel the pulsing rhythm, moving her hips. "That's it, my girl. Take your pleasure, love." He felt the flood of moisture and knew she was close. He kissed her and intensified his touch, focusing his own mind and skillful touch right at the center of her. Thunder roared in his ears when he felt her let go, coming in great waves against his hand. He wanted to taste it. Wanted his tongue on her. Wanted to be deep inside her. Wanted everything. But there was time, and he'd wait until she was ready. Then he'd have her forever. This was just the beginning for them.

Sean came home after a long shift, expecting to see clothes strewn across the chairs in a path leading to the bedroom. It wouldn't be the first time. But William appeared, groggy and wearing his boxers. "Christ, man, would you cover that up!" Sean yelled. That's when William noticed the tent protruding from his undergarments.

"Sorry," he said roughly, grabbing a pair of sweatpants and a long shirt.

"Is Katie here?" Sean asked plainly.

William looked annoyed. "Of course not. I walked her back to her friend's house last night. Give me some credit."

He knew how much William liked this young, fair-haired beauty. "So she's not the one? Surprising. I thought she'd be the one causing you to break our deal."

Sean's brother looked at him like he was an idiot. "Quite the contrary. She is the one. I'm going to marry her."

Sean gave a short laugh until he realized that William was serious. "You barely know the girl. Listen, forget our deal. If you want to be with her, don't give that stupid conversation another thought. I was talking rubbish."

"It wasn't rubbish. It was about finding our mates. I love her, Sean. She's like the air to me. I don't need a year or a decade to know that. I knew it immediately, like some sort of cosmic puzzle was fitting together in an instant. I'm desperate for her. And because I love her, I'll wait. She's innocent. She's been sheltered on that island, and she needs to get her land legs before I'm dragging her off to bed or to the altar. Blue balls be damned." He looked down at his barely concealed problem, wanting to choke the life out of it. It was weakening his resolve, the bastard.

Sean's throat was thick with emotion. Everything was going to change. "I'm happy for you, brother. Jesus, Willy. I'm so very happy for you. And she feels the same, I hope?"

He smiled so tenderly, it made Sean's heart ache. "When she looks at me, the love shines out of her eyes. I've seen lust from a woman, but never this. I'm not sure she knows it yet, but I see it. When I'm with her, I feel loved. I feel it to my soul."

Sean swallowed hard. "Then she'll be my sister until I'm in my grave, brother. She'll want for nothing. And Mam will love her. You need to let them meet her."

"I will. Soon, I will take her to meet the family. Maeve already loves her. She is working on another poncho for her as we speak."

"Buying her love with knitwear. The way to a teenage girl's heart." They both laughed, the seriousness of their conversation easing. "I picked up a day shift tomorrow, so I'll see you in the morning, brother." He slapped William on the back. "Sweet dreams, loverboy."

William grinned. "You're next, Seany. She's going to hit you like a ton of bricks."

"From your mouth to God's ears."

FOUR

Petruchio: Come, come, you wasp. I' faith, you are too angry.
Katherine: If I be waspish, best beware my sting...

—William Shakespeare: Taming of the Shrew, Act II: Scene I

Sorcha laid her cheek against the cool glass of the bus window. She'd had a near miss with her brother, as she'd come home early from her shift. John had been working late, and by the time she'd finished packing and crawled into bed, it was too dark in her room for him to see the bruise on her cheekbone. Her hair covered most of it when she wore it down, and she had no purpling under her eyes, as she'd feared would happen. With a bit of makeup, she'd not look like an abuse victim.

Now she was headed toward Dublin, gazing out over the dewy landscape. As the bus left the city, she felt the sadness seep out of her bones a little at a time. Ireland was so beautiful, once you cleared the razor ribbon and armored trucks from your sight. There were no buildings with pockmarked concrete, scarred by the blast of RPGs. There was no graffiti. She saw no cars hulled out from fire because they'd been used to create a mobile bomb. Last month, there had been a bombing in Derry. Last February, the Provisional

IRA had detonated another explosive device at a restaurant on the outskirts of Belfast.

She remembered the first bombing that she'd been old enough to understand. She was twelve years old when the Ulster Volunteer Force orchestrated a bombing in Dublin. Was any place truly safe? Were there places in Ireland where people didn't have to worry about killing and destruction? She knew there were, deep down. She looked around now and saw the rolling green hills and small cottages of her homeland, and she knew that some people lived in modest comfort and safety. But what was she on about? She was a city girl. Born and raised in the concrete jungle of Northern Ireland's capital. What the hell would she do in some small village with only the sheep and the old folk to talk to?

Likely, she'd spit out child after child, not having time for anything else. She'd be married to a farmer or a fisherman who'd drop into their marriage bed exhausted and for just long enough to get another child in her. She shook herself, banishing the thought. Despite what her mother thought, or that cowboy of a doctor she was now studying under, Sorcha Mullen need not ever marry. She had a career to fulfill her.

Suddenly the idea of walking the streets of Dublin with her cousin seemed like a fine idea. Maureen was a sensible girl, despite what her brother thought. A good Catholic, too. Maybe Maureen would take her to a nice restaurant or a museum. Or she could explore the university. She'd always wanted to tour Trinity College.

At the end of the two-hour bus ride, Sorcha was stiff and grateful to be within the city limits. She followed the signs to the city bus pick-up and boarded one headed for Kevin Street in Dublin 8. She was pleased that her accommodation was so close to some of the places she'd like to visit. Most of them were located in Dublin 2, which she could easily reach on foot. She grabbed her bag at her stop and stepped off the bus. According to her directions, Maureen was one block from the bus stop. When she reached the building, she used the doorbell. A stern-looking woman came to the door, mouth pinched. "I'm here to see Maureen Mullen, if you please. I'm her cousin, Sorcha."

"Aye, she told me to expect you. She's up in her room, likely sleeping the morning away. Come in, Miss Mullen. I have a few ground rules to cover, if you are to be a guest here."

It suddenly made sense. As strict as her auntie was, Sorcha had been shocked that she'd let Maureen live in downtown Dublin, but her cousin lived in a boarding house. Likely an all-female boarding house, hence the rather unfortunate-looking keeper of the gate.

The woman didn't introduce herself, instead putting up a plump finger. She began ticking off the house rules. "Number one: There will be no men permitted past the front step. There's no exception to this rule unless the building is set afire and the man has a firehose in his hand. Not even the parish priest gets by that threshold." She arched her finger in a semi-circle as if to draw the invisible boundary. "Number two: Curfew is at eleven pm sharp. If you come after that time by even a minute, you will be locked out until six in the morning. If you come without your hostess, you will also be denied access. Number three: You will respect the other guests in my home by not making excessive noise. Record players are allowed between the hours of four and eight at a reasonable volume. And the final rule: There will be no food of any kind in the rooms. Each girl has a shelf in the kitchen cupboard for essentials, and there is shared milk in the icebox. I prepare a hearty breakfast each morning. As you are not a resident, you will be required to pay fifty pence for this service or go elsewhere for your breakfast." Sorcha hadn't uttered a word since she started. She bit back her caustic comments as they occurred to her, afraid she'd be out on her ear before she ever saw her cousin. "Now, let's go fetch your hostess. She's on the ground floor just this way."

Sorcha followed her, feeling like a soldier marching in step. She wasn't sure that the reasonable offer of a fifty pence breakfast was worth it, at the cost of meeting this woman's sour face across the table.

The young woman who answered the door was a shock. At

first, Sorcha was afraid she'd gotten the rooms mixed up. The girl had smeared make-up, bleached blonde hair, and had obviously slept in her bra and slip. She peered out of the one eye that wasn't glued together with day-old mascara. "Sorcha! Oh, love, I'm sorry. I overslept!" She glared at the woman next to Sorcha. "Problem?"

"Yes. Clean that room, or you'll both be out before teatime. I won't abide a lazy slattern for a boarder." The nasty landlady departed with a sniff of disgust.

She pulled Sorcha in and said sweetly, "Yes, Miss Kerrigan. So sorry."

Then she closed the door, letting out a frustrated breath. "The old cow. For what she's charging my parents, she should bloody well clean it for me." She took in the sight of Sorcha. "Aren't you a picture? I must look a fright. I had to sneak in last night after the old bat went to bed. She's very fond of her rules."

Sorcha smiled, scooting aside some clothing to have a seat on the bed. "I noticed. I received a thorough briefing. Now, get dressed and show me your city, if we're to be back by eleven. It's silly really. By the time I finish my shift and my home visitations, and then take a bus across town, I'm lucky to get home by midnight. Especially with all the checkpoints."

Her cousin sat beside her. "Is it too awful? I can't imagine."

"No, not too awful. There's been trouble brewing and they've increased the number of checkpoints and searches since the bombing in Derry, but I'm fine, cousin. How are you? Ye look very different. You've gone blonde, I see."

She grinned. "Aye, and my father almost keeled over with a stroke at the sight of me. But he can hardly say anything since my mother's been bleaching her hair for thirty years. I can't imagine why. My hair was mousy brown, but she had lovely red hair like you. There's a fair number of redheads in Cork."

"I can tell you why she likely bleached it. She probably got called carrot top one too many times. It got rather old by the time I reached twelfth year."

"I'll bet those doctors are chasing you plenty." Maureen was fishing, Sorcha knew, but she was a kind-hearted girl.

"Hardly. It only takes a few minutes of me opening my gob to dispel them of the notion," Sorcha said, almost proudly.

"You always did have a temper. And how is your brother? You should have brought him. I've got friends in the city he could have stayed with."

"He works a lot. I barely see him, even though we live together. And I hate that he works at the mill. He's smart. He should have gone to university. He took a summer job at that damn mill last year and never left."

"Well, I can ask around. Maybe there's work here that's a bit more to his liking. Something safer, at least. I can't believe you didn't move out of that ghastly city when your parents did. Mam says they have a lovely little house."

"Yes, well, it's too far to both work and school. Once I've finished my schooling, I'll consider it. I've been given a great opportunity, though. I think I'd like to stay at the Royal Jubilee if they hire me on after I complete my internship."

"Well, now, that sounds promising. But if you ever decide otherwise, Dublin has some very good hospitals."

Maureen got dressed and washed up as Sorcha tried to make some order out of her messy room. Then they left, deciding to enjoy the campus of Trinity College before they ate. Sorcha walked through the city parks, smiling at the changing leaves and fragrant blooms. It was so open. So much cleaner. They spent the entire morning and through lunchtime walking around the college campus and surrounding areas. Maureen was now sitting next to her, sprawled on the cool grass of St. Stephen's Green. "I slept through breakfast. Why don't we take an early tea? There's a nice little bakery a few lanes over, which stays open all day. Do you fancy some cake or sandwiches?"

Sorcha answered, "I could do with a bite to eat. Lead the way." As they began to walk, Maureen seemed nervous. "What is it?"

"Did a patient's husband really put that mark on your face?" Maureen asked.

Sorcha eyed her, grinning. "Do you think I'm the sort to let a boyfriend put his hands on me?"

Her cousin smiled. "No, I don't suppose you are. I just wanted to make sure you weren't covering for someone."

"I'm not. There's no one to cover for even if I had a mind to do so. I haven't even had a date in almost a year. This was a clear case of injury in the line of duty. It's the first time. Unless you count the time a patient kicked me in the never-you-mind. She didn't mean it, of course, but she had a shot of pain cut through her, and her left foot landed a good one right in my baby-maker."

Her cousin was laughing now, the mood lightened. "Who knew being a midwife was so dangerous?"

Sean whistled down the road as he caught sight of his brother. William approached, the apology clear on his face. "Sorry. I got a call right as I was heading over. Public urination in the rose bushes at St. Ann's."

"Lovely. Did you catch him?" Sean asked.

"Aye, I did. Smelly bastard. The vicar told me to let him go and gave him a sandwich. I don't know why he bothered calling. So, where to, brother? I'm famished."

"You are always hungry. How about Granny Nan's? She won't be too crowded, and she likes me," Sean said proudly. Granny Nan was a tough old bird.

"It's the uniform. Women can't resist it," William said with authority. "Especially the older ones."

"She wants me to meet her daughters. Christ, that's all I need. She's heaven in the kitchen, but she'd be hell on a son-in-law, I suspect," Sean said with a grin.

· · ·

Sorcha smelled fresh scones as she followed her cousin into Granny Nan's Cafe. The place was sparsely occupied, as the hour was between lunch and teatime. Maureen made introductions, and Granny Nan looked at her with an appraising eye. They were discussing the specials when the bell over the door gave a tinkling ring. Sorcha stiffened as three men walked into the place. They looked to be about her age, but they were glassy-eyed and unsteady on their feet. She moved closer to her cousin, giving her arm a squeeze in warning. Maureen looked at the men.

"No bother, cousin," she whispered. "They've likely been watching the match at the pub down the road. The pub won't be serving food just now."

One of the men, with dark, unkempt hair, went to the counter, ignoring the fact that Sorcha and Maureen were trying to order. He slapped a hand on the counter. "Look here. We need three ham sandwiches and some Cokes."

Nan bristled with insult. "Don't you go banging on my counter and expect me to come running! These lasses were here before you, so behave yourself or there will be nothing for you!"

As if they'd just noticed them, the three men turned in unison. The dark-haired one raked his eyes over Maureen. "Well, well. Pardon me, ladies. Where are my manners?"

His voice made Sorcha's skin crawl, and she felt Maureen tense beside her. Sorcha said, "Nan, we'll have two bowls of soup with bread, a pot of tea, and a banoffee pie to share." She approached the counter, refusing to cower to the creep. "How much do I owe you?"

The man slapped a fiver on the counter. "I'll get this, Nan."

Sorcha slid her own money toward the counter. "No, thank you."

"Think you're too good for me, do you? How about your friend? I bet she's game for some fun."

Nan shouted, "Get out, now. Get your sorry selves back to the pub!"

He pointed menacingly at the old woman. "Shut your gob, old woman."

Maureen said calmly, "Nan, lock yourself in your office and call the guards."

Sorcha jumped as a voice came from behind her. "If you don't want her, I'll have a go. I've got a thing for redheads. Tell me, love. Does the carpet match..." Sorcha didn't give him a chance to answer. She rounded on the man with a napkin dispenser, knocking him upside the head. Maureen screamed and grabbed her arm, pulling her toward the door. Then, the third man tried to block their way, and Sorcha struck him in the nose with the heel of her hand.

They were quickly out the door. Sorcha looked behind her to see if they were following and ran right into a brick wall, or so she thought. Strong hands grabbed her by the elbows, keeping her from landing backward on her bum. She screamed, jerking away. She had an unclear image of two hulking giants in dark clothing, then she shifted her attention to the three men piling out of the restaurant. They were spitting mad as they lurched toward her.

It was a blur of quick and sure violence. One man was shoved face-first against the brick wall; another had a leg swept out from under him by the same assailant, landing him on his back with an *umph*. She turned just in time to see the other man clothesline the dark-haired one with a long, thick arm, sending the poor sod ass over teakettle. He flipped him on his belly and put a large boot on his neck.

"Wow." That was all Maureen said. Sorcha took in the two men, realizing they were both in uniform. The one man whose leg had been swept out from under him moaned and tried to get up, which cued an equally large boot right on his chest. "Stay down, ye little bastard." The voice was smooth and deep, the threat in his tone obvious.

· · ·

Sean O'Brien wasn't struck stupid very often, but as he looked at the woman before him, he barely found his words. He had one piece of shite shoved up against a wall, the other under his boot. His brother, his oldest ally on the earth, made short work of the third, pinning him underfoot.

"Are ye hurt, lass? Did they do ye harm?" He didn't even speak to her friend. All he saw was this small, young woman; hair in rich shades of auburn, pale skin, and fiery green eyes. She ignored the question. "Is anyone hurt, madame?" His voice was more forceful.

Sorcha's temper flared. "Don't get a tone with me, officer. I've had enough of brutish men for the week. Now, let the wee fiend go so I can teach him a little respect!" Sean heard William chuckle behind them.

Granny Nan made an appearance, then. "Those two were playing the bully with these nice young girls. Filthy suggestions in my tearoom. I've never seen the like!" Nan said something particularly cutting in Irish.

Sean's brows went up. "Nan, jump on the police box on the corner and call for a car."

That's when the jackass with Sean's boot on his chest started popping off at the mouth. "That little twat is the one who started it. All high and mighty. She wouldn't let me buy her lunch, all conceited like, then she hit my friend with something, punched my other mate, and ran out before we could have her arrested. Stupid, daft cow..." Sean pressed harder with his foot, causing the man to squeak.

Sorcha said calmly, "Let him go. Take your foot off him this instant."

Sean looked at her like she was insane. Sorcha repeated, eyes piercing, "I said, let him up."

Sean exhaled. "Christ. Why do women always protect their abusers? Did he put that bruise on your face, which you've tried to cover?"

He let the man up, disgusted. Sorcha answered the question.

"No, I don't know him. And no, he didn't put this bruise on my face. That's another matter altogether." The man stood up, indignant. "And I did assault the other two men. The only problem I can see is that it appears I forgot one." They all watched in horrified fascination as Sorcha Mullen kicked her sensible loafer right between the man's legs. He doubled over, wailing in agony. "That's what you get for opening your filthy mouth in Nan's shop!" Then she cuffed him above the ear. "And that's for calling me a twat! Ye get yer belly full o' drink and try to play the ass with three respectable women. I should twist yer wee bollocks off with a pair of tweezers!"

The man dove at Sorcha and ended up right back where he'd started, Sean's boot back in place. Sean looked at the most beautiful woman he'd ever seen, steam coming out of her ears. "Are ye done, madame?"

She exhaled, then looked at her cousin who was speechless. "Maureen, would ye like a crack at him?"

"No, cousin. I think these officers have it all under control." Her cousin looked like she was having the time of her life.

"Aye, so it appears," she said lightly. Sean and William were handcuffing the men. "Let's get that tea, then. Good day, lads." She started walking away as if she'd just changed her laundry from the washer to the dryer.

Sean called to her, "I need written statements." She started walking back into the cafe, behaving as if she hadn't heard him.

A patrol car was there within minutes, and the three men were loaded into the back. "Charge them with drunk and disorderly. I'll meet you back at the station," William said to the transporting officer. Then he looked at Sean. "And you'll get the ladies' statements, I assume?"

Sean took statement forms from the patrol car, thanking the responding officer. "Thank you, Officer Sullivan. Maybe you can meet us after work for a pint." Bill Sullivan was new to the Gardai, but Sean had taken an immediate liking to him. He also played the piano as well as any Irishman ever had. They'd done a few open mic nights together in the city.

Sullivan answered, "Thanks, but I'm taking my lass to the pictures tonight." William patted the roof of the car, signaling Sullivan to leave.

As he walked toward the cafe door, William said over his shoulder, "Be careful, brother. She looks like she might bite." Then William started the walk back to the Garda station.

Sean smiled, rather liking the idea of that little fireball sinking her teeth into his skin. He shook himself, feeling like a rotter. She'd just had a hard time from those three eejits. He was in no position to be gawking at the poor woman.

He opened the door to the cafe, and all his good intentions flew right out the window. Christ, she was beautiful. Her cousin was a looker as well, but in that done-up way that wasn't as pleasing to his eye. She'd obviously bleached her hair, and she wore a lot of makeup. Excessively teased, plucked, painted, and dyed. The other, though... she could have been on canvas. The Pre-Raphaelite coloring, the lush mouth, the pale skin. *Get it together. You're here for a reason,* said the angel on his shoulder. But the devil weighed in on the matter with all sorts of vivid suggestions. Jesus, he was losing his bloody mind. As if she could read his thoughts, the woman's back stiffened, and her knuckles were tight as she gripped her tea mug.

He said, "I'm sorry to disturb your tea, ladies. I'll need to get written statements." He slid a paper to Nan over the counter.

Then he turned back to the table just as Sorcha stood. "Nan, could I have a scone for takeaway? There's a shop next door I'd like to visit." Sean watched her with interest. She didn't meet his eyes. She slid two pounds toward Nan and took the bag. "Maureen, I'll be next door."

Sean knew instinctively not to push. He went and took a seat next to the blonde. The wood was warm where she'd been sitting. "Is it something I've done? Did I scare the lass? I didn't mean to."

He couldn't make sense of it. She'd gone head-to-head with three full-grown men.

"It's nothing you've done, Officer... O'Brien? That's the same name that was on your partner's shirt."

"Brothers," he said, simply. He held out his hand and said, "Sean O'Brien. Pleased to meet you. I wish it was under lighter circumstances. My brother, William, is the other brute." She smiled at that, the moment easing.

"Don't take it personally, Officer Sean O'Brien. She's fierce, it's true. And she's got a dreadful temper. It is likely just the uniform that put her off. They make her nervous, I think. Where she's from, the relationship with the military and police force is a bit... strained at the moment."

"Derry?" he asked, his heart squeezing in his chest.

She shook her head. "No, Belfast. She's from West Belfast, on the Catholic side of the wall. It's..." She paused, trying to think of how to say it. "It's a different life. People who become informers to the police put a target on their back. She's a good girl. She doesn't involve herself in *the Troubles*, but it doesn't mean it doesn't blow back on her and her family. It's hard to hide from it, I suppose. Now, if you've got a pen, I think Nan and I can give you a full account. Ye'll get no statement from Knuckles Malone, I'm afraid." Sean laughed at that.

"I think I'll go try to apologize at least. For being a man, if for nothing else. It's not the impression she should get of our city. I understand, now. At least, I think I do. How long is she visiting?"

"She leaves on Monday. She's only been here a few hours, and this happens." She shook her head, disgusted. "She came to get away from crime and mayhem. I'd try to dissuade you from going over there, but I think you'd ignore the warning." The woman's eyes were knowing. "Is your brother single?"

"He's not married if that's what you mean, but he's not single. He's head over heels for an island girl. Sorry." Sean winked at her and left to find the green-eyed beauty.

. . .

Sorcha heard him come in. She felt him come in as surely as if she'd seen it. Big men in big boots couldn't walk softly, even if they had wings on their backs. She went on the defensive, turning on him. "Have you finished with my cousin? Daylight is burning, and I have things to do."

The officer smiled at her, damn the man. He was so beautiful, it almost knocked the wind out of her. She took in the weapons on his belt. A nightstick that made her palms sweat. How many times had she seen young lads beaten with those sticks? He watched her eyes dart to the impact weapon and his face softened. Damn him. "Well, don't just stand there grinning at me."

"You don't need to fear me, lass. I'm just coming to apologize." Sean thought that would sweeten her up a bit, but Christ, was he wrong. She put her fists on her hips.

"Is that what she told you? That I'm scared of you? You are an arrogant one, aren't you? I cut my teeth on that sort of violence."

"Aye, in Belfast. I heard." His brows were up, mocking her. It infuriated her. "I thought your speech was a bit different. You don't sound like a Dubliner. Regardless, I am sorry. Not for my own actions, but the behavior of those men. That's no way to treat a lady. I'll talk to the judge about letting them cool off in jail for a week or two."

She wasn't sure what to say. "You don't need to apologize for someone else's actions, and for the record, I was handling it fine. It's not the first time a belligerent drunk has tried to sweet talk me out of my knickers. You should let them go. They'll likely lose their jobs otherwise."

"You'd speak up for them, after the way they behaved? And not just toward you, but toward an old woman? Is that what you did when your fella struck you? Told them to let him go?"

"You don't know what you are talking about, ye thick-headed lout!" She spat the words in a fit of frustration. "It wasn't a lover that did this. It happened at work. Haven't you ever had someone take a swing at you while you were on duty?"

"What sort of job puts you together with such men?" Incredulity marred his perfectly masculine face.

She said smartly, "I'm a midwife. Not that it's any of your concern. So, Officer..." She peered at his nameplate. "O'Brien. I don't need to be rescued, because I'm not a battered woman. What are you smiling at, for pity's sake!"

Was he smiling? Yes, he was. Like a smitten boy, no doubt. He asked, "You deliver babies? Christ, now it makes sense. It's not a job for the faint of heart. I went to an emergency call with a woman in labor. I had to wait there with her until the ambulance came. She damn near dropped the child in the bread aisle at the grocer's. All the while I'm praying to the Virgin Mother, *please don't let me have to deliver this child.*" He put his hands together as if praying, looking up to the heavens. It made her smile, which pleased him. "So, lass, are you going to tell me your first name or do I have to assign you one of my choosing? I need it for my report," he said innocently.

"And what name would you give me?" she asked. Despite her best intentions, she rather liked sparring with this Sean O'Brien. "If you were to choose, what name would it be?"

He lifted a shoulder, saying smoothly, "That's easy. Katherine. It's from my favorite play."

He enjoyed plays? This hulking giant of a man liked the theater? Then it all fell into place. She narrowed her eyes at him. "That wouldn't be a Shakespeare play, now, would it?"

His eyes sparkled with mischief. He was deliberately baiting her. "Oh, you've heard of it. Well, Elizabeth Taylor certainly played the part well, but she's got nothing on you."

Zing. Contact. Sorcha closed her eyes, reining in the impending explosion. *Taming of the Shrew.* The anger coiled in her belly, and she pushed it back, only to cause a wave of another sort which threatened to overtake her. She couldn't help it. The giggle burst out of her before she could call it back. She opened her eyes, and he winked at her. The infernal man actually winked, flashing her with perfect teeth and a rakish grin. When she gave a full belly laugh, his face showed surprise and wonder. He took in every inch of her face. It was unnerving. Her skin flushed under his gaze. Then, her cousin was behind him. "I see you two have made up. If you've gotten all you need from us, we'll be on our way."

Not by half, Sean thought. *I haven't gotten nearly enough.* He turned to Maureen. "She won't give me her name. She's rather tight-lipped when she's not in a temper."

She handed him her statement. "It's in there."

He scanned the page. "Sorcha Mullen," he said softly. And he pronounced it perfectly, a hard k-sound and a rolling r. She felt it to her toes.

Maureen boldly asked, "What time are you off work, Officer Sean O'Brien? We owe you a drink, at least, for aiding us. I thought I'd show her the city at night."

Sorcha was horrified. Whether it was fear that her cousin was trying to make a pass at the officer, or fear that she was trying to play matchmaker, she wasn't sure. She started to argue over them exchanging plans, but he answered her.

"I'm off at four. I'd like to see you both again." Her cousin smiled, and Sorcha wanted to scream.

"Around half six. And invite your brother and his island girl. It'll be a grand time. I'll even let you choose the pub."

Sean approached her, and it became undeniable where his interest was aimed, and it wasn't her cousin. His eyes burned with it. "If ye don't want me to come, hen, I'll not bother you. I'm no brute who'll push his way into a place where he's not wanted."

Sorcha's jaw was so tight that it ached. "Please yourself. It's no business of mine where you find your pint." His eyes bore into hers, and she wasn't sure what she wanted.

He seemed to decide something. "Make it six o'clock at Tom O'Shanter's for a start. The food is better, and it won't be so crowded. Ye've got to feed the girl. She hasn't got anything but a cold scone for her tea."

Sorcha's face softened a bit, despite her best efforts. He was quite beautiful to look at, and he wasn't a brute. Not really. "Six it is," she said. His face lit up at the small gift, and she felt the absurd urge to cry.

"Eat your scone, Katherine. Ye likely burned off your breakfast beating on those three unsuspecting lads," he said with a grin. Then he was gone.

FIVE

"I don't know why you had to invite him out! I'm not the sort to go on the piss all night. He'd likely have more fun if he went out with his mates." Her cousin looked at her like she was an idiot.

"Sorcha, sweetheart, he's got no interest in going on the piss with his mates. Didn't you hear him? He'd rather go somewhere quiet and feed you. He's darling altogether."

"Then you go to eat with him!" she snapped.

"He doesn't want me, and apparently his brother is head over heels in love. If anything, I'll be the fifth wheel. But he likes you, Sorcha. Surprising, given he watched you kick that fella in the ballocks. He must like them feisty. And what was all that Katherine business?"

When Sorcha told her, she was on the bed in fits of laughter. "Aye, he must really like them feisty. You have to work on that shrew tongue of yours, Sorcha, dear. You can practice tonight by being a good girl at dinner. I've called a guy I've been seeing off and on. I hope he can come, too. I'll hate seeing two other women with such fine specimens gazing into their eyes while I play the spinster."

They finished dressing. Maureen had tried to give Sorcha some of her clothes, but Sorcha put her foot down. "No, Maureen. I won't go playing dress up to try and impress a man that I'll likely never see again after tonight. It's cold, and I'm not comfortable in those sorts of clothes."

Her cousin dressed like something out of a discotheque. Lots of blue eyeshadow, glittering lips, and a thin, low-cut dress. She looked at herself in the mirror and fixed her sweater. It was soft and dark green. Her skirt was thick, dense cotton with pretty buttons going all the way down to mid-shin. Her boots were plain, but quality leather. She thought she looked rather good. To hell with everyone else. She decided to keep her hair down. It covered the bruise that Mr. Fitzpatrick was thoughtful enough to give her. She hid it with a good bit of powder and glossed her lips with some strawberry flavored lip balm. That was as good as it was going to get. What did she care what some copper from Dublin thought of her clothes? She pulled on her long coat, grateful for the fuzzy lining. Then she slid her calfskin gloves onto her hands. She thought about a hat but decided against it. She had a hood, after all. Then they started the walk to Tom O'Shanter's.

As Sorcha approached the establishment, she was pleasantly surprised. It was well lit and had big glass windows. It wasn't a pub at all, more of a bistro. Then she saw him, and the bottom dropped out of her tummy. She heard her cousin make an appreciative sound under her breath. He was half a head taller than any other man passing by. They both were. They looked alike, Sean and William. William had his arm around a stunningly beautiful young woman. *His island girl,* Sorcha thought. Her eyes went back to Sean, and his eyes were only full of her. He took in every inch of her. She suddenly cursed herself for not borrowing something of Maureen's. She straightened her back, determined not to make more of this evening than what it was. It was simply a night out with strangers before she went back to her own city. But she had to admit, in the privacy of her own licentious thoughts, that those blue eyes were heaven. Like the sea at midday.

Sean's voice was rough and aching. The sight of her punched right through him. He nodded at Maureen and introduced her formally to William and then to Katie. "And this is Sorcha Mullen." *My future wife or I'll die trying.* He leaned in and gave Maureen a peck on the cheek. "It's good to see you under better circumstances." Then he turned to Sorcha. He moved so gently as if he feared she would run. He was giving her a chance to discreetly reject him. When she didn't pull back, he pressed a big palm over her shoulder and leaned in. His lips were featherlight on her hair. "I'm so glad you're here."

Sorcha clearly didn't particularly care for Maureen's date. He was arrogant and spoke like an idiot. Like he was playing a part. His hair was stringy and too long, and he was trying and failing to grow a beard. Some men looked more masculine with long hair. But those sorts of men had likely died alongside their squires in the Middle Ages, or drowned on a longship, far from home. This man, Greg, didn't pull it off at all. He'd been watching too much television and fancied himself a pretty boy. He wore an ugly satin shirt, unbuttoned too far down his chest, and a gold chain with a medallion. A fake leather jacket. A small thatch of dark hair showed on his scrawny chest. He made up for his inadequacies by trying to be smarter than everyone else in the room. Right now, he was rambling on about Andy Warhol. Sean gave Sorcha a knowing grin.

"I don't suppose someone in your profession would have a grasp of the fine arts." That did it. Sorcha watched William's face shift. He gave Sean a chiding look that said, *Don't beat the little turd half to death in front of your pretty date.*

Sean just laughed, which caused old Greggy-boy to bristle.

"Fine art? Andy Warhol copies soup labels and a murdering dictator's photograph repetitively over the canvas, and you think that's fine art? Che Guevara was a bastard, and Warhol was a hack. But to each his own," he said with a wave of his hand. "I always preferred the pre-Raphaelites." He gave an affectionate glance at Sorcha.

"I suppose if you have archaic notions about art, you would like that sort of thing. Chubby angelic children and women coming out of seashells." He did everything but roll his eyes. This guy was too much.

Sorcha stiffened, offended on Sean's behalf. She was ready to let her mouth fly when the dark horse surged into the lead. Katie spoke up. "The cherubs were done by Rubens, and he wasn't a pre-Raphaelite. He was from the Baroque movement. And *The Birth of Venus* was painted by Sandro Botticelli, from the Renaissance period. I thought you said you were studying art?"

"I study modern art," he said defensively. He was starting to squirm under the scrutiny.

Katie smiled sweetly and said, "Ah, that explains it. Sean, why don't you tell us why you like the pre-Raphaelites?"

Sean was trying like hell not to laugh. Maureen was so uncomfortable and embarrassed as she picked at her dinner, either by her jackass of a boyfriend or because of the way they'd just chopped him off at the knees. His parents might be from the country, but they were cultured and educated. And just because his collar was blue, it didn't make him an idiot. He answered Katie's question. "Well, their art is timeless, isn't it? It's a celebration of lush, feminine beauty. The paintings are perfect, even down to the petals on the flowers and the fruit in Persephone's hand. What was beautiful then is still just as striking now. It might be more beautiful now because it's so rare to get a glimpse of such beauty." He looked at Sorcha while he spoke.

William chimed in then. "And an uncommon amount of redheads, if I remember." Katie kicked him under the table.

Greggy-poo had his knickers in a bunch now. There was no

help for it. "Let's go, Maureen. I've got some mates meeting me at the club in fifteen minutes."

Maureen looked at Sorcha, whose eyes dared her to ditch her. "You don't mind, do you? We only have a couple of hours left and it looks like everyone has finished their supper."

"I'm not leaving, Maureen. That's very rude." Sorcha was shocked at her cousin. Maureen had been the one to invite Sean and William, and now she was expecting Sorcha to just get up and leave them before they'd even cleared their plates?

Katie reached across the table and took Sorcha's hand. A warm exchange of reassurance. "Don't run off. We'll see you get home by eleven."

Maureen had a stab of conscience until she saw Greg's face. "You'll be okay, then?"

William answered, "I'll guard her like my own blooded sister."

Sorcha met Sean's eyes. He said simply, "It's your choice. I'd like to bide for a few hours with you, but I won't put you on the spot. If you need to go, then go."

Sorcha took one more look at Greg's pouty face and decided. "Eleven sharp. Do not lose track of the time." Maureen gave her a swift kiss on the cheek and was off.

As they went through the door, William shouted, "Nice to meet you, Greg!"

No sooner were they out of sight than the giggling started between Katie and Sorcha.

The time passed swiftly. They switched to a smaller booth, giving up their big table to a larger group. Katie and Sorcha sat next to each other, like two little hens. William was more relaxed than Sean had ever seen him. He ordered a bottle of white wine for them to share, and they nibbled on a couple of shared desserts. When Sean told the story about how they'd met, Katie was covering her mouth, eyes wide and filled with mirth. She told them about her small home on the island. About her father and mother, tending the sheep and selling the wool. About her attempts to update the clothing line they sold to the tourists.

"That is wonderful, Katie. I'd love to see some of your work. I wish I had more time to visit, but I'll be going back on Monday, I'm afraid." She pushed that thought aside. "I can't imagine living in such a small village. Does it get lonely in the wintertime?" Sorcha asked.

"Aye, it's a bit close in the house. But I don't lack for warm garments. Sometimes I walk for hours, just taking in the sea air. Dublin is fun and all that. I'm glad I came to study here. I just..." She looked shyly at William. "I can't imagine living here long term."

"Your island sounds very beautiful, Katie. And what about you two?" she asked the brothers. "Did you grow up in the city as I did?" So Sean told her about Doolin, their little village in County Clare. "I've seen those cliffs. In a book, mind you. Not the real thing." She gave a little laugh. "So, no barricades or hand grenades, then? A pity. You haven't lived until you've smelled the sweet scent of tear gas blowing dreamily through your bus window." Their faces fell in unison. "Jaysus, would you look at you three? It's fine. I'm used to it. I'm only teasing."

Katie said, "I see it on the news sometimes. It seems to be a very troubled place. I'm sure you love your city, but it must be difficult being stuck in the middle of all that."

"It is. The IRA has tried to recruit my father and, more recently, my brother. They act like you're failing your bloodline if you don't join the fight. But I've had enough of that to last me a lifetime. All I want to do is bring life into the world. To help young mothers deliver their sons and daughters. When you live with war long enough, you realize that it will never truly end. So, you just endure it."

She knew she'd said too much, but there was something about Katie that loosened her tongue. She felt like an old friend.

Sean's heart was in his throat. He wanted to jump across the table and shake Sorcha. He wanted to scream, *you don't have to endure it. You shouldn't have to live like this!* But he knew his words wouldn't be welcomed.

William broke the tension. "Tell us about that shiner. Did you get a fighting woman in the delivery room?" Sorcha smiled, glad for the distraction. So she told them, from start to finish, how she'd come to get knocked sideways by Mr. Fitzpatrick.

She'd kept the tone deliberately light, realizing the conversation had gotten way too serious. "So, you see where channeling my inner Katherine Minola landed me in a bit of trouble." She looked at Sean, expecting a wink or for him to agree with her. She saw something else entirely.

He said tightly, "You acted foolishly, Sorcha. When you told me you got that while doing your midwife duties, I assumed you got kicked in the head from a woman in the throes of birthing pains. What the hell were you thinking, taking on a grown man like that? For God's sake, woman—he'd already struck his pregnant wife."

"Aye, and I wasn't going to let him have another go at her. I was thinking I needed to get her to a hospital. And I've already had a tongue lashing from my supervising physician, so I don't need one from you. What would you have had me do, Sean? Wait there in their home until he came back? Is that what you would have done?"

Sean rubbed his eyes with his thumb and middle finger, the fight going out of him. "Of course not. But you lipped off to him when he was drunk and his blood was already up. He could have knocked you out and continued beating his wife. He could have hurt all of you. That old woman has to live in the same building. Did you think of that?"

"No. My concern was for Sinead." She sighed. "I know you're right in part. But you don't understand what that city is like. The police are so overrun with trouble. They aren't going to break their necks to rush over for a domestic dispute. Quite often, we're left to our own devices. And she wouldn't have pressed charges. She still won't. If taking a shot to the face put him in jail for a few months, then maybe it was worth it."

Sean gave her an impatient look. "Don't say that. You're no

good to your expectant mothers if you are laid up in a hospital bed. Promise me you won't take chances like that anymore, or like you did today. What if William and I hadn't shown up?"

She gave him a tired look in return. "Soon, I'll be a world away. You can't play the hero for everyone. I learned to take care of myself a long time ago." Then she smiled, changing the direction of the conversation. "You should have seen them, Katie, love. They had those three lads laid out in ten seconds flat."

Katie kissed William on the cheek. "You're a real hero, mo chroí." Sorcha cocked her head. Katie said, "You don't have the Irish, then?" Sorcha blushed. Katie stuttered over her words. "I didn't mean..."

"It's okay. I know. And no, I don't speak Irish. I know a little, just from the music mostly. But they aren't allowed to teach it in the public schools, and the nuns at my school were too busy trying to drill Latin into my thick head to bother with Gaelic."

Sean's eyes were soft. "Well then, if you ever have need of an interpreter, all you have to do is ask."

She wanted to tell this man that she had no need, for one thing, and for another, that she'd likely never see him again. But when she looked into those blue eyes, she didn't have the heart to pop the bubble they'd created around them. She liked Sean. And she liked William and Katie. And it was almost time to go. "Well, we've chatted the night away. I need to settle my bill and start back toward the boarding house. It has a very strict curfew. Thank you all. It's been a wonderful evening."

She took out her wallet and Sean's face twisted in feigned insult. "Surely you don't think my mother raised me to let a woman pay for her own supper? I've already settled with Tommy."

Sorcha put her wallet away. "Thank you, Sean. I won't forget what you did for me today." She stood, and they all stood with her.

Sean slid on his coat. He knew what she was doing. "And if you think I'm the sort of man to let a woman walk the city alone, your opinion of me is worse than I feared." He nodded to his brother. "I'll see you at home, brother." He leaned over the table to give Katie a kiss on the head. "Katie, love."

Katie's eyes suddenly misted with tears. She gave William a shove and said, "Oh, move, you big ox! I need to give her a proper goodbye."

She hugged Sorcha so fiercely, Sorcha found herself feeling a bit weepy as well. "I don't want this night to end. Please keep in touch, Sorcha, dear. Come back and visit. This can't be the end of it."

William put his hands on his hips. "There, now. She's only going to bed. She doesn't leave until Monday." He looked at Sorcha. "Right? Ye've got until Monday. I have to work tomorrow, but..." he looked at Sean's face and stopped short. "I suppose that is for you two to decide. Fair enough. I'll butt out. But at least give her our phone number and Katie's information."

"I will. Now, we do have to go. She's got a curfew. Tick tock," Sean said as he pointed to his wristwatch.

"Sean, you can stay here. It's only a few blocks," Sorcha said.

"And what will you do if that she-bear of a landlady won't let you in? Do you really think old Gregory is going to arrange his plans around her?"

"She would never do that to me," Sorcha said, but she'd been concerned about that very thing ever since Maureen had left her.

"Nevertheless, I'd feel better if I was sure you got home safely. Call me old-fashioned. It may not be Belfast, but you saw today that there's still mischief pouring out of the pubs. Let's go. You can argue with me on the way."

As they walked briskly toward Kevin Street, Sorcha said, "I like Katie. William is obviously smitten. How long have they been together?"

"A little over two weeks," he said.

Sorcha stopped, and he coaxed her forward. "Two weeks? But they seem so in love."

"They are in love. Very much so."

"But it's impossible. You can't love someone after only two

weeks." Sorcha said it, but after seeing the two of them, even she didn't believe her own words. She'd seen the tenderness and love between them. It was different from the lustful glances that went on between new couples. Even her cousin, with that prat she'd brought to the dinner party, was sending steamy glances his way.

She took in the sight of Sean O'Brien, walking slowly to match her pace. The way he looked around for potential trouble. The way he held the door and had refused to let her pay for her dinner. She'd seen that tosser Gregory conveniently go to the toilet and stick Maureen with the bill. Her brother would never have done such a thing. John had the same protective nature. Old for his years. And that was only the beginning of the differences. Gregory's outfit had been too much. She looked at Sean with his thick turtleneck sweater, navy blue and setting off his eyes like a beacon. Simple blue jeans and a pair of well-loved high-top sneakers. It was simple and masculine, like he had nothing to prove.

As if reading her mind, Sean asked, "So tell me about your brother. You share a flat?"

Sean watched as Sorcha's face softened at the mention of her brother. "Yes. My parents would never have agreed to it otherwise. I mean, I am grown and capable of supporting myself. At least, I will be at the end of term. My parents bought a house about ten miles north of the city and it just didn't work for a reasonable commute. It's twenty minutes or so if you drive straight through, but the checkpoints, the parking, it doesn't work. I don't even own a car."

"Can you drive?" Sean was genuinely curious. It wasn't that uncommon for a city dweller to forego getting a driving permit.

She shrugged. "A little. We boosted my best friend's father's car one night and went on a joyride. She stole the keys, I did the driving." Then she remembered what he did for a living. She gave him a daring look from under her lashes. "Are you going to arrest me, officer?" He stopped at that.

Sean moved in close, keeping his hands in his pockets. He looked down at her, aroused by their difference in size. The top of her head came to his chest, and she'd fit perfectly against him if he held her. "Although it might be a grand time if you decided to resist arrest, it's out of my jurisdiction," he said. Her eyes flared.

Sorcha was not practiced at flirting. And she had been... flirting, that is. She was teasing him and he liked it. She liked it, too, but he was very close right now. She wasn't sure it had been a good idea to poke the beast. Then he stepped back, and she was almost disappointed.

"More importantly, I'm no hypocrite. William and I were quite the handful at that age. I boosted my father's car more than once as a lad."

She grinned. "And did he catch you?"

"Not the first time. We were very stealthy. Put it in neutral and wheeled it down the road before starting it."

"An advantage to being built like a rugby player. You can push an entire automobile. "

"We were both forwards, thank you," he said cockily.

"Aye, well I'm no forward and I've lifted a woman pregnant with twins on my own. Don't get too fat headed about it." He smiled at that, taking in her petite form. He could picture her brow furrowed with the effort. He'd like to see her at work. "Smart and strong. A useful combination."

Their conversation halted as they stopped in front of the building. She saw Sean check his watch, and she did the same. Five minutes until the curfew and her cousin was nowhere in sight. She was going to kill her. They made idle chatter, Sorcha looking down both sides of Kevin Street, willing Maureen to appear.

"Maybe she took a taxi," Sorcha said weakly.

"Why don't we knock? Maybe she's already home," Sean offered, but she could tell by his face he was just trying to make her feel better.

She walked to the door, and as if summoned from the depths of spinster hell, Miss Kerrigan opened it while her hand was poised to knock. "You have two minutes. She's not sneaking through the window this time either."

Sean spoke then. "I don't believe we've met. I'm Officer Sean O'Brien of the Dublin Garda. It appears Miss Mullen will be without accommodation tonight if her cousin is running late. Is it possible that you could bend the rules for this nice, law-abiding lass? She's far from home and..."

The stupid cow slammed the door in both their faces. Sorcha darted down the steps and looked both ways. No one in sight and no taxis. "Damn that girl. She really has had a moral decline since I last saw her." Then she winced as she heard the bolt slide home on her accommodation.

Sean didn't bat an eye. "Well, let's wait a few more minutes. If she doesn't show, she's probably not going to. If she told you she crawled through the window, she may think that's an option."

"She wouldn't do that. She wouldn't just not come home with me visiting," Sorcha said with diminishing confidence.

"Well, since you know her very well, we'll wait an hour and then I'll call the station." His eyes were tranquil, but she wasn't fooled for a minute.

"You think you're clever altogether, don't you?" Those fists were back on her hips. "You can go, Sean. I'll wait for her. You shouldn't have to stand here all night." He said nothing, which infuriated her even more. "Is this the part where you offer to take me to your place?"

He didn't bother with feigned offense but said calmly, "No, we'll wait. I've got nowhere to be. She's probably running late." After five minutes in stressed silence, she smacked him on the arm. "What was that for?" he laughed.

"That was for being so bloody agreeable. You know damn well she isn't coming and you are just patiently waiting me out!"

"Well, I am a patient man, Sorcha, but don't push your luck." His voice grew more animated as he continued. "Aye, I don't think she's coming. Aye, I think she's probably piss drunk and content to leave you to your own devices. Aye, she'll likely have her ankles pinned behind her ears by old Greggy-boy before they both pass out. And aye, I wasn't going to say all of that because she's your cousin and it wouldn't help your mood. But, since you seem the sort to push a man to the breaking point, Sorcha Mullen, then yes... I'm. Waiting. You. Out."

She turned away from him, frustrated and angry and knowing he was right. She exhaled and nodded to herself. "I'll go to a hotel. I'll just call a cab."

"I'll take you. There's no need to call a taxi," he said.

"You've fulfilled your gentlemanly obligation. I'll handle this." She paused, as did he, as a cab came into view. When it passed by them, carrying a passenger that wasn't Maureen, Sorcha ground her teeth and screeched out an angry, high-pitched growl. Sean just went and sat on the steps in front of the boarding house. Almost lazily, he said, "A hotel and a taxi at this hour is going to cost you about fifty pounds. And that is for a dodgy hotel. The hostels are likely full, but we can check. And it's communal living. You'd just have a bunk in a room full of broke, smelly backpackers."

Sorcha put her head in her hands. Then she ran her fingers through the auburn waves, gripping tight to contain her frustration. "That is nearly all the money I have with me for this trip. I'm going to kill that little trollop."

He continued, "And I wouldn't take advantage of you in this situation by trying to take you back to my place, despite your unkind accusation. I'm a stranger, more or less, and I would question your judgment if you did agree to it. I would never lay a hand on you, but you don't know that. I'll pay for the hotel. Come on, love. It's cold. Let's go call my brother. He and I share a car. He'll bring it here, and we will figure something out."

"You already paid for dinner. You are not going to humiliate me by paying for my hotel room. I'm not poor," Sorcha said pissily.

"I didn't think you were, Sorcha. I just want to help." His voice was so gentle, it did her in. She turned to him.

She took in his face, the anger leaking out of her. It was replaced by tenderness for this beautiful, caring person. "You're a good man, Sean O'Brien." She struck on a thought. "How about this..." she said before she lost her nerve. "Collect your car and just stay with me. Show me something that's better at night. Show me a Dublin I'd never see otherwise. I mean, you don't have to work tomorrow and…" She started doubting herself. "It's okay, we can try the hostels."

The smile she got was worth all the headaches Maureen had caused. "I'd love to show you around town. Are you sure? You must be knackered." He approached her now, slow and steady. He could call Katie, but the thought of staying with her was too tempting, so he didn't offer it outright. When he stopped, he smoothed a hand over her hair.

Sorcha's heart pounded as their eyes met, and she thought he'd kiss her, but he didn't. "I want you to be safe. I wouldn't sleep a wink until I was sure of it. If that means keeping you with me, then I'll do it. I just don't want to push you in a direction you aren't comfortable with. I'd love to show you Dublin. Truth be told, I'd love to get in that car and drive you to my cliffs. Show you the small village where Willy and I grew up. I don't like that cousin of yours very much right now." Another idea came to him. "Sorcha, you know I'd drive you home, right? You could send for your things later. If you want to leave, I'll take you. It's your choice. You're in control."

She searched his eyes, knowing that he meant it. He'd get in the car and drive her to Belfast this instant if she asked it of him. "I don't want to leave. I'm enjoying myself. I don't want my holiday to end like this. Maureen is a chit, but I wouldn't have it be over."

He nodded. "Then let's start with the car and a drive around town. You've already blown your curfew most scandalously." He grinned, rubbing a thumb along her cheek. "I'll show you parts of my city that are much better at night. We'll take it an hour at a time."

She smiled at that. A whole night out with him. He really was breathtaking to look at, and his voice was a sexy, smooth baritone, but it was the eyes that did her in completely: blue, like the sea on a foggy morning. "Thank you, Sean. That sounds perfect altogether."

Sean had trouble breaking away from looking at this woman's face. Beautiful green eyes and that wavy, auburn hair. Her sweet, curved lips were shaped perfectly to draw a man's gaze. Pale, creamy skin that continued down the column of her throat. He didn't know what good deed had earned him this reward, but he was going to make the most of it. An entire night with Sorcha Mullen was going to change his life. He knew it down to his bones.

They drove for hours. Sean knew all the secrets of Dublin. He'd lived here for eighteen months, working a lot of night shifts. He knew all the people who ruled the city after dark. Security guards, all-night petrol stations, and twenty-four-hour corner stores. They drank instant coffee out of takeaway cups, and he showed her everything.

Their first truly daring adventure was when he gained access to the catacombs under Christ Church by bringing the night-watchman some pastries. It was still, dank, and perfectly eerie. She walked lightly like she'd wake the dead otherwise. She came across an old stone sarcophagus, most likely unearthed decades ago and put on display within the bowels of the church for theatrical effect. The top was removed and splayed alongside it as if some supernatural force had raised the occupant from the dead, and the corpse could be walking just up ahead, dragging one foot. She loved the spooky element as she let her imagination take flight. She peered inside just as Sean growled behind her, catching her around the waist. Her ear-shattering scream was followed by a few unladylike, juicy curses that made Sean belly laugh in her ear until they were both overcome with fits of laughter.

"You're a devil, Sean O'Brien. Ye nearly gave me heart failure!" She'd have seemed a little more believable if she hadn't been in snorting, laughing hysterics a minute earlier. His eyes sparkled with mischief, his face flushed from laughing. He was absolutely breathtaking, and that's when she knew she was in very big trouble.

After the catacombs, he drove her to see the various statues around the city. Then he illegally parked and took her across the Ha'penny Bridge. She giggled as he took her hand, running over and back on the arching bridge, and then jumped back into the car with a wave to the parking services officer. He also took her to places where he'd had some big arrests, but he never let her get out of the car, as if he was afraid the stain of evil deeds would somehow reach out and hurt her. At their final stop, he got a blanket out of the boot, and they left the car parked on a spit of land called Howth. They walked for a long time. She saw lights from the port and the stacks from the powerhouse where the steam coiled out and then slowly dissipated in the night sky. As she swept her gaze along the coastline, she caught the flashing illumination of a nearby lighthouse.

When Sean began to lead her up the path to the lighthouse, she shivered with excitement. The keeper was likely asleep, so he walked her around the great, expansive base of the towering structure, then spread the blanket open and around her shoulders. They sat there, silently taking in the vast sea, illuminated by the city lights. At this view, she could very well have been on a ship. "You're right, Sean. This wouldn't be the same during the day. It's just what I wanted. Thank you."

"You haven't seen the best part. Just wait a while. It's going to be perfect," he said, almost on a whisper. So she did. She didn't even feel herself doze off, so warm was she in the shelter of the blanket and the heat they shared under it. She woke when he nudged her, probably an hour later. "It's almost time," he whispered like he was telling her a great secret.

She looked ahead just as it started. Her throat was tight with emotion—the sun was coming up. "Now it's perfect," he said softly. But when she turned to see his face, he wasn't looking at the sunrise, he was looking at her. "I knew it would be."

"You knew what would be perfect?" she asked. His eyes were so sincere when he answered her that it nearly stopped her heart.

"The sunrise on your hair," he said with a smile. Then he bent and kissed her. It was soft and sweet. Undemanding. Yet it was like a lightning strike. She trembled as he pulled away. Then he came back to her, winding his hand in her hair. He spoke to her, whispered words against her mouth that she couldn't understand, but affected her, nonetheless. It was more to do with the reverence in his tone. The wanting and tenderness he spoke to her, with his voice and his lips. The kiss went on and on, small aching noises coming from her throat. He finally broke away, his breath harsh against her neck. His voice was strained. "I'd better get you back, love. The curfew is lifted at the boarding house. We'll check to see if she's back." With that, he stood and walked her the long way back to the car.

Maureen was back and extremely hungover. It was Sorcha's angry shrieking that woke her after she'd ignored the knocks from her landlady. She came to the front door in her clothes from the night before, smeared makeup and all. The landlady barked at her before Sorcha had the chance. "You've broken the latch on the window, for pity's sake. That is it. I've had enough of these antics of yours. You've been warned repeatedly, Maureen. If you leave without causing trouble, I won't call your parents. They write the checks, so I have a mind to do it anyway, but I'm giving you a chance to slink away quietly. By noon and not a minute later."

Maureen looked at Sorcha, the tears starting. Sorcha snapped, "You don't have time for that. Stop this instant. Get dressed and start packing." She turned to Sean, who was tall and stoic as he watched. "Maureen, where should we go? We need to get relocated so Sean can go home."

"We can go to Greg's. He's got a townhouse," she offered with a weak shrug.

Sean butted in then. "Aye, and how many male roommates does he have? Where would she sleep?" he asked, not sparing her an angry tone.

"Five. But I think they have a sofa." She tried to muster a smile.

Sorcha groaned. "I love you, Maureen, but you really are an idiot. I'll change my bus ticket and head back today."

"Please don't! My mother will talk to your mother, and they will want to know why you left so early!"

This was the final straw for Sean. "Jesus Christ, woman! Is that all you're worried about? You left your cousin with virtual strangers last night, stayed out all night even though you knew she'd be turned away! You are unbelievable."

Sorcha put a hand against his chest. "It's okay. I'll just go back early."

He shook his head. "You shouldn't have to. I'll see what I can do. If I can find you a nice place to stay until your departure, would you stay? I'll start with Katie. You liked Katie, yes?"

"Sorcha, I'm so sorry." Maureen looked like a whipped dog.

"You weren't sorry last night when you left me without a bed to sleep in!" Sorcha said, spitting the words like gunfire.

"I thought you'd end up sleeping at his place! You seemed to be getting on. Jesus, Sorcha, I said I was sorry."

"You're sorry? For what exactly? Insinuating that I'd shag some man I just met, so that you could be free to go home with that badly dressed, pompous fecking prat!"

That's when Maureen slammed the door in her face. Sorcha screamed, "I need my clothes, you selfish cow!" Then she was back, opening the door and tossing her luggage on the front step. "And my mother won't need to call her, because I'll tell Auntie exactly what you've been up to!"

It took a while for Sorcha to calm down. Sean just drove quietly, finding his parking garage and unloading her things. "You can shower and take a nap. I'll call Katie. She's staying with a friend, but the girl is very nice and won't bat an eye. She's rarely even there."

"Thank you, Sean. I'm sorry." Her voice sounded so small. She was humiliated.

"You're welcome. And you have nothing to apologize for. She's obviously not the girl you knew. I can't believe that little..." He bit back the nasty name he was going to call her and said, "I can't believe she'd ever considered being a bride of Christ. Are you really going to tell her mother?"

She rubbed her temples, suddenly exhausted. "No, I'm no snitch. I'm thinking I won't have to. Despite what she said, I am sure the landlady will be eager to tell her mother how many times our young Maureen hasn't come home."

Sean was opening the door to the apartment, and she saw that his shoulders were shaking. "Are you laughing?"

He let it go, then. "I'm sorry. It's not funny, but... *badly dressed, pompous fecking prat?* It was too perfect." Sorcha smiled, then let out a little giggle. He said, "I think I fancy that look. I might get myself one of those shirts. Do you think they come in men's sizes?"

"Stop trying to cheer me up. This is a mess." She was smiling when she said it.

"It's not a mess. It's the better plan. Going home was a terrible idea." He kissed her on the forehead, leading her into the flat. "Are you hungry?"

"No, just knackered. I'd love a hot shower and a nap on your sofa."

"You'll not take the sofa. You can take my bed. I'll have William's room. We both need some real sleep. The linens in the bath are clean. Use whatever you need."

Sorcha took her bag into the bathroom, took a quick shower, and put on her nightgown. When she came out, she was a little embarrassed. A full-length flannel nightgown with long sleeves and a high neck didn't exactly scream sophistication, but it was Irish flannel and deliciously soft after so many washings. He approached her, taking in the get-up.

"I wasn't expecting anyone to see me in this but my cousin. I'm sorry. I can't fall asleep in my clothes. I've had them on for over a day."

He fingered the sleeve, his eyes intense. "I like flannel. It's soft.

And you're beautiful in anything, Sorcha. Now go on. Sleep as long as you like. I'll be getting up in four hours."

"Thank you again. Did you call Katie?"

He smiled. "I did. You have a pull-out bed for as long as you need it. Her roommate left for the weekend and said it was fine. Go on, now. Lie down before you fall down. You can lock the door if it makes you feel safer."

"I feel safe with you. My mother would have a stroke if she saw the predicament I was in, but I feel safe."

"I like your mother already," he said, and he closed the door behind him.

Sorcha came awake to men's voices. She'd fallen asleep hard, having had only five hours the night before. She dressed quickly, made the bed, and tried not to think about how good that pillow smelled. Heaven. He smelled like heaven, spicy and masculine. She'd slept like the dead, but the last thoughts had been about that kiss. She'd never been kissed like that before. She'd never been affected by a man's kiss so completely. He hadn't kissed her since. In fact, it had taken great effort for him to pull himself away. Now, after some rest, her mind was clearer. Exactly what did she think was happening here? She had a life in Belfast. The last thing she needed was to get hung up on someone who lived across the border. The complications of this entanglement were insurmountable.

She thought about William and Katie, and her shy confession that she couldn't imagine living in Dublin full time. Were they doomed as well? Or would William transfer out, leaving his brother here? She didn't think so, and it made her sad. Two wonderful men, too far out of reach to consider anything long term. She shook her head, pushing her thoughts aside. It was only a kiss. And if she got more kisses, they'd be a fond memory for the days on which she needed something good to think about.

. . .

Sean's whole body went into overdrive as Sorcha emerged from his bedroom. He'd had a miserable four hours in William's bed. All he kept thinking about was that kiss. About the sun on her hair. About that damned nightgown. How could something so conservative and downright granny-like be such a turn on? She'd slept in his bed, and he'd done the honorable thing and left her alone. He'd be the worst sort of bastard if he had tried something. They were alone in his flat, and she had no place to stay and no transportation. He was raw from the restraint, and one kiss would have led to him being less than a gentleman. Less than she needed.

"Good afternoon, Sorcha," William said. He was still in his uniform. Sorcha was expecting him to say something stupid about her sleeping in their flat, but he didn't. All she saw in his face was kindness and genuine affection. "I heard about your cousin. I'm sorry for it, but I'm glad you'll be with us longer. Katie's over the moon about having you stay with her. She's out buying nail polish and snacks and likely dusting off her records. She's got a thing for American music."

Sorcha was blushing under Sean's gaze. She said to William, "It's very kind of her. I'll have to find a way to repay her. Maybe I could make dinner? Does she have a proper cooker?"

"Yes, she's got a small galley kitchen, but it has everything you need. She's on her way over right now. She just lives a few blocks away—for now, anyway."

"When she's done with her fashion course, how will you deal with the distance? She's across the country." Then she thought about how that sounded. "I'm sorry. It's none of my business."

"A couple of hours in the car and a ferry ride aren't enough to keep me from my girl." His smile was so genuine when he talked about her, it made Sorcha feel good for having known them both.

"Well, I think this worked out just fine," Sean said. "What are your plans today, after you get moved to Katie's? Is there anything else you'd like to see?"

Sorcha thought about it. "There's a chorus group having an

open practice at St. Patrick's at four o'clock. I think I'll take a walk around the city and end up there."

"Would you mind some company?" he asked.

"No, I wouldn't mind. Don't feel like you have to. I don't want to interrupt your whole weekend. You've all been so nice."

Sean didn't dignify any of that with a reply. If she thought he'd rather be anywhere but with her on his day off, he was going to have to make his intentions a little clearer. Not with words, but with actions. Then something occurred to him. "Are you a musician in between catching babies?" Sean felt a wave of pleasure at the thought.

"Yes, actually. My mother taught me piano and fiddle, and I've been known to sing in the privacy of my own flat."

The two men exchanged glances and Sean said, "That's quite a coincidence. Our mother teaches piano. Not so much anymore, but she used to give lessons. She taught us and Maeve when we were still in nappies. What are the odds?" Sean shook his head.

Sorcha said, "Well, I suppose it's a good job to do from home, if you've got babes underfoot." Before Sean could reply, there was a knock at the door. Katie came inside, and William gave her a chaste brush of the lips. Then she came to Sorcha, a genuine joy and anticipation plain on her face. "We'll have a grand time, you and I. We'll eat chocolates, play records, and tell secrets." She gave William and Sean a direct look. "No boys allowed."

"Sorcha wanted to go to St. Patrick's for the rehearsal evensong. Why don't we bring back some takeaway before you toss us out in the cold?"

Sorcha reminded him, "No, I want to make dinner. I'll go to the grocer's on the way back, then I'll make us all something."

Katie said, "I love that idea. A real night in. But we still need our girl time. The lads will get tossed out on their ears after dessert."

William caught her around the waist. "You seem eager to be rid of me."

"Oh, aye. We're having some new fellas over as soon as you're out the door." He tickled her and she squealed.

"Take it back." More squealing. "I can do this for days. Take it back."

"Okay, I take it back!" she said, laughing.

He kissed her soundly on the lips. "Okay, that's better. Now I'm off and back to work. I'll see you all at six."

SIX

Sean led Sorcha out of the church, putting a hand on the small of her back to guide her through the nave and out the front entrance. He was happy about the peaceful smile on her face. These cathedrals had changed hands so many times, fluctuating with the politics of the time. And sadly, some of the most beautiful cathedrals were not Catholic, but Church of Ireland, the Irish branch of the Protestant Church. They were breathtaking, however, with stained glass, dramatic arches, and beautiful artwork. The type of acoustics that made the chorus sound like angels who had come down to earth, stirring the soul. "Do you sing in the church chorus at home?"

Sorcha shook her head. "I haven't got the time, I'm afraid. I work dreadful hours. The training for midwifery is intense. I was trained as a nurse first, and I thought I wanted to work in emergency medicine. But the first baby I ever delivered hooked me for good. Giselle Aurelia Ramsey, six pounds and two ounces. She had the fine, black hair that some babies are born with. Lively dark eyes."

"A silkie babe, aye. Do you remember every child?"

Sorcha nodded. "I keep a journal. I remember them all. Even the ones I held after they'd left the earth. Especially those."

"Does that happen a lot?" he asked sadly.

"Not on my watch. There have been a couple of cases where the child was already gone when the mother came into the hospital. Some miscarry early on, though. In those instances, there's nothing to be done but hold her hand. It's terrible, but I try to be more than a nurse in those circumstances. I treat them how I'd want to be treated. Learning from nuns has its advantages."

"And now that you're at the Royal Jubilee? Do they have Anglican nuns and priests who are in service to the hospital?"

"Yes, they do. Mostly Anglican, but yes. And there are things there that can be obtained, that you wouldn't get from a completely Catholic hospital."

"You mean birth control? How do you contend with those conflicts?" Then he thought better of it and said, "It's too personal. You don't have to answer."

"It's okay. I'm a nurse and a midwife. It's a fulfilling life. But my practice doesn't mix with politics. If a woman wants to control how many children she has, and there's a safe alternative that I can offer her, then it's my duty to put her needs above my own. I would never condone terminating a pregnancy, and my superiors would stand by that decision, but if they want to discuss family planning, I will aid them."

Sean thought about that for a long while, and he felt Sorcha's appraising gaze on him as they stood at an intersection. She walked forward. "I see I've shocked you. Well, I suppose it's easier to see the matter as black and white when you don't have to live with the consequences."

Sorcha's face flushed with irritation. She marched across the intersection, ignoring him as he called her name. Then he stopped her by firmly taking her elbow. "Would you slow down, woman? You aren't giving me a chance to even think."

"What's there to think about? You're here in Ireland where some small village priests would still send the lass to a convent and then take her baby away and adopt it out to another family without her permission. I'm a good person, Sean O'Brien. I'm an even better midwife. And I'll be damned if I will ever tell a woman no to condoms or a diaphragm or even a tubal ligation referral if it's going to keep her from ending up with another mouth she can't feed. You don't know what it is like to see that kind of poverty!"

He leaned in, pissed off in his own right. "You think I don't know about starving kids and the woes of a broken woman? Well, let me tell you something, Sorcha Mullen. You don't know shite about what I've seen! You think because we don't have bombs going off on the street corner, or weekly protests, that Ireland doesn't have its own hard cases?" He snorted. Then he was the one to walk off in a huff.

Her voice was soft. "You're right." He stopped, not turning around for a minute. "You're right, Sean. What I said wasn't fair, and I'd like to hear your stories. I'm sorry, I get defensive about my work."

He turned around and stalked back to her. "You get defensive about a lot." She lifted her chin and the corner of his mouth turned up. She was adorable. "I don't think less of you, Sorcha." He looked down, hating some of the memories he had in his mind. "When I was new to the Garda, I went to a call of a DOA. That's a…"

"Dead on arrival, yes. I know."

He gave a nod. "Yes, I suppose you would. Anyway, they thought it was a homicide. It wasn't. It was an eighteen-year-old girl who had bled out from trying to do it herself. She was pregnant." He swallowed hard, the gore fresh in his mind. "She'd used something to…"

Sorcha understood, putting her palm on his arm in comfort. "I understand, Sean. Jesus, what a thing to see. I've never dealt with that, and I hope I never do. I'm sorry. I wish I could take that memory away from you."

"She was barely out of a school uniform. She died scared and alone because she had no one to turn to. You're the only one I've ever talked to about it. I had nightmares for weeks." His eyes closed at the onslaught of memory.

He felt her take him into her arms. "Thank you for trusting me with it." He pulled back, finally looking at her face. He cupped the back of her head and kissed her between the eyes. Then he started down a narrow alley.

She didn't follow. She said, "You haven't touched me since we left the lighthouse." There was a question in her voice.

"I know." He inhaled, fighting himself. "This thing between us, it's powerful. I couldn't touch you while we were alone in the flat. You know I couldn't. I ached to touch you. To curl up with you in my bed and feel that soft nightgown. To smell your hair and your skin. But I'm not that strong, Sorcha. It had to be nothing."

"You can't tell me you've never been with a woman, Sean. I'll not believe it."

"But you haven't been with a man. I wouldn't take advantage of you like that," he said firmly.

"You can't possibly know that!" she said, pulling her eyes away from his gaze.

He came so close, she felt his breath on her hair. "I can know that," he said more softly.

"Was my kiss so amateur?" she snapped at him, starting to feel a wave of embarrassment.

So he did the only thing he could do. He pulled her tight against him and kissed the hell out of her until she felt the brick of a building behind her. His hands were in her hair, his hips fused to hers. She moaned against his mouth. He took her mouth in waves, his firm lips so skillful that it made her knees weak. His tongue tasted her. She could barely stand as he held her. That's when he pulled his mouth away, his arousal brushing her as he did. He tilted her head to look at him. "You see? Now do you see, you stubborn, pushy, little peahen! I'm ready to lift your skirt right here in the street. I can't be trusted if we get started. If I felt less for you, I could. But I can't. I'm desperate for you, Sorcha. My whole body aches to get inside you."

Sorcha was completely addled. Her heart was pounding and she was flushed with arousal. He pulled her face closer, such wonder in his eyes. "You should see how beautiful you are right now. You can't imagine how beautiful you are to me."

And suddenly she knew he was right. She rested her forehead on his chest. "Sean, you don't understand. Where can this possibly lead? I leave in two days. You're right, I am not experienced. And in two days, you and I will be light years away from each other."

"It's two hours, Sorcha. It takes me longer to drive to my home-town. And there's the bus that you can take to come here. This doesn't have to be it for us."

"It does. This weekend is all we can expect, Sean. You and I exist in different worlds. I have my work and you have yours. This is doomed to fail. Come Monday, this will end, whether we like it or not."

He took her hand, leading her down the road. "You're wrong, Sorcha." He said the words without hesitation. "This is just beginning."

Sean looked ahead as he felt her warm, small hand in his. The tenderness that rolled through his chest nearly made him want to tear up. He barely knew her, but he felt the pull just the same. The rightness of her hand in his. Of sharing meals together and sitting next to her in a church pew. Of kissing her like his life depended on it.

He remembered the night William had met Katie. His brother had looked shell-shocked. Now Sean understood it all too clearly. He'd just have to make her understand it, too. This wasn't a weekend fling for him. She was as stubborn as a pint-sized mule, however. Words weren't enough. He had to show her. Convince her with the only thing she seemed to respond to. The heat between them was like nothing he'd ever felt before. They were going to be perfect together.

Sorcha and Sean washed the dishes as Katie put on another of her records. She had loads of American music, a lot of Motown and folk music mixed with just a little rock and roll. Right now, she and

William were slow dancing to *When I Need You* by Leo Sayer. Sorcha watched them, feeling her heart squeeze in her chest. She looked at Sean, who was watching them as well. His heart was in his eyes. "They're beautiful together, aren't they?" she said.

"Yes," he answered. His voice was rough with emotion. "It's enough to make you believe in love at first sight. He knew, you see. He knew the first night he met her. She was his mate."

"His mate? That's a bit animal kingdom sounding, isn't it?"

He just smiled. "I suppose it would sound odd to an outsider. It's what we've called it in my family for centuries. We've got a long history, does the O'Brien family. As do you." He changed the direction of the conversation to her. "The Mullens come from the O'Maolin clan in County Cork—I'm sure you know that." Sorcha nodded, conceding the point. He continued. "There's a legend about the men of my line, passed from one generation to the next. But that's a tale for another time, I think. If there is another time."

"Are your parents like that?" she asked, motioning to Katie and William.

He smiled. "Oh yes." He put the drying towel down on the counter. "But that's an even longer story and also for another time. Come, love. Dance with me." He held his hand out to her and she took it, letting him lead her into the living room.

As they lost each other in the ending to the song, Sorcha forgot everything but him. The height and width and strength of him consuming her every sense. The song ended, and she heard Katie take William out the front door. They said something about pulling the car around. But all she saw was Sean. His hand was at her back, the other folding hers against his chest. He looked down at her, his gaze growing hungry.

It was she, this time, who initiated the kiss. She pulled his head down and his mouth came willingly. The kiss was soft at first, and then it wasn't. It was deep and silky as he slid his tongue against hers. "Sorcha," his voice begged, pleaded. It said, *please, stop this, because I can't. Please don't stop this, because I need you.* He waged war with his body and his heart.

To hell with that, Sorcha thought. No way in hell was she stopping this. She wrapped her arms around his neck until she was practically dangling off him. He moaned and lifted her at the waist. He had her against the wall in a flash, his hips pressed into her as he lifted her hands above her head, holding them shackled at the wrist with one big hand as he fused their bodies together. He kissed her neck, her collarbone, then back up to her mouth again.

Then they heard the doorknob jiggle. A little too vigorously, like Katie was sending off a warning bell before she came inside the flat. He pulled away with a curse. "We need to stop." It almost killed him to say it. Sorcha kissed him again, rough and demanding. Then she pulled away as she savored his bottom lip.

"You're right, Sean. This isn't done between us."

"You look like you're ready to do murder, brother. What happened in the five minutes I left ye alone with her?" William said, fascination warring with humor on his face.

"She is the most frustrating, stubborn... Why are you laughing?" The look Sean gave his brother could have pierced his flesh.

"Jesus, she's the one. I knew it! You've got it bad, brother," William said with a self-satisfied grin that made Sean want to punch him. "What's the matter? This is a good thing. Won't she have you, then?"

"That's not the issue. The problem is I think she would have me." Sean rubbed his eyes, suddenly spent from the strain of this battle with himself.

"What do you mean? She seemed..." William searched for the right words. "A bit untried for someone her age. Katie said she's twenty-one."

"She is. I mean, she hasn't. But she's a passionate woman, nonetheless. There's a fire between us. Jesus, William, I feel like I could burn up from it."

"Then what's wrong? It sounds like a good problem to have."

Sean answered, "The problem is that she's headed back home

on Monday with the idea that this is our only weekend together. She's not looking for an entanglement, William. She says we're doomed to failure. I can't just have her and let her go. It can't be like that. If I have her, I want all of her." He looked at his brother. "Have you and Katie talked about the future?"

"Not really. But we will. Soon. It's gotten serious, and she needs to know how I feel. I can't hold it in anymore. I feel like I'll burst if I do. She's got a few more weeks here, then she'll go back to the island and settle in for the winter. She's it for me, Sean. *Mo mhuirnín dílis*. I don't know how to breathe without her."

Sean understood. The thought of Sorcha leaving on Monday made him break out in a sweat. He cared about her. He didn't like the idea of her riding back over that border to a life which didn't include him. They'd only just found each other.

SEVEN

Sorcha sat with her back propped against the sofa, her legs stretched over the pull-out mattress. Katie climbed over her, settling in after changing the record. Their fresh toenail polish was drying and they were both in their pajamas. Katie said, softly, "Can I tell you a secret, Sorcha? I mean, can I tell you something without you judging me?"

Sorcha turned, setting down the magazine she was using to fan her toes. "Of course, Katie. Anything."

Katie took her arm in hers and linked them. "I don't have a good relationship with my sisters. I mean, they're okay and all. It's just, I'm the youngest. They're all married and starting families. They wouldn't understand this."

She tightened her arm, giving Katie a reassuring squeeze. "Go ahead, Katie. You can tell me anything."

"William and I made love last night. Sean had called him and said that he was going to drive you around the city. He told him what happened with your cousin. And, well, we finally did it. We were together."

Sorcha smiled, patting her hand. "How did you feel afterwards? Are you happy that you did?"

Katie's smile was so sweet. "Oh yes. He was so..." She blushed, not having the words to explain.

"Attentive?" Sorcha offered.

Katie giggled. "Yes. He was. He was gentle at first. The things he makes me feel, I can't even describe. It's wonderful. And when I was ready, we came together. I love him, Sorcha. I know it's a sin and I should've waited until I was married. My parents would be so disappointed. But I love him. And I think he loves me, too. It was a perfect night. I can't bring myself to regret it."

"That's good, Katie. That's how every woman's first time should feel."

"Have you ever done it?" Katie pried.

"No, I'm afraid I haven't found my William," she said. "I'm very focused on my career. I love nursing, so I don't want anything to mess that up. I don't want to do something that can't be undone."

"You mean like getting pregnant?" Katie asked. Sorcha nodded.

"Have you thought about how to avoid that, Katie? I know you love him, and it seems like he feels the same way, but it's only been a couple of weeks. You need to be careful if you're going to continue to be together. Did you use any... methods?" she asked as tactfully as she could.

"Well, he didn't finish." She struggled over the words. "I mean, he did, but not..."

"Do you mean the withdrawal method? He pulled out of you before he ejaculated?" Katie's face turned crimson. "I'm sorry, Katie. I'm a midwife. I'm used to using blunt and precise language." Katie just nodded. "Yes, well, that's good, but it's not reliable. I know you can't get birth control very easily down here, but there's another way I can tell you about in addition to the withdrawal method. Times to avoid during your cycle. It's still not foolproof, Katie. You need to know that. Something like condoms would be better."

"I can ask him, but those things aren't easy to get. They want women to be married and have a doctor's prescription. It'd be so embarrassing to ask him."

"Katie, if you're close enough to him to make love, you are close enough to discuss birth control."

Katie sat up, lifting her chin. "You're right. I'll talk to him. Until then, could you tell me more about the times to avoid?"

"Yes, I can. Do you have a calendar?"

They talked for hours, Katie asking questions and growing more comfortable with the conversation. They talked about their hometowns, their families, and Sorcha shared stories about her work.

"I think what you do is amazing, Sorcha. What a beautiful calling. The women in Belfast are lucky to have you. Do you ever get scared, living so close to the trouble?"

"Sometimes I do, but it's my life. I can't stop living it because of bloody-minded men. Most of the time, I am safer than most. When I go into a building to visit a patient, I'm greeted with gratitude and respect for the service I provide. Incidents like this..." She motioned to the fading bruise on her cheek. "This is a rarity. Most of the time, they're pouring me tea and sending me away with homemade biscuits."

"Sorcha, you know there's work for midwives in Dublin." Katie's face was so hopeful, it made Sorcha want to cry.

"I know, but I have a life in Belfast. My brother, my parents nearby, my colleagues and patients. It's enough. For me, it's enough. I can't be derailed by romance any more than I can be derailed by the fighting and violence in my city. I'm almost done with my training, and I will make a life that fulfills me."

Sean walked toward the building where Katie and Sorcha were staying, William alongside him. "I'm going to take Katie back to our place. It'll give you this last evening alone with her. Maybe that's what will make the difference. Take her to dinner and then go down to the Strand and walk on the beach. Convince her, Sean. You can't let her go without a fight."

"I know that!" Sean snapped. Then he sighed, eyeing his brother. "I'm sorry. I didn't mean..."

"I know you didn't. She's a stubborn woman. That red head of hers is no lie. And it's better me than her. She'll take it out of your hide if you snap at her like that—it's one of her better qualities." William's grin was playful. "She seems quite the handful."

"She is. Christ, she's stubborn."

"You would know. Like minds and all that."

Sean's mouth turned up at that. He couldn't help but wonder how all of that fire would translate in the bedroom. He wasn't going to say that to William, however. They rang the bell for Katie's apartment, and she unfastened the window above. "I'll be down in just a minute!"

She came down, opening the secure door to let Sean in the building. "She's ready. She borrowed a dress from my roommate's closet. Hold on to your hat." She gave William a swift kiss and they were off.

Sean thought Katie had prepared him for the sight of Sorcha, but he was wrong. When she opened the door, the breath shot out of him. Holy God. He stood there stupidly, until she started fidgeting nervously. "I borrowed it. If it's too much I can just change."

Sean took one step in and shut the door. All he managed to get out of his mouth was, "Shut up, woman." Then he was on her. She softened against him, letting him take her weight in his arms. "Jesus, Sorcha. You're so beautiful." More kissing, desperate kissing. "How in the hell am I supposed to leave this flat with you looking..." He couldn't even finish the sentence. He kissed her again, until he couldn't kiss her anymore. Until neither of them could catch their breath. Until he had to stop or he'd drag her to the closest bed, honor be damned.

He broke the kiss, backing up until he hit the wall with his back, getting himself away from her for a moment. The sight of her was almost too much to bear. The dress was a deep forest green, snug, wrapped across her and tied at the side. It showed every curve. Reaching just below the knee, it also showed a beautiful pair of legs. She'd even worn low heels.

"You are the most beautiful woman I've ever clapped eyes on," he said hoarsely. And she was. Her hair was auburn waves that spilled over her shoulders and kissed her breasts. Her skin was ivory, from her fragile, heart-shaped face and graceful neck to the skin that smoothed down her collarbone to her chest. She'd pinned the dress at the V so as not to show her cleavage, but he knew it would be creamy swells of heaven. Her stomach would be smooth and soft. She took a step toward him, and he pushed himself off the wall, side-stepping her. "I'll just get your coat."

Sorcha was convinced that Sean O'Brien was the strangest man she'd ever met. He was also, ironically, the sexiest. It wasn't something he'd own or admit to. He didn't try. He just was. Big, strongly built, too handsome for any woman's peace of mind. And much to her frustration, he was a gentleman. He fought his urges gallantly, and won. Not one in twenty men could make that claim. Most of them were all too happy to help a woman out of her knickers. Even a virgin. She hadn't expected him to react the way he had. She hadn't dared hope for it. She wasn't sexy, she knew this. She wasn't tall, leggy, or blonde. She didn't look like those American models every young man had on their bedroom wall—Farrah Fawcett or Cheryl Tiegs. She was short and pale with red hair that was neither curly nor straight. She'd been called cute. On a few occasions she'd been called pretty, but no one had ever made her feel sexy until now. She slid her arms into her coat and turned her face up to his. She grabbed his ears and brought him to her, nose to nose. "Thank you, Sean." Then she kissed him sweetly.

He smiled against her mouth. "For what?"

"For making me feel beautiful."

He brushed her mouth, his breath shaky against hers. "You are as you are, mo chroí. I've done nothing." He kissed her once more, then took her hand and led her out the door to dinner.

. . .

Dinner was perfect, Sorcha reflected. Sean was a wonderful storyteller. His recollections of antics with his brother were comical. It was obvious that he was the more serious of the two. William was a bit wilder, more charming, and a hell of a fighter when it was called for.

"I couldn't ask for a better wingman. We had to fight to stay together on the force."

She said, "I'm close to my brother as well. It's probably different, though, for two men. It's not like he's going to discuss women with me or back me up in a pub fight. But he's mature for being younger. He's..." She paused, looking down at that scar on her arm. "He's my hero."

Sean followed her gaze, reaching across the table to take her wrist. He ran a thumb over her scar. "How did you get this?"

She wasn't going to tell him. The story was an awful one. And Sean had little true understanding of life in West Belfast. He'd grown up in a small fishing village. "I tripped and put my arm through a windowpane. He treated the wound until the ambulance came. He was very brave." She felt sick about lying to him, but he didn't want to hear the truth. It wouldn't serve either of them.

"Well, he should have gone into medicine like you did." Sean didn't let go of her wrist, and his smile warmed her.

"He should have done a great many things. He's smart. I wish he'd quit that blasted mill. There's always trouble between the union and the owners. The working conditions aren't what they should be."

Sean withdrew his hand when the waiter brought the bill. "Would you like to go for a walk? You're not dressed for the beach, but I have a blanket in the boot of the car."

"That sounds heavenly."

. . .

They'd discussed everything but the subject that was on both their minds. It was maddening. Sean had tried to guide the conversation, only to be thwarted by this stubborn, pigheaded peahen at every turn. He couldn't take it anymore.

"Now that you've got the layout of the bus terminals, discussed your favorite biscuits, and commented on the weather, can we just get down to it?"

Sorcha stopped short, her eyes defiant. "I don't know what you mean."

He cupped her head, pulling her face toward his. "Sorcha, why are you doing this?"

She shut her eyes. "Sean, we've discussed this."

"No, we haven't. You've decided for both of us. Is this how it's to be with you? You decide and I stand like a helpless sap and have no choices?" He let her go, walking ahead. "If you don't want me, Sorcha, you should have just said so. I'd still have helped you. You would still have gone to Katie's and we could have just…" He shook his head. "We could have parted ways."

"That's not why I'm with you, Sean! You know it isn't!"

"I don't know anything. Actually, that's not true. I know that you have no reservations about walking away. I know that whatever I'm feeling is one-sided. Other than lust, that is. I feel that from you. I'm familiar enough with it. I thought at first…" He cut off the words. "It doesn't matter. It's getting late. I'll see you home." He walked toward the car park.

"Sean—" But he cut her off, slicing his hand through the air. After that, she was silent. The drive back was tense.

He parked in front of Katie's apartment building. He was angry, but he still got out of the car and opened Sorcha's door. He said tightly, "Goodbye, Sorcha." She paused in front of him. "I can't do this. I can't pretend, even for you."

"You don't understand, Sean."

"You're right, mo chroí. I don't." He didn't look back as he pulled away.

. . .

Sean felt mortally wounded as he opened the door to his flat. William stood, his face grim. "I can't talk about it right now, Willy. I just can't."

"I'm sorry. Katie just called. She said Sorcha looked just as bad. Apparently, she's in the bathroom crying with the water running. She thinks Katie can't hear her."

"Of course that's what she'd do. God forbid she take any comfort or advice from anyone." His words were bitter, but the news that Sorcha was crying didn't offer any sort of victory.

William put a hand on his brother's shoulder. "Work starts at eight. Goodnight, Seany. And maybe we should go home during our next days off. I could use some time away from Dublin and I think it would do you some good as well. I want to introduce Katie to Mam and Da." Sean nodded, heading to his own empty bed.

EIGHT

An ounce of mother is worth a pound of clergy...

—Rudyard Kipling

Aoife O'Brien knew both of her sons better than they knew themselves. O'Brien men weren't skilled at hiding their feelings, whether they be steeped in joy or misery. She said, "Your brother seems very happy. Do you like Katie?"

Sean started, coming out of the haze he'd been in long enough to answer her. "I do. I adore her. It's a good match—he loves her and she him. A man couldn't ask for more."

"Or a mother. I'm of the age where I'll start to see my children pull away. I'll have to give them over to another woman. Or man, in Maeve's case. Eventually, you'll all find your way to your mates."

"Well, one out of three isn't bad. And I'm sure some likely lad will sweep Maeve off her feet when she's a bit older."

"And what about you, Sean? You haven't told me her name."

His eyes darted to her. "Have you been talking to Willy?"

"No, I'm afraid you sufficiently sealed his lips—not that I didn't try. What else but a woman could put you in such a state?" his mother said.

"Aoife, leave the lad alone." Sean's father came into the kitchen, refilling his cup from the kettle and stealing another biscuit.

"Like your father left you alone? If I remember correctly, his advice was for you to *get your arse back to Donegal and don't come home without her*. Do I have that right, my love?"

David smiled at her. "Close enough. I wasn't as stubborn as this one. You have to trust the process, Aoife. Trust the process and it'll all be grand in the end."

Sean spoke up at that. "Can ye please stop talking about me like I'm not in the room? And what bloody process would that be?"

"The blood, sweat, and tears it takes to finally get the girl. O'Brien men like pigheaded women. Don't look at me like that, Aoife. You can't deny it was a good bit of fun fighting it out." Sean caught a flash of humor in his mother's face.

Sean said, "What about William? He and Katie haven't had any issues. It was easy for him. Are you saying she isn't his mate? Because I won't hear it. They're perfect together."

His father thought about that. "Aye, I have to say he's been rather lucky, and she's definitely the one. Let's hope it stays that way." Sean didn't like the look on his father's face. It was a quick flash of something that looked like foreboding. Then he hid the expression behind a smile. "Now, whoever this lass of yours is, best start laying on the charm or Maeve will end up beating you to the altar."

As if summoned, Maeve came through the kitchen. "Don't count on it."

Sorcha pulled the chicken out of the oven, then moved aside for her mother to inspect it. "Maybe ten more minutes, love. Thank you. You know I love help in the kitchen."

Sorcha mustered a smile, but Edith Mullen knew her daughter. It didn't reach her eyes. "Are you going to tell me the whole of it? What happened in Dublin last week?"

"You heard enough from Auntie, I suppose. Maureen is back in Cork, and Dublin was a failed experiment." Sorcha hated the lie. Her mother was no idiot.

"Yes, I know all that. I also heard about the bruise on your face. When were you going to tell me that you were attacked by a patient?"

"It wasn't a patient. It was her bastard of a husband." Sorcha accepted the admonishing look. "Sorry, but he was an awful man."

"You're very brave, my dear girl. Sometimes too much so. You have no children, yet. When you do, you'll understand how I beat myself up every day for not selling that flat."

Sorcha's eyes shot to hers. "You can't, Mam. Please. John and I both need a place to live. The work is in the city. That's the reality."

Edith said, "I won't. Not yet. But if there's another incident like this, you'll have to relocate. I understand that you're almost done with your studies. After your training is finished, you won't need to live right in Belfast. John could easily find a roommate at the mill. I want your word that you'll be safe, and I want you to stay open to alternatives once this final stage of your training is complete. Promise me, Sorcha."

Sorcha thought about Sean, and she felt tears prick the corners of her eyes. She turned away. "I promise."

"Now, tell me what sort of bastard has broken your heart." Sorcha had just taken a sip of tea, and she spit it across the space between herself and the cabinetry, leaving a brown splatter like a crime scene.

"Mam, really. I know you're trying to relate to me woman-to-woman, but the profanity doesn't suit you."

Edith gave a one-shoulder shrug. "It got your attention. Now, tell me who's got you in such a sorry state. I can feel the sadness rolling off you, my sweet girl. Only a man can put that look on a woman's face. Who is it and what's he done? Is it a doctor at the hospital?"

She gave her mother a long, calculating look. Edith was a

wonderful woman, honest and strong. She'd always celebrated Sorcha's independence. She also had a rock-solid marriage. Not perfect, but loving and true. So, Sorcha started from the beginning. She started at Granny Nan's tea shop and told her everything. Well... almost everything. She left out the searing kisses and knee-buckling temptation to toss her well-protected virtue at Officer Sean O'Brien. If he hadn't been so damned restrained, she may have done just that. It was scandalous, even for her forward-thinking, independent mother. So, no. She didn't tell her everything. She did, however, decide to give her one glimpse into the sort of man that Sean was. That kiss. The first one at the lighthouse. He'd stayed out all night with her, been an absolute gentleman. Then in one perfect moment, he changed her life forever. She could search Northern Ireland to every guarded border, and she'd never find someone who looked at her the way that he had when he said, *I knew it would be perfect... The sunrise on your hair.*

Her mother actually sighed like a schoolgirl. Then something occurred to her. She laughed. "Katherine Minola. Well, now, that's promising."

Sorcha folded her arms over her chest. "And how, pray tell, is that promising?"

"He's assessed that temper of yours, and he's still smitten." She cocked her head. "Dublin is not so far, Sorcha. He seems a good sort. A lot of men would have taken advantage of that situation. A Garda officer, you say? Well, that's something, isn't it? I don't see the problem."

"The problem is, I don't want a relationship right now. Especially one that will take me out of the city when I'm at a crucial time in my career. This opportunity is grand, Mam. I was chosen for this and I'm working with some world-class doctors. I can't get distracted."

"It's not like he's proposed, Sorcha. If you like him, don't push him away before he even has a chance."

Her mother didn't understand. Sean was a force. Her pull to him was visceral as well as physical. She already felt like she'd been gutted. They'd spent one weekend together. If she kept this thing between them alive, she was doomed. Her mother read all of this and more in her face. "Well, well, I see." She squeezed Sorcha's hand. "You are in trouble. It was the same for me, when I met your father. It was like a bolt of lightning. Then the hum of electricity that was always there, even after the strike. My poor girl. You are in a pickle, aren't you?"

Her mother did understand, at least partly. "Well, I won't tell you what I think you should do. You've always needed to sort these things out in your own time. You won't be pushed. I'll just say this. That sort of connection is rare, Sorcha, dear. Most would treasure it. And doing without it doesn't seem to have made you happy."

Sorcha walked the familiar lane, feeling her palms start to sweat even though it was late October. She stopped at the familiar blue door, steeling herself for whatever treatment she was going to receive from her patient. Sinead was a sweet, quiet woman with a gentle manner, but Sorcha's good intentions had ended in Mr. Fitzpatrick being jailed for assault. If he hadn't been well-respected in his trade, he'd have been fired. Lucky for him, his union lawyer had stepped in, pro bono, to get him a reduced sentence. Ten days in jail and probation because it was a first-time offense. That part was laughable, given the abuse he regularly heaped on his wife. It wasn't Sinead who answered the door, but the older woman who'd driven the getaway car that afternoon of the assault. "Hello, Nurse Mullen. Please, come in."

She led Sorcha up the stairs, talking over her shoulder. "We were afraid we'd scared you off. Sinead is resting, but you're welcome to wait and see the baby. I'm helping her until she is ready to leave." She opened the door as she said it, and Sorcha was surprised to see that there were boxes in the living room. "She's not taking much. Just things that were her own, before she moved in with him."

"I don't understand." Sorcha's throat tightened, wondering

how much her interference had destroyed. "I didn't mean to cause so much trouble. I just wanted to protect her."

"And you did. She knows that, deep down. She's going to stay with her sister across town. It's not the first time she's left. I'm just hoping she'll stick to it this time, for the sake of the child." She left the room, and that's when Sorcha heard the cooing sounds of a newborn. She knew that Sinead had delivered a healthy little girl, and Sorcha's tears finally surfaced as she took the tiny pink bundle in her arms. "Oh, you are a beauty, aren't you? Yes." She hadn't even noticed when the old woman had gone down the hall, leaving her in the apartment alone with Sinead and the baby. When she returned, she had company: five other women whose faces were familiar. Some had been patients, some she'd just seen in passing.

A dark-haired woman with kind eyes spoke for all of them, as Sorcha took in the heaping basket of goods. "We wanted to say thank you. For Sinead and for all the women in this district. It's not much, but we all added something. There's Mary's jam, and some strong tea from me, and Bridhe put in some homemade bread. There's some face cream and a pack of pretty hair ribbons." Sorcha's vision blurred as she became overwhelmed by the simple gifts. She didn't relish humping that large basket onto the bus, but it was so very kind that it took her aback. "Some don't have anyone to rely on other than other women. We just wanted you to know that we all admire and appreciate you. Our menfolk, too. They'll likely beat that wee mongrel half to death when they let him out of the gaol. There are certain people who are protected, no matter what the trouble. Our men would no more strike one of our midwives than they would a nun."

Sorcha wiped her eyes and noticed she wasn't the only one shedding tears. "I know that. And thank you. I'll treasure every bite and every drop."

She left, wondering if Sinead had just been hiding from her. They'd assigned another midwife to do the home checks, but she had just hoped to see her one more time. It didn't matter. Maybe her neighbor had been right. Maybe this time she would stay gone, for the sake of the child. And if she didn't do it for that little girl, Sorcha wasn't sure she wanted to know.

Sorcha was exhausted as she walked away from the bus stop, ready to be done with the day. The hospital ward had been outrageously busy today. She'd delivered one baby on her own, without a physician's aid, but instead with the help of another nurse. She'd also assisted on another birth, in addition to her regular prenatal appointments. She liked being busy. The last week and a half would have been murder, otherwise.

He hadn't called. She was such an idiot. She'd taken Katie's information both in Dublin and on the island, promising to write to her. She also had phone numbers. Some silly, traitorous part of her had hoped Sean would ask for it. That he'd reach out and call her, even though she'd given him no reason to hope. It was ridiculous. She wasn't a tease. She'd meant what she said at the time. She'd foolishly thought that once she was back home, the blissful bubble they'd created around their small group would prove to be just that —a bubble that was not based in reality. That the spell Sean O'Brien had worked on her would be broken. But it hadn't happened. Now she was heartsick, missing him, and cursing herself. She reminded herself repeatedly that he hadn't called. Obviously, the distance had worked for him, if not for her. She supposed that was a good thing. She certainly wasn't going to call him. She had her pride. She'd made her bed. She was going to lie in it. Or not, in this case.

She had two more home visits and she'd be done for the day. Something in the air had triggered multiple labors. Some midwives blamed the moon and others the weather. Low pressure storm systems were notorious times for early labor. No sooner did the thought occur to her than the heavens opened up and a downpour unleashed on her head. *Blast.* She'd left her umbrella in the hospital locker room. Of course she had. She opened her coat and put her midwifery bag close to her chest, running through the alley that led to her next appointment.

She was met by two things in rapid succession. The first was a familiar shriek. The next was a door flying open, a ten-year-old boy named Oliver pulling her in unceremoniously. "What is it, Oliver?" Stupid question, but he'd caught her off guard.

"The baby's coming! I was just going to the phone on the corner," he said.

"Hold off, love. Let's see what we have before you call an ambulance." Sorcha tried to sound calm, but the shrieks told her all she needed to know. Then she opened the door. Mrs. Kelly was close. Too close. "All right, now. Let's get you to the bed and have a look. When did your pains start?"

She took that inopportune time to break her waters all over the living room carpet. The woman gave her a panicked look. "The others weren't like this. It's in my back. I thought at first I'd twisted it."

Back labor. Damn. That could be painful. "Come now, Mrs. Kelly. Let's go have a lie down and let me check you."

"It's not moving as much today. It's got me worried."

Sorcha said, reassuringly, "The baby is getting into position. He's likely resting before his journey. Now, when did the back pain start?"

She groaned. "Around lunchtime. Maybe five hours ago?"

Sorcha helped her recline, then removing her undergarments, she looked between the woman's thighs. Dread washed through her. "Okay, dear. I'm just going to have Oliver call the hospital. You don't have a phone?"

"No, the line has been broken for two years. There's one on the corner. What's wrong? Why are you not checking me?"

"Just a moment, dear. That's it." She patted her knee. "Don't get up. I'm just going to ask you to get on all fours with your rear in the air. Do you understand? Get on your hands and knees like..."

"The way I was when I ended up in this condition? I'm gonna

kill him!" Sorcha swallowed her reply. She helped the woman get into position, then left the bedroom.

"Oliver, is your father nearby?" Sorcha asked.

"No, ma'am, he's in London. The baby wasn't supposed to come until next week."

Idiot. Sorcha bit back the word. "Are you a good reader, Oliver?"

He nodded. "Yes, I'm the best in my class. I get all high marks."

"Okay, that's a good lad. I need you to call this number." She took the paper out of her bag that had the number, staff names, and a place for comments. She'd made these after the first time she'd had to play a game of telephone between the hospital and an untrained and hysterical family member. "Can you read this?" She held it out to him after filling it out.

He read, "Female, thirty-nine weeks pregnant, pro..." He looked at Sorcha.

"Prolapsed cord."

He continued, "Prolapsed cord. Send an ambulance." His eyes shot to Sorcha's.

"Be brave, my lad. Go on. And tell Dr. Stirling to prep for surgery." The boy's eyes almost broke her heart. "She's okay, Oliver. Run now. I won't let anything happen to her or the baby. Hurry, lad." On cue, his mother screamed.

Sorcha ran back into the bedroom, glad to see her patient was being compliant. The bulging, pulsing cord was visible like a discolored organ. The woman screamed at her, "I want to push!"

"I'm right here, love. I'm sorry, Theresa, but I'm going to have to insist that you don't push." Sorcha's voice was so calm that it caused the mother to be suspicious.

"Something's wrong." She was quiet now. "Tell me." Her voice was thick with pain and emotion. "Is it dead?"

"No. Your baby isn't dead." She wasn't sure about that, but she wasn't going to even entertain that possibility. "Your baby didn't descend far enough into position within the birthing canal. When your water broke, the cord came down before the baby. It's why you have to stay in this position and why you can't push. It will cause the baby's head to restrict the umbilical cord, and cut off blood supply to the child."

The woman started to weep and Sorcha said, "No, Theresa, don't do that. You have to stay alert and calm. We are going to make sure your baby is just fine. I am going to help you, but you must listen to me very carefully."

When she explained what she had to do, the woman's eyes bulged. "You've had a baby before this one. This is going to be uncomfortable, but it will work. You have to relax and trust me. Can you do that, Theresa?" This was tricky business out of the confines of a hospital. The surgical team wasn't one floor up on the elevator. Sorcha scrubbed her hands thoroughly, then put on her gloves. "Bum as high as you can get. That's it. Now, I'm going to put my hand in, and I know it's not going to be comfortable, but it is the only thing to be done until we get you to the hospital. I won't let go, my dear. As long as this takes, I will hold this position and protect the child. Once the next contraction is done, tell me to go."

The next one was seconds later and had the woman moaning and whimpering. "It's done." Her voice was pain-laden and exhausted, like the fight had gone out of her. The urge to push had to be terrible. Sorcha slid her hand to the left of the cord and into the mother's vagina. The poor woman hissed at the invasion. "Easy, Mam. Relax as much as you can. I've almost got it." She felt the woman's cervix around the child's head and wedged a hand between the head and the compressed cord. She'd only ever seen this done, but she didn't have time to doubt herself. A sigh of relief came out of her as she made room for the cord to expand. The child's head was as warm as the mother's body. She said a silent prayer: *Please let this be enough.* She felt the next contraction. They were so close. Dammit. Oliver made an appearance in the door and choked on his horror at the scene before him. "They said ten minutes, Nurse Mullen. There's a roadblock the short way."

"Of course there is!" She snapped the words and immediately regretted it. "I'm not mad at you, darling. You did a fine job. Your mammy would like a bit of privacy. If you could go to where the lane meets the road and guide them down, that would be so helpful. You're so brave, Oliver. Your father would be proud."

Theresa had gone to some place in her head, breathing slowly, fighting like hell to stay still and not succumb to the urgency of her labor pains. Sorcha's back was killing her as well, her wrist and hand bruising against the woman's pelvic bones and the need to keep the pressure off that cord. She was really going to have to start exercising more. Her muscles were already tired. "Breathe slow and deep, Theresa. You are doing so well." The woman shook with pain as the next contraction stole her breath.

Sean went through the next bloody checkpoint, cursing this blasted city and all these hell-spawn barricades. Directions were useless when you had to keep detouring. He finally found the place where John Mullen had agreed to meet him. He gave a wave, and the younger brother of Sorcha Mullen got into his car without hesitation. He'd thoroughly vetted him on the phone, finally insisting that he'd meet him and escort him to the hospital where Sorcha worked. Sean had pointed out that this wouldn't do if Sorcha left from her home visits and returned straight to the apartment. John had been unbending, however. He wouldn't guide him to their flat. Given the fact that Sorcha only had a postbox for an address, he was at the boy's mercy.

"Sean O'Brien. It's a pleasure to meet you, John. I've heard a lot about you."

John shook his offered hand as they pulled forward. "I can't say the same. Turn left just there." He pointed and Sean obeyed. "Sorcha didn't mention any copper boyfriend."

"I'm not her boyfriend. We are just friends and I'm here because it's rather important. She's coming up on her days off. We need her in Dublin."

"Need is a strong word, Sean." This kid was extremely paranoid, and he understood it. Sorcha was mistrustful of uniforms, and it made sense that being a police officer wouldn't put the lad's mind at ease. "One man's need is another man's wish. You've got five minutes. Once she hears you out, if she doesn't see the emergency, you're on your way. I won't have you pestering my sister or following her home."

He was starting to like this kid. "You're a good brother. She told me as much."

"Did she? And what did she say?" John asked.

"She told me you were her hero." Sean's smile was respectful, not mocking in the slightest.

"Sorcha told you about what happened?" John seemed surprised.

"She told me about when she sliced her arm open on a windowpane. She said you treated her and called an ambulance. I know some grown coppers who swoon at the sight of blood. Full marks, John. Truly." A look shifted in the young man's eyes, and Sean started wondering if there had been more to the story.

"Up about half a mile on the right. Park in the patient area to the left of the ambulance chutes."

Sorcha was shaking, her whole body tight with purpose. When the paramedics had tried to get her to remove her hand, she'd almost hissed at them. Thank God Dr. Stirling had thought to send Angelina in the ambulance. *She can't. Her hand is the only thing keeping the baby's head off the cord. You'll have to transport them like this.* Now they were screaming through the city streets as fast as they could go in downtown Belfast.

When they pulled up to the emergency entrance, Dr. Stirling was waiting at the bay doors. "Jesus Christ," he muttered. "You're very hands on, Nurse Mullen. Now, why don't we get you out of there?" *There* meaning the ambulance or *there* meaning her patient's birth canal, she didn't know.

She said, "I've got the child's head in my palm and off the cord. Angelina says the heart rate is good. Mrs. Kelly has done marvelously, but it's time to get this child out. Is the operating theater ready?"

The paramedics worked without pause, bringing the gurney down while Angelina held Sorcha steady. That's when she saw Dr. Childs come through the bay doors. "Jesus, Nurse Mullen. You do like to stir up trouble, don't you?"

It was a statement, not a question. Dr. Stirling let out a whoop. "Off to the races!"

John spoke to the nurse in charge, charming as much information as he could about his sister's whereabouts. Then he approached Sean. "She's on her way in an ambulance. Apparently one of her patients is in trouble." They walked toward the emergency wing and had just reached the main intake area when the bay doors leading to the ambulance chutes burst open. John and Sean almost called out, but then froze, jaws dropped. Sorcha was utterly focused, not even seeing them. She was yelling, "I'm not leaving you, Theresa. I'm rock steady back here."

Sean looked at John and shook his head. John said, "Did she just have her arm up that woman's..." He put his hands forward. "You know what? It's better I don't know." But Sean knew, despite the hospital sheet covering the woman's business end, that Sorcha was in some sort of birthing crisis. Her face had looked like a warrior's. Intense, focused, ready to do battle. Jesus, what a career she'd chosen.

Sorcha was rolled into the operating theater, adrenaline high. It was just in time. Her fingers were starting to go numb. If she couldn't feel, she couldn't know for sure that the cord was being protected.

"Sorcha, it's okay. You can pull your hand out. We're going to get this patient under anesthesia. Everything is ready." Angelina's voice was soft. "Dr. Childs, I think she's going to need you to stand by."

Sorcha didn't understand until her arm was free and she tried to get off the cot. She started shaking then, her muscles completely spent. She had trouble even standing. They got on either side of her. "I want to assist."

"You aren't sterile, Nurse Mullen. And we can't let you have all the fun. You're going to put us all out of a job," Dr. Childs said lightly, knowing how hard it would be for her to abandon her patient after what they'd been through. "It's time to rest, Sorcha. You did well. Like a seasoned professional."

"Don't try to sweeten me up, doctor. I'm not as frail as I look."

He chuckled as he helped Sorcha out of the room. Once they had her seated, he slid off her glove and examined her wrist. "That's going to be bruised, I think, but no harm done. How long were you like that?"

Sorcha looked at her watch and answered, "Twenty-one minutes."

"Well, you can skip your exercises this week." He turned to Angelina. "How did you know she'd need help walking?"

She smiled and Sorcha saw the stars in her eyes for this man. "My first prolapsed cord was during a home visit as well. I was in that position for a while, but I think Nurse Mullen has broken my record."

"Bloody roadblocks," Sorcha murmured.

"Well, you two are a regular pair of superheroes. I'll have to buy the first round if we ever get the same night off." Was he flirting? Sorcha took in his face. Oh yes, he was definitely flirting. She'd done a little fact gathering. He was only twelve years Angelina's senior. She wasn't on his staff or under his training program. Nothing inappropriate to stand in their way. Another nurse came then, interrupting. "Nurse Mullen, your brother is here."

"John? That's odd. I'm not that late. Thank you, Janet. Tell him I'll be right out. I just need to get cleaned up." She looked down at her uniform. Blood smears. "I'll at least wash my hands. Give me three minutes."

She stood, stretching her neck and removing her other glove. "I'm off for the next two days. Call me and tell me..." The words were still on her tongue when the theater nurse poked her head out. "The doctor wanted me to tell you that the baby is perfect! No problems."

Sorcha croaked, "And the mother?"

"She is stable. Well done, Nurse Mullen!" Then the nurse retreated into the surgical room.

Sorcha walked into the waiting room, looking for her brother, and froze. Holy God. Was she hallucinating? Sean O'Brien was standing by the soda machine, buying her brother a cola. She looked a fright. She should have changed! She should have fixed her hair. Sean glanced up and his face was tight. The greeting died on her lips. He didn't look happy to be there.

"Hello, Sean. This is a surprise." She looked at her brother.

"He called the flat. I wasn't going to let him come looking for you on his own. You never mentioned you met a man in Dublin." His tone was just a little accusatory. "Says he's a copper."

She gave Sean an apologetic look. "Yes. A very good one, actually. It's okay, John. He's not a pervert or murderer. I'll be fine."

John eyeballed Sean. "Yes, well, see that he gets you home soon. There is trouble brewing tonight."

She nodded. "Aye, the ambulance had to detour around some new barricades. We'll be home directly."

John left, and she just stared after him. "I didn't think I'd ever see you again." Her voice was hoarse. She gazed at him and his face was grim. "What is it, Sean?"

"It's Katie. She's a mess. I don't know what's the matter, but she said she wanted you. She's not a hysterical woman, so it must be serious."

"Katie? Why would..." Then she stopped the words. *Oh, Katie.*

It could only be one thing. "Take me to the flat. I'll need to pack a bag." She stopped, looking down at herself. "Wait, I need to get a few things."

Sorcha was back in a few minutes, carrying a medical bag, her purse, and a heavy coat. "I'm ready."

They headed toward the flat, Sorcha directing him west through the streets of Belfast toward her side of the separation walls. Sean looked around, taking in the scenes anew. Military vehicles, armed men, pedestrian and vehicle checkpoints. There was a public bus being boarded by two soldiers carrying weapons. "Has that ever happened when you ride the bus?"

"At least once a week." She said it so matter-of-factly that it caused him to look at her. She seemed so tired.

Sean changed the subject. "Was that woman in distress? It seemed like you had..."

"My whole hand and wrist in her vagina? Yes. A prolapsed cord. The baby didn't descend, her water broke, and the cord came ahead of the baby. Very dangerous for the child because the cord becomes compressed and cuts off the blood flow. They're both fine. A Caesarean is the only safe method of delivery in that circumstance."

"And you were holding the child away from the cord?" He noticed her discolored skin and said, "Your hand and wrist are bruised. They're going to have to start sending you to those home visits in protective armor."

"I missed you." Her words sounded pathetic to her own ears. "I had no right to, but there it is. I missed you. I know you didn't come here to see me, but I wanted you to know. I didn't want you to think that our time together had meant nothing."

Sean had stopped at a light. "I missed you, too. Like a chest wound. Every day. Every night."

Sorcha put her hand in front of her mouth, her eyes tearing. "I don't know what to do, Sean. I can't think right now. All I know is that I don't want to feel the way I have for the last ten days."

"We'll take it one week at a time, Sorcha. That's all we can do."

He pulled forward with the traffic, smiling wider than he had in days. Then he took her other hand in his.

NINE

Sorcha slept the whole way. Sean had given her a jumper of his to use as a pillow, and she was out in seconds. She was a fighter, but the stress and physical demands of her job had left her exhausted. She came to just as he was parking.

"This is your place?" It wasn't a question really, more a statement of surprise.

Sean answered anyway. "Yes. Willy didn't want her to be alone. She cried herself to sleep. I can't imagine what's got her so upset. The only thing I can think of is... maybe she's got another fella. But then why ask for you?"

"Katie loves William. That can't be it." She said nothing else, the unease coiling in her belly. She and William had only been together a month, but that's all it took when you were in love. Sorcha noticed Sean was staring at her. *Trying to read my mind, blast the man.* But she was not going to speculate.

Sean unloaded her overnight bag and noticed that she still had her medical bag with her. She watched the realization wash over his face. His eyes darted to hers, but he said nothing. They walked up to the flat in silence.

Katie was still asleep. Sean took Sorcha's bags and put them in his room. "I'll sleep on the sofa, I think." He paused. "I just would feel better if we all stayed together. I think Katie needs it."

Sorcha went into the darkened room, hearing Katie stir. She looked up from the bed, her face caving in on itself. A sob broke out of her. Sorcha went to the lamp, turned it on, and closed the door behind her.

She sat on the edge of the bed and pulled Katie to her. "Oh, Katie, please don't cry. You're going to get me started."

"I can't help it." She hiccupped the words.

Sorcha rubbed her back. "Then go ahead, love. I'm here. You cry all you want. When you're ready, we'll talk."

It was a few minutes before Katie regained her composure. Wracking sobs shook the bed. Finally, she sat up and Sorcha handed her a tissue. Katie said, "I tried. I did the counting, and I talked to William. The last week or so we did use something. He managed to get some..."

"Rubber condoms? That's good. I know that wasn't an easy conversation. Can you tell me what has you so upset?"

"I'm late, Sorcha. I'm four days late. I'm never late." The hysteria was creeping back into her voice and Sorcha tried to stay calm. *Pretend she's your patient.*

"I see. Well, when we talked about the calendar and your ovulation cycles, I'm afraid that the first few times you were together weren't ideal. I couldn't turn back the clock for you, so I decided not to cause you undue panic. Perhaps this is just stress."

"I thought so as well. My breasts are sore, but nothing has come," she said miserably.

Sore breasts were a sign of menses, but also of pregnancy. "Katie, the best way to handle this is for us to test your urine. It's the quickest way. And I think you should tell William. He's really suffering out there. If you get this news, negative or positive, I think he should be by your side. If you love him, then you need to walk this road together."

Katie took her hand. "I'm so glad you're here. I feel stronger with you beside me. You're like a sister to me, more so than even my own blooded sisters. Does that sound silly? I mean, we don't know each other that well."

"Love of a kindred sister isn't much different than loving a man. Sometimes it happens fast. It isn't silly, Katie, I feel the same way about you." The two women hugged, Sorcha offering her new friend some courage for the conversation to come.

Sean and William stood up as soon as the two women opened the bedroom door. Sorcha's throat was thick with emotion as she watched William take Katie in his arms. He looked at Sorcha, giving her a silent thank you. Sean was quiet, but they must have talked when Sorcha left them.

"Whatever it is, Katie, I love you. Forever." Sorcha gave him a pitying look. Then he pulled back to look in Katie's face. "Are you pregnant, Katie? Is that what's got you so upset?"

"I don't know." Katie started shaking, as if the words being spoken had unleashed a fresh wave of terror.

"Can we find out today? Do you have something with you, Sorcha?" he asked calmly.

"Yes. I have my test kit. We'll give Katie a bit of privacy in the toilet and then I'll do it."

She watched Sean go to Katie then. He said, "I'll leave if you want."

Katie said, "There's no point, now that you know. I'm so ashamed, Sean."

Sean put his palm on her shoulder and tipped her chin up. "You've done nothing to be ashamed of, Katie, love. You've made my brother happy. You've loved him. We will not abandon you, mo deirfiúr." Then he gave her a brotherly hug.

Katie went into the bathroom and Sorcha asked him what it meant. "My sister. I called her my sister." If Sorcha wasn't already half in love with him, that sealed the deal.

Sorcha set up her mobile test kit, test tubes, a dropper, and the beaker of Katie's urine. When she looked up from the test, after she'd done her magic, her face was as calm as she could make it.

Sean knew as soon as he looked in Sorcha's eyes. She'd gone into her professional mode. Jesus wept. This was unfortunate. He'd fancy being an uncle, just not like this. Not with Katie's fearful eyes watching every move. "The test is positive, Katie. You are pregnant," Sorcha said gently. She gave her a little smile, but it didn't help.

Katie looked at William, expecting him to be as terrified as she was. Or worse, cold. Like he wouldn't claim it or something. Instead, they all saw something in his eyes that they hadn't expected. A warm smile and the misting of tears. He got off the couch and knelt in front of Katie. "We're going to have a baby."

"I'm going to have a baby. I'm going to bring shame on my family." Her face was tight, getting ready for William to retract the warmth and run for the hills.

"No, Katie. We are. You and I. I wouldn't have had it happen so soon, my love, but I can't bring myself to be upset. I love you, Katie Donoghue, and we're going to be a family."

Sean and Sorcha left for a walk, leaving them alone to talk now that the worst was over. William was so positive, so supportive. Katie shook her head. "You don't understand. My community is so small. It's not my parents. It's the others. It's not like Dublin. Those people would send their daughters off to a convent and the nuns would take the baby and adopt it out. I'm not saying my parents would ever do that, but they would be shamed by the community were it to get out. People would stop going to the shop or buying livestock from my father. This is going to ruin them."

William said, "Then we'll get married before anyone finds out. I'll put in for a transfer to County Clare or one of the neighboring counties as soon as I can manage it. We'll tell our parents tomorrow. I won't hide it like we did something wrong, Katie. This is our baby."

"They're going to be so disappointed," she said.

"Aye, well, if either one of them wants to take a swing at me, then I guess they're entitled," he said resolutely.

Katie's eyes were so sad. "I love you, William, but I never wanted to trap you into marrying me. I didn't want it to happen like this. I'm so sorry. I feel like I'm ruining your life."

"It's not your fault, Katie. I was the experienced one. This is on me. I should have been more careful. Besides," he said with a grin, "how do you know I didn't trap you?"

She smiled, nudging him. "You're an eejit."

"But I made you smile." He kissed her hands. "And I'll keep doing that until we are old and grey. Katie, I knew I was going to marry you after the first night we met. I was just letting you warm up to the idea."

She kissed him then, soft and sweet. It whirled into something more heated and urgent, a tangible need that bound them together. He picked her up and took her to his bed.

Sean walked alongside Sorcha, breathing in the crisp air of autumn. St. Stephen's Green was mostly deserted. "It's enough to make you forget you're in the city. This is a lovely walk." Trees towered overhead, and there was a calm, natural pool that gave the park a soothing feel. Despite the surroundings, things were a bit tense and unnatural. They hadn't parted well, and in the wake of that, she wasn't sure how to behave.

"It is a lovely walk," he said, uncharacteristically awkward. "What are you thinking right now?"

Sorcha kept her slow pace, staring ahead. "I'm thinking that this was harder than the patient with the prolapsed cord. I knew how to fix that. I could take action. I don't know how to help with this."

"You are helping by being here. She didn't have to go into the hospital and do this alone. Was it your idea to tell William before the test?"

"Yes. He loves her, and she shouldn't have to bear this alone."

"She won't. He'll marry her. You know that, right? He'd marry her tonight if he could."

"And your families? How will they treat her?" Sorcha really wanted to know. There was no accusation in her tone.

"William has met her parents twice. It's difficult this time of year. The ferry will stop running from our dock this week. It'll run sporadically out of Galway for another month or so. I'm not sure how we are going to pull a wedding together, but we'll do it."

"But how will they treat her?" Sorcha repeated.

"My family will support them fully. And I can only hope her family feels the same. William says they're good people."

"That's good. Katie's young. She's going to need the support."

He said, "She's not that young. People get married all the time at our age." Sorcha shrugged, conceding the point. Sean stopped, putting a hand on a large old tree. "This tree is a sort of lovers' spot. It's been here for over a hundred years. It's said that if you pass the tree and don't kiss your sweetheart, you'll be cursed."

"Sean O'Brien, you've just made that up!" Sorcha was laughing now. His eyes were as mischievous as a boy's as he pulled her to him, covering her mouth with his. The kiss was playful at first, but that didn't last. He had his hands in her hair, leaning his back against the tree.

"Christ, I missed this. I missed you." He deepened the kiss and Sorcha was lost, consumed by the passion that she'd tried to turn her back on, but hadn't been able to let go.

Katie and William were gone when they returned to the apartment. When Sean started making the bed on the sofa, Sorcha used the time to ready herself for some much-needed sleep. When she came out of the bathroom, Sean had been expecting a whole lot of flannel. He was surprised to see her instead in a pair of track pants and a boxy fleece jumper.

"Springfield Junior Rugby?" His eyes held amusement. "Let

me guess. Your brother wouldn't let you out of the house with that nightgown?"

Her grin told him everything. "I'm not sure he believed me about not staying here, but it's not like flannel is the new lace. I don't understand it."

"Don't underestimate how fetching you look in that gown. It's soft and feminine. I've been thinking about it ever since. I look at you now, and I can't help but see your brother's disapproving face. An idea that wasn't lost on him, I assure you."

She put her hands on her hips. "My little brother has little to say on the matter."

Sean took her by one wrist, folding it behind her and pressing it against her back, a show of dominance as he lowered his head and took her mouth. It was deep and possessive. His other hand cupped her face, rubbing a thumb along her jawline.

Sorcha felt his hard arousal against her belly. Her hand smoothed up his chest, feeling his heart thundering through his shirt. His muscles were thick and smooth, and she knew without seeing them that he'd be magnificent without his clothes. Her body responded, wanting more. She moaned his name as he kissed down her neck. Then he broke away, cursing. "Don't pull away, Sean." She leaned back into him, brushing up against his hard cock.

His hips jerked. "Sorcha, we need to stop."

"Just because I'm a virgin doesn't mean we can't do anything. Why does it have to be all or nothing?" He raised a brow at that, his eyes lighting up. His grin was devilish as he kissed her again. She squeaked against his mouth as he palmed her ass and pulled her up to wrap her legs around his waist. It was followed by a very feminine sigh.

Sean struck on an idea as soon as the words came out of her mouth. She was a virgin, yes. And he absolutely would not take her fully unless she understood that it would be forever. He'd never been with a virgin, and he wouldn't be unless he intended on marrying her. Just like William would have never slept with Katie if he didn't feel the same.

Sorcha was bloody-minded. She'd fought this connection tooth and nail. One thing that worked to his advantage was that she was curious about her own sexuality. She also wanted him as badly as he wanted her. There was an emotional connection, yes, but the physical pull between them was a force all its own. This was how he'd get to her. This was how he'd win her forever. He'd make her crave him to the point of madness while he waged war with her stubborn spirit. He'd seduce her body on the way to winning her heart. He didn't have to take her virginity in order to do that.

He closed his bedroom door with his foot, never letting go of her hips. His cock was hard and thick against her core, and her kisses became more urgent. He started with a slow urging of his hips as he guided her up and down against the ridge of him. He knew right where she needed him, and she shuddered against his mouth, making urgent little noises. "Feel me, Sorcha. Feel what you do to me." His voice was hoarse as his own arousal grew edgy.

He took her down to the bed, his hips moving and seeking. She broke the kiss and arched against him. That's when her brother's shirt got tossed out of sight. She slid her hands up his shirt tail, grazing her nails on his chest. His hips pressed against her as she slid the T-shirt over his head. He nuzzled her nipple through her bra and she pushed a hand in his hair. God, he wanted his mouth all over her. He wanted to taste her lush arousal, but he had to take this slow. He'd likely lose his head otherwise. "I need to touch you. Will you let me feel you, darlin'?" He took in her face, looking for any sign she wanted him to stop.

What he got instead was hooded eyes, a flushed mouth, and: "Yes. Touch me, Sean. Please, touch me."

He pulled the cup of her bra aside as he teased circles around her nipple. Then he slid his hand between their bodies, searching for the heat between her legs.

As soon as Sorcha felt his fingers make contact, she couldn't hold back the gasp. His eyes never left her as he stroked her aching sex. She fumbled for his trouser button. "You need to let me touch you, too, Sean. I want us to be together in this." He bit back a growl, because there was no way he was going to tell her no. Then she took him in her hand and he groaned. He felt a new flood of moisture between her legs as they each found a rhythm. He could have come with a few strokes, but he needed to hold back. He needed to slip over the edge with her. Look in her face as he watched her fall apart in his arms. He drew her nipple in his mouth, pulling as he watched her face. He felt her hips take on a faster pace. He closed his teeth lightly on her nipple and a cry ripped from her. He plunged his finger inside her as he felt the pulses of her climax. She met his eyes as she lost her ability to breathe, but she cupped his balls on the downstroke and he couldn't deny her. He kissed her hard as they stifled each other's cries, writhing against each other as they rode out the pleasure together. He thrust his hips against her palm and whispered her name as he joined her.

The blood roared in Sorcha's ears as she lost herself in the orgasm. It was her first orgasm unless you counted sex dreams. Whatever she'd been expecting, whatever she'd read about in her human sexuality textbooks, she hadn't been prepared for the force of the pleasure. Then, as if it wasn't perfect enough, she felt him let go. Felt the power of what she did to him. Her climax doubled back and crested again, and she wondered how she'd lived without this for so long. The connection of two people who cared for each other. The intimacy and vulnerability and the trust. Now they lay together, their breath harsh and their hearts pounding. No awkwardness, no desire to move or clean up. Nothing but blue eyes meeting green in adoration and wonder.

"You're so beautiful. I don't want to let you go." Sean rubbed his lips, featherlight over hers. "I don't know how I'm going to let you go."

· · ·

They tried to sleep, but it wasn't easy. The energy hummed between them. "I want you to come with us tomorrow," Sean said. It wasn't a question. He knew she didn't have to work for two days. After all, she'd worked ten days in a row. "I'll get you back up north in time for work, I swear it. Please."

"It's such a private time for your family, Sean. Maybe I shouldn't intrude."

"We won't be there when William and Katie tell the families, we can make ourselves scarce, but I think it would ease her if you were close by. That aside, I'm selfish. I want you with me. I want to show you where I grew up, and I want you to meet my mam and da."

She put her chin on his chest. "You're trying to woo me, Sean."

"Yes, I am. How am I doing so far?" She smiled and then she closed her teeth on his nipple.

"Ouch!"

"Payback," she said.

"Did you mind it?" he asked. But he knew, the cocky bastard.

"I loved everything you did to me. Couldn't you tell?" She did it again, using her tongue, then grazing with her teeth. Quick as lightning, he pulled her astride him, taking her mouth. He threaded a hand in her long hair, kissing down her neck. She was wearing one of his shirts now, and he nuzzled her through the cotton. He slid his hand down between their bodies, palming her sex underneath her panties. She rocked her hips as she arched her neck. He crooned, his words vibrating against the bare skin of her throat, "Come again, hen. I need it again."

In the end, he'd gone to the sofa. Katie's roommate was home, and William would be back. No sooner had he reclined on the old cushions, than he'd heard William's keys. He sat up as William came inside the apartment, and said, "I'm sorry I woke you."

"Not at all, brother. Come and sit with me a while. I know you're knackered, but we should talk."

He sat, and Sean's heart squeezed. He patted his shoulder. "I'm sorry. I know you love her, but I'm still sorry. This isn't how you wanted this to happen, I know."

"It's my fault. I know better. She said that she and Sorcha talked last time she was here. Sorcha told her about the rhythm method, but that it wasn't a failsafe. Neither is pulling out. I got hold of some condoms after that, but it must have been too late." He rubbed his short hair. "How can a man my age be so stupid? It's a wonder it hasn't happened before this."

"Yes, well, more experienced women usually have their own methods. Two of the three women I've been with had IUDs and the other had a diaphragm. They get the stuff somehow. But you're right, it's no excuse. We have to do better. Be better."

"Well, since you're sleeping out here, you obviously have more self-control than I do."

Sean laughed. "I wouldn't say that, but your situation is its own sort of birth control. It made an impression."

"Do you love her?" William asked, and he couldn't keep the fatigue or sadness out of his voice.

Sean answered, "I barely know her." Which didn't answer the question.

"That doesn't always matter, Sean."

"No, I don't suppose it does."

Sean and William took the front seat as Sorcha sat in the back, holding Katie's hand. The tears seemed to ebb and flow, Katie only forgetting their mission for small periods of time as the group tried to find new ways to distract her. Finally, Sorcha squeezed her hand.

"Katie, snap out of it. You are going to walk into this situation with your head held high. You are not the first woman to have this happen, and you won't be the last. William will stand by you through everything. Some women don't have that luxury. You are going to get this over with swiftly and then start planning your wedding." Katie blinked, then swallowed. "Katie, are you happy about having William's child? Do you love him enough to raise a child with him? Grow old? Spoil your grandchildren?"

Katie searched her mind. Sorcha saw it plain as day. She also felt the weight of this question hang in the car as William tensed. Katie seemed to indeed snap out of it. "Of course I do. I love him. I want all those things. He's the love of my life." Bold words for a twenty-year-old.

"Well, that's a relief. William, you can take a breath now," Sorcha said plainly. "And it doesn't matter one bit how you got here. It's happening. You are going to have William's beautiful, blue-eyed baby and live out your life being disgustingly happy, so stop punishing yourself. A child is a blessing. You're both smart, capable people from happy families. This child will want for nothing. All you need to do now is paint the nursery and pick a wedding date."

She said the words so forcefully that Katie hiccupped on a laugh. Sorcha winked at William, and Katie finally let go. Her laughter was like a balm. William looked at her, love shining out of his face.

"We are going to be happy, aren't we?" she said, finally.

"Disgustingly happy," he said, grinning at Sorcha. But she wasn't looking at him. Her eyes met Sean's in the rearview mirror, and her throat tightened as she saw the same depth of emotion in his eyes that she'd seen when William looked at Katie. It warmed her, and at the same time it scared the hell out of her. She was such a bloody hypocrite.

Sean pulled over just long enough to let William boot Sorcha out of the back seat so that he could hold his beloved Katie. Sorcha was finally able to relax and look around as they got farther away from the city. She remembered Nurse Betty's advice about taking a drive into the country. It was so green. On occasion, she'd pass an old farm and see ruins of some ancient structure embedded in the plowed fields. Despite the crispness of the autumn air and the trees that had begun shedding their greenery, the landscape was beautiful. They'd left before sun-up, and she felt the sun start to rise at their backs as they made the journey west to County Clare.

"Where will I stay? Should I go to a bed and breakfast?"

"No, my mother wouldn't hear of it. You can stay in Maeve's room. William and I share a room, and Maeve will stay on the sofa or at Gran's. It's all arranged, no doubt. I called this morning. It's not an imposition."

"I don't mind sharing Maeve's room. She doesn't have to leave." Sorcha didn't have a sister, but she wasn't much older than Maeve.

"She's got a single bed. It's no bother. Just relax, Sorcha. My family is delighted—I've never brought a girl home before."

"Are you more the love 'em and leave 'em sort, Sean O'Brien?" she asked. He smiled at that.

"More like the other way 'round. I've been used and discarded more than I care to admit. As for you? Once we get there, we'll lock you in the dungeon until you agree to wed me."

She shot right back, "Dungeon? Surely I rate the tower and not the dungeon?" But the humor masked her nerves. Was he serious? Surely not.

Sean knew she didn't think he was serious. More was the pity, but she couldn't say he didn't warn her. He didn't have a dungeon or a tower, but he had other ways of convincing her. He'd use any dirty trick he could. Then something occurred to him. Something wicked... because he did have a tower after all.

Doolin, Co. Clare, Ireland

Sorcha smiled as Sean drove into the small village. The downtown area was a single street, Fisher Street, with a row of traditional buildings, pubs, shops, and other establishments. She liked the look of this charming stretch of land. To her left were rolling hills and sheep, lined with a creek that ran along the road. There were signs for the pier, and she guessed this was where Katie would ferry over to her island. Inis Oirr was the smallest occupied island of the Aran Islands and the closest to Doolin.

Katie pointed out a pub, commenting that she'd met William there. "Oh, yes. They had every girl in that pub swooning in her knickers."

"Can we go there, do you think? I don't frequent the pubs in Belfast. There's usually too much trouble."

"Yes, of course. Maybe not this weekend, but next time. Mind, ye'll have to sit at a table. Women don't sit up to the bar."

"Yes, it's the same in Belfast. Ridiculous, but most restrictions on women are."

"Well, I hope you don't find my home too awfully old-fashioned." Sean's tone was teasing, but his face held a bit of insecurity.

"Your home is lovely, Sean. It's like a storybook, really. A far cry from Dublin or Belfast. Especially Belfast. Not a barricade or checkpoint in sight. No armored vehicles. It's green and peaceful. Maybe you could take me to see your cliffs today?"

His eyes were warm. "I'd love that. And O'Brien's Tower will be there as well."

"Any relation?" She smiled at the thought of Sean and William on horseback several hundred years ago.

"A distant connection. It's a common name in these parts. Just like you'll find a Mullen or Mullins on every corner in Cork or a lot of people with the surname Kerr in Donegal."

Sorcha turned back to Katie. "Are there a lot of Donoghues in Aran?"

Katie nodded. "Yes, on the islands and the rest of Galway. So how did a branch of the Mullen clan end up that far north?"

Sorcha shrugged. "Marriages, the search for work, and some excitement during the blitz."

They all knew what she meant. The rest of the world knew about the London Blitz that happened during World War II, but the bombing of Belfast during the same time got little more than a side note in the history books, if even that. She thought about her city, with its old buildings pockmarked by one war or another, military roadblocks, raids, and the poor living conditions of much of the Catholic housing. Had there ever been peace? It seemed hard to imagine. The only people that prospered up north seemed to be mill workers, factory workers, and ship builders.

She wondered about the conversations that took place, not only in these village pubs, but also around the dinner or post-Mass tea table. Did they ever speak about the troubles in the north? In her own life, she always seemed to overhear the men speaking of the fight for independence, the different conflicts, and words like Ballymurphy Massacre or Bloody Sunday spoken with bowed heads and boiling resentment. Did people in Doolin speak of the internment of political prisoners? Sons, nephews, and fathers jailed for years, leaving their families to suffer as if they'd died. Leaving the women worse than widows, because she'd be shunned if she ever tried to leave the man. Prisoners' wives were in a unique sort of cage. Had any of these people had friends, siblings, or sons who'd died at the wrong end of a UVF pistol? Had any of them built car bombs that sat parked at the entrance to a shop or pub?

She looked around at this small, quaint village and thought not. She tried to imagine what life would be like for Katie and William if he managed to transfer back to County Clare. Katie would likely fit right in. Her village was even more secluded from those sad, troubled happenings than Doolin.

As they wound down the narrow road, Sorcha saw the freestanding homes. Modest, yes, but land rich. Everyone had at least an acre with outbuildings, sheep, and the occasional cow or donkey. The remains of tilled earth and this year's harvest lay fallow. There were trees that had shed their leaves but had the occasional shriveled apple still holding onto a twig.

Still, she was surprised to see the house when Sean entered the drive. It was lovely, as well-kept as her parents' home in Glengormley, but far more traditional. The cottage was a vision, with empty flower boxes and rows of rose bushes waiting for spring. Peat smoke rolled out of the chimney, making it seem cozy and inviting. The thatched roof, if it had ever had one, had been replaced by slate, but the white-washed stonework gave it such a picturesque look,

Sorcha thought it could've been a home from a storybook. A wave of nervous excitement went through her.

"Maeve is at school. Once you talk to Mam and Da, will you head to Galway?" Sean asked, his face trying to stay void of any grimness or pity for the path ahead.

William answered, "Yes. Why don't you come in and get settled, then you can take the car out for a drive? Mam and Da won't appreciate an audience at the start of it. Give us an hour or so, then head home. I'll need the car."

Sorcha's belly jumped with nervousness as an attractive, forty-something woman came to the door. Her hair was brown and neatly arranged to fall at her shoulders. She was tall and slim-figured, and Sorcha could see some familiar features in the set of her brow and jaw. Her frock was simple, with clean lines and handsome buttons. Her eyes landed on Sorcha, and she gave a broad grin. "You must be Sorcha. Welcome, my dear. And Katie, it's so good to see you."

Katie's face was pale and tense, but she replied politely, "And it's good to see you, Mrs. O'Brien."

The inside of the cottage had been renovated beautifully, but didn't look too modern. There was no linoleum or shag carpeting that seemed to be the latest fashion. Nor did they have the trendy mustard yellow appliances that baffled Sorcha. Such an ugly color, yet many people favored it. Instead, the home was classic and lovely. A crisp white interior with warm wood beams and tongue and groove flooring. Aoife's tastes were more like her own, with botanical fabrics and hints of blue here and there. It was calming and inviting. The temperatures by the coast were ever-changing this time of year, and David had a fire going in the rustic-looking hearth in the sitting room.

Their exit had been delayed by a pot of tea and some home-made lemon tarts. David O'Brien was a large, well-built, handsome man who looked so much like Sean and William that she was taken aback. This is how Sean would age, she thought. Strong and beautiful, blue eyes sparkling with intelligence and a hint of mischief. A full mouth which smiled easily. As they made their excuses, Sorcha felt at least a little of the tension release in her body. These people were good, honest folk. Any fear that they'd verbally assault Katie with the usual nasty comments reserved for unwed mothers dissipated. They'd be worried and a bit disappointed, but they wouldn't turn their backs on William or his intended bride. And apparently the parish priest would be prudent enough not to ask a lot of questions with regards to a rushed wedding ceremony. Sorcha prayed that Katie's parents were equally loving, for William's sake as well as hers.

Sorcha had seen the Cliffs of Moher on television documentaries and in magazines, but nothing quite prepared a person for the real thing. It was a massive landscape, too grand to take in all at once. The sprays and mist clouded up from the crevices as the sea bashed away at the base of the cliffs and treacherous nooks and crannies. There was a sea cave, dark and mysterious, as well as freestanding rock formations that jutted from the sea. "It's magnificent. Truly. I've never seen its equal. Even on the Antrim coast, there's nothing of this scale."

Sean warmed at the words, pleased she liked his home. She'd taken in even the most minor detail of their surroundings. When he thought about the dangers of city life, even in Dublin, the thought of letting her go back home sent a fresh wave of panic through him. He felt like every goodbye would be the final one. Not just due to the dangers of urban life, but due to Sorcha's own inability to picture a life outside of Belfast. He watched her now, staring out the window of the car, and the sight broke his heart. She was a strong woman, brave and skilled at her trade. Did she even know what life could be like if she'd just give him a chance? Now he headed toward one of his favorite spots: a ruined tower located just on the outskirts of the village proper.

She said, "And what is so special about this particular tower?"

"Are you wondering whether I intend to lock you in it?" His smile was teasing, his eyes mischievous. She remembered the discussion about dungeons and towers and smiled back at him. He said, "This one would make a poor prison. It's fallen to ruin with no roof. It's the last part of an old estate and is creepy altogether in the nighttime. There are no streetlamps or other unnatural lighting. When the stars are bright, ye feel like you could be looking up from ancient times." Then he confessed, "It's a bit of a local trysting spot, truth be told, at least when I was a lad."

She narrowed her eyes at him. "Oh, is it now? How many unsuspecting young women have you lured here?" She sounded almost miffed, which both amused and delighted him. "And don't look so satisfied with yourself."

He cut off her protests with a palm that started up her corduroy-clad leg, sliding between her thighs. "None yet," he purred. Yes, she'd be his first and last. Her education would continue, and he was an eager teacher. The beauty of it was, he learned something new every time he touched her.

She scissored her legs, not sure whether she wanted him to stop or give her more. Then, she was out of the car, pulled by the arm until an old stone structure swallowed them whole. He kissed her and was so achingly thorough that she could do nothing but slump against the stone wall. He nibbled her neck, and she panted his name. The light came through the top of the ruin, and she was aware of every nuance. Light catching the lush moss and tangling ivy. Of the stones, cold and rough against her back. The smell of the earth, the decaying wood, and of him. Most of all, him. Spice and soap and his own unique, masculine scent. A fragrance that deepened as his arousal grew.

He pulled his mouth from hers, hovering with his lips just a breath away. He towered over her, but she knew that with a word, he'd back off. She didn't want him to, however, and she arched into his mouth. His fingers were skilled as he undid the buttons of her shirt, spreading the sides apart to reveal the pale skin of her breasts and stomach. The cool, damp air was a blessing on her scorching skin. He lavished her body with kisses, then nibbled her shoulder, grazing with his teeth and tasting her skin. He kissed her collarbone, her breasts, the curve on the underside as he knelt before her. He met her eyes.

"I need this. I need you right here." He gave her open-mouthed, hot kisses down her navel as he unbuttoned her trousers. "Your taste. Your heat and slickness against my tongue." His words were slow and slurred with desire, and the power he had to seduce her with those words was unsettling and exciting. He paused. "Do you want that, Sorcha? Do you want to feel my tongue and lips against you while you come? Do you know how a man can please a woman like this?"

"Of course I know. I'm a midwife, not an idiot." She said it peevishly, trying to gain control of the conversation. She wanted this. Had fantasized about it, actually. But her fantasy had never been like this. With the cool autumn air on the trail of skin where his mouth had been. Her nipples hard and aching, with the ocean roaring in the background, the baseness and earthiness of this union making her wild. The arousal pounded in her ears as she bloomed under his hands and mouth.

He said, "Aye, ye can know a thing, but not really know it. Let me show you, mo chroí. Will you give me this? Will you give me your taste?" He'd unzipped her pants by now, pulling them low as he nibbled her through her panties. "You're going to be perfect, I know it. Please, say it. Tell me you want this." He nuzzled her and she cried out, her hand pressing into his hair. He mouthed her over her panties, loving the feel of her hips as they urged forward, seeking what she wanted. But he needed her to say it.

"I want this." She could barely catch her breath.

He freed one leg from her pants, then he slid down her delicate pink panties. The first touch of his mouth was light, seeking, exquisitely soft. Her hips jerked. He pinned her to the wall as he hooked her freed leg over his shoulder. He had to fight the urge to drop his trousers and dive into her delicious heat, but this was enough for now. He slid one finger in as he teased the very center of her sex. When he slid the second finger inside her, he drew her deep into his mouth, covering her as he fluttered his tongue along the sensitive nub. The cry grew in her belly as she started to climax. She looked down at him, watching. Then she fell into an endless, catastrophic abyss.

TEN

William came back to the house close to dinner time. He looked exhausted. He also had a small cut and swelling at the corner of his mouth. "Jesus, Mary, and Joseph!" Aoife crossed herself. "Is she okay?"

"She's fine. I wouldn't have left her otherwise. Her da got one shot in before her mother called him to heel. I can't say I blame him. What would Da have done in his shoes?"

"If some lad brought my sweet girl home in the family way, I'd have throttled the wee mongrel. You were lucky it was only one shot to the gob," David said plainly.

"Yes, well." William rubbed his jaw absently. Then he shrugged. "After things calmed down, he poured us both a stiff drink. I told them I love Katie with all my heart. We're to be married here, to keep the local busybodies away."

Aoife said, "I called Father Michael. It's early enough to get married on the island, if she'd rather. She shouldn't have to hide."

"I'll ask her. She worries about a scandal, because it's a small community."

Aoife looked at him, smiling. "You're a good man, William. The circumstances aren't ideal, but I saw it that first time we met her. She's the one, forever and always. This is no scandal. It's a blessing, despite what the others might say."

Sorcha watched this beautiful family and her heart swelled with love and admiration. Her mother would have said something very similar. Every woman in Katie's position should have this sort of support. She wasn't sure whether to add anything to the discussion or not, but she wanted to say something.

Aoife didn't miss a step. "What is it, Sorcha?"

"I was just wondering if maybe it wouldn't be prudent to keep the pregnancy quiet from the rest of her family. Apparently, her sisters can be quite..."

"Self-righteous?" William offered. She nodded. "Yes, Katie said as much. They agreed. I'm sure there will be speculation when the child comes, but it's none of their business, sisters or not."

Aoife stood, wanting to have the conversation over. "That's enough for now. Sorcha, dear, I'd love to hear about your work." The men groaned.

"Why do women abhor violence or bloodiness in a rugby match, but have no issue with discussing childbirth at length?" William said just as Maeve came in from school.

Maeve said, "The perfect way to clear the room of men: talk about our girly bits." They all laughed, the tension of the day easing.

Sorcha and Maeve hit it off so well that Maeve ended up forgoing the sofa and slept in a sleeping bag on the floor of her room. "I'm headed to uni next fall semester, although I'm not sure where to yet. NUI most likely. Mam doesn't want me in Dublin. Of course, my brothers are no help."

"Yes, well, seeing where you've grown up, I would have to agree. City life has some advantages, but there are a lot of disadvantages."

"You must see a lot in Belfast, given *the troubles*. Is it all nationalists where you live?"

"Yes. The city is divided into segments. You don't see much crossover. That's what the walls are for."

"They talk about it in school, but it's hard to imagine. Walls and barricades don't seem terribly peaceful."

"Yes, you're right. It isn't very peaceful at all, I'm afraid."

Maeve cocked her head, appraising Sorcha. "Are you one of the freedom fighters? I've heard there are some women."

"No, not at all. I support my family and neighbors. I'd love to see a time when we are free to live our lives in peace. No walls, no occupation. I can't fault the cause, it's the methods I can't condone. For every bombing, there is some sort of retaliation. It doesn't matter who threw the first punch. Talk doesn't seem to work, but I just wish we could sort it all out without guns and fighting. The UVF often targets civilians, it's not just the IRA. They really don't care who they hurt—it's like they don't see us as humans."

Maeve thought about that. "It's the mob mentality. Atrocities are more palatable in groups."

"You're very smart, Maeve," she said, meaning it. She liked Sean's sister. She was sharp and witty and very pretty. She had the same blue eyes and pale skin, with just a dusting of freckles over her nose and under her eyes.

"You know, Willy and Katie are going to try moving nearby. It's a good place to raise a family." Sorcha kept her own counsel, so Maeve added, "They think I'm a child, but it's obvious why they're getting married so quickly. I personally love the idea. I think I'd fancy being an aunt. The only thing left to do is marry Sean off to a nice girl."

She looked at Sorcha, who dodged the shameless probe. "So, Maeve, what do you think you'd like to study at uni?" And the conversation continued on to less dangerous waters.

Sean and William had to return to work a day earlier than Sorcha. She'd offered to take the bus, but they wouldn't hear of it. After a leisurely drive up to Kilcar, near Donegal, for lunch at their grandparents' house, they drove along the Antrim Coast. Sorcha's brother had warned them not to stop in Derry, or Londonderry as the loyalists called it. Derry met Belfast blow-for-blow when it came to armed conflict, and no one wanted to spoil the day with the heavy reminder of the turmoil that awaited Sorcha in her home city.

It was like a mini holiday. None of them, other than Sorcha, had ever seen the Giant's Causeway, and the peculiar rock formations stunned and amazed all three of them. Sorcha's heart swelled with pride. Finally, she could show them something beautiful and unique to Northern Ireland. Something that had nothing to do with barbed wire or political unrest.

It was a gray, late autumn day, with a cold, damp breeze whipping off the water. The kind of wind that cut into a person, right through their clothing. But the weather only added to the allure of the landscape. Formed by a volcanic fissure, the interlocking basalt columns seemed too geometrical to be made by nature. Yet, it was indeed a God-made wonder that towered above them in some places and in other places paved their footsteps before disappearing into the cold and shifting sea.

The puffins were in rare form today, hopping along the stones to Katie's delight. "They're adorable. There are so many. We've got them on the island, of course, but I've never been able to get this close."

Sorcha's victory was short-lived as they drove into the city. At the first checkpoint, Katie held Sorcha's hand so tightly that she almost yelped. "It's okay, Katie. They'll just use the mirrors to check under the car and maybe look in the boot."

Once they came to the building on Springfield where Sorcha lived, there were no places to park. Debris cluttered the roads as always, and for the first time she could remember, she felt a pang of embarrassment. She hated it. This was her city. These were her people. She would not make excuses, and she hated that the urge to do so had almost won out. She heard Sean speak to William. "Get in the driver's seat. I'll walk her up."

"You don't have to," she said, a little too shortly.

"Christ, woman. Don't make everything a struggle." But he was grinning when he said it, teasing her. He waited as she opened the main door to the building and started climbing the stairs. "Is John home? I'd like to say hello."

"Yes, he is," she said over her shoulder. Before she got to the door, he pulled her into his arms and kissed the hell out of her. Kissed her until she stopped thinking. Kissed her until he felt the sweet submission as she melted into him.

He pulled away just enough to speak. "When we're old and gray, you and I, I will remember that time we went to the old tower. I'll take it to my grave." Then he took her key out of her hand and opened the door to the flat.

John was doing the washing up. And if he noticed the state of Sorcha after being kissed senseless, he didn't comment. "I've warmed some stew. There's enough for you both."

Sean smiled, marveling at how a young man could be so self-sufficient. He liked that the lad had a warm meal waiting for Sorcha. "I've got to go. We're double-parked. Thank you for the offer, though." He turned to Sorcha. "I'll see you at the wedding if not before." When Sorcha's face looked confused, he said, "Surely you'll come. It'll be a small affair, but Katie will want you there."

"I'll have to look at my calendar. I guess I could try. I'll have to take the bus to Dublin, then again to the nearest big town, but I'll manage it if I can."

"Get yourself to Dublin, and I'll get you to the wedding," Sean said. "It was good to see you again, John." He kissed Sorcha on the forehead and was gone.

Sorcha avoided the inevitable conversation for a while, but John was a Mullen, after all—stubborn as the day is long. "Does Mam know about Sean?"

Sorcha lifted one shoulder. "Sort of. Not everything."

"Is he good to you?" John asked, his tone gentle. He was such a man of worth, beyond his years.

"Yes, he truly is. He's a good man, John. So, I'm sure I'll make a mess of things and run him off." She gave her brother a crooked smile. "What about you? Have you got your eye on someone?"

She saw a flicker in his face of something. Then he shook his head. "No, there's no one."

She put her arm around her brother's shoulder. "We are a sorry pair, aren't we?"

ELEVEN

Dublin, Ireland

It was late evening, halfway through their shift, when Sean got a call to a domestic disturbance. He was partnered with Sullivan tonight, but when William was free, he always found his way over to Sean for backup. Sean did the same. Despite the rules about siblings not partnering up, the department couldn't seem to keep the O'Brien brothers apart.

Sean walked at the back of the line, Sullivan between himself and William. The shift was shorthanded tonight. Officer Sullivan was a smart kid, a couple of years younger than Willy, but he had the makings of a fine officer. Sean could see his leadership potential, even at the bottom of the seniority pool. You couldn't teach it and you couldn't beat it out of a man.

William signaled toward the door they were trying to find. He heard the man ranting, out of his head, just like the neighbor had reported. They should really have more men, but there was a huge pub brawl in Ringsend and a nasty pile-up on the byway. The three of them were on their own.

Sean hated druggies and the dens they usually inhabited. They were unpredictable. With the influx of not only heroin and cocaine, but LSD and PCP into the Irish urban scene, they never knew what they were going to be dealing with. Sean palmed his nightstick, ready to back his brother up if he needed to, and hoped like hell that the insanely stoned piece of shit inside this apartment wasn't armed. Being the senior responding officer, he should be in the lead, but William was a good point man. You used your assets where they were most well-placed.

There was a smack, then a moan from another person. A woman. William kicked the door in before Sean could stop him. They piled in, the woman bleeding from the lip and sprawled on the couch. The man was thin, disheveled, and his eyes flashed madness. William had him underfoot in a flash. "Check the other rooms, Sean. Sullivan, cuff her until we can sort this out." Better to secure them both. Domestics often went sour when the husband was arrested. A sobbing, injured victim could end up turning on the officers in defense of her wife-beating husband.

Sullivan swiftly handcuffed the woman. She was high as a kite. There were pills on the table that had been crushed for snorting. "Looks like angel dust," Sullivan said. "Ma'am, how much did you take?" PCP and LSD were a nasty business, with hallucinations and psychotic behavior common. She looked up at him. "My baby. They took him, the bastards. They left that thing in his place."

"What thing, ma'am? Where is the child?" Sullivan's face was wary as he exchanged a glance with William, then looked down the hall where Sean had gone.

"They left that thing in his place. Have you seen my baby?" She was unfocused, drooling.

William said, "Where the hell is Sean? We should call an ambulance for her at least."

William had a bad feeling. He'd searched and cuffed the man, so he went down the hall to find his brother. He yelled, "Sean! Oh, there you are." His face blanched. "What is it?"

Sean's face was destroyed. "I need you to call an ambulance." William walked forward to go into the bedroom. "No, Willy. Just go and call an ambulance. There's no need for you to…"

The words exploded out of William. "What the fecking hell is back there? Answer me, Sean!" He pushed past Sean and went into the still, dank room that had a shroud of death hovering over it, an unholy mix of smells and sorrow. The moan of despair that came out of William made the hair stand up on Sean's neck.

It had taken both Sean and Sullivan to pry William off the man. And, in the end, it hadn't been him who had done it. But he'd been the one to buy the drugs. To keep his girlfriend strung out on PCP, despite the fact that they had a child. All she kept repeating was that they'd taken her child. Left that nasty thing in its crib. *It squeaked and shit and... after all... didn't rats give people the plague?* The baby had been so thin, you could see its ribs. Cracked lips from vomiting and no fluids. Not at all like the soft, pink, chubby babies Sean had seen in his lifetime.

The still, blue figure lying in its own feces and vomit would haunt the three officers until the day they died. As would the rat poison in the kitchen, set next to a dirty baby bottle. When they held their own children in the years to come, they'd shut down the memories, wishing they could burn them away.

Sorcha ran to the phone, not expecting the voice that came over the line. "Hello, Sean. How are you?" The long-distance fees were a bit dear. They'd agreed to speak once a week for five minutes, but this wasn't a pre-arranged call.

"I'm glad you're home. I just..." He sighed, sounding so tired. "I just wanted to hear your voice. You have such a beautiful voice."

"Sean, tell me what's happened." She could hear that something was off. "Did someone get hurt at work?"

"It's nothing, love. Just some long work days. I'm fine. How is your work going? Have you had any more excitement?"

"Sean, don't change the subject. Please, tell me. I promise you that whatever it is, I have likely seen worse. Let me be the one to support you for a change."

"Sorcha, it's..."

"Sean O'Brien, start talking, or I swear to you I will call your mother right after we ring off." She leaned into the phone, twisting the cord nervously.

"You are a pushy little peahen, you know that?"

"Aye, it's my Mullen blood. I've got a dreadful temper besides. Best get used to it. Now talk."

He told her, choking back the urge to cry like a child. Holding back the curses and the awful, putrid things he wanted to say.

"Oh, Sean. I'm so sorry. Christ, I take it back. I'm not sure I have seen worse."

"I shouldn't have told you," he said sadly.

"That's nonsense. I want you to talk to me. Even the horrid stuff. It's the only way this is going to work. I need to be a friend to you, Sean."

"Is that what we are, Sorcha? Friends?"

"In part," she hedged.

"And the other part?" he said, his grin coming through in his tone. Finally, a smile.

But she wouldn't give him false hope. She'd done a lot of thinking the last couple of days. A dangerous habit. "I don't know, Sean. I just don't know." The phone was silent. "I'm sorry, Sean. I want to support you, but I won't lie to you."

"Aye, but you'll lie to yourself." She heard his dismissal as if he'd slammed a door in her face, the fleeting smile gone. "Anyway, thanks for the chat. I needed to talk, I suppose. I'll see you soon."

"Sean, wait."

"No, I don't think I will, Sorcha. I'll see you this weekend. Katie's been asking for you."

"How is she? Any morning sickness?" She was happy for the change of subject.

"No. She's pale, but no sickness. She hasn't seen a local doctor yet. You'll have to ask her the rest. I'll be at the bus station on Thursday. Goodbye, Sorcha."

John came to the door and Sorcha cursed. She hadn't heard him come into the flat. "I'll get up and warm some dinner for you," she said, turning to sweep the tears from her cheeks before she faced him. "It's just some leftover roast from yesterday."

He caught her elbow as she tried to walk past him. "I'm no child, sister. You can talk to me."

Sorcha's face trembled with suppressed tears. "I know, John." She leaned into him and he wrapped his arms around her.

"You don't have to be so bloody strong all the time, Sorcha. You deserve some happiness. Why, love? Why do you feel like you can't let this man into your life? Keeping him away isn't making you happy. You're miserable. Why are you so at odds with yourself all the time?"

She nestled into her brother's embrace. She wished she knew.

Royal Jubilee Maternity Hospital, Belfast, Northern Ireland

"Nurse Mullen, room seven, stat." The words came over the intercom and Sorcha shoved her cup of tea at one of the nurses. "Here, have my cup. There's no need wasting it." It was awful tea, but it was caffeine. Nectar of the gods for an overworked nurse. She came into the room on a skid, blinking twice at the scene before her. A nun, her favorite at the hospital. She was a Catholic sister who volunteered there, even though it wasn't a Catholic hospital. "Sister Barnabas, can I be of some assistance?" The scene before her was like one of those American westerns. *A stand-off,* she thought. That's what the Yanks called it.

On one side of the rolling table was a very pregnant woman. On the other side was Sister Barnabas in full habit. She moved quite well for a woman of advanced years, her spritely build and direct gaze cutting a formidable figure. "Now you listen to me, young lady. Ye'll give me that cigarette this instant or I will call the orderlies and have you restrained!"

The woman spat back, "I'll be done with it by the time they get here, *aul wan*, so knock yourself out!" Then she took a drag and blew the smoke out in an act of childish defiance.

Sorcha almost laughed at the slang *aul wan, old woman,* but the sister was right. "Mrs. O'Cleary, I am certain we talked at length about this. Your baby is underweight. There are new studies out that have linked…"

"To the devil with your studies. My mam smoked with all five of us and do I look like I'm low birth weight?" Point taken, because she had some heft to her. Nonetheless, Sorcha nodded to the sister and sprang at the woman, latching onto her wrist as the sister pried the cigarette from her hand. Sorcha watched the sister go to the sink and put out the ember.

"And if you don't care about your own child, let me remind you that we have tanks of oxygen on this floor. There is no smoking!" Sorcha said firmly. Just as she finished the last word, the orderlies came piling into the room. Sorcha went to the woman's handbag, rifled through it, and took out her lighter and remaining cigarettes.

"That is my property!"

"Well, I'm sure we'll find them a good home. Now, get in that bed or I will call your husband down here from the docks. I'm guessing you've kept these"—she wiggled the pack—"a secret. I distinctly remember you promising him and me at your last appointment that you'd quit. I remember the relief on his face, as he is concerned not just for you but for his firstborn child." That did it. The woman burst into tears. Sorcha handed the cigarettes and lighter off to the orderlies and helped her into bed. Sister Barnabas pulled up a chair, sitting on the other side of the bed so that she could take the woman's hand. "You were doing so well, Mrs. O'Cleary. What happened?"

She was rather unfortunate looking when she bawled, wiping her nose on the clean bedding. "It's the stress. Ned is working dreadful hours. There's talk of a strike with the dock workers. Our tub has been clogged for a week, so I'm washing myself in the kitchen sink! I don't know what I'm going to do when the baby comes!"

"Well, now. How about we start with an exam? And then Sister Barnabas is going to help us find a good-hearted handyman from your local parish to work on that tub."

Sorcha smiled from across the table at the old nun. She explained, "She is quite a handful. She's not all bad, ye mind. It's just that she's been smoking since she was fourteen. It's not so easy to give up, once it takes hold. She's under a lot of stress."

"Do you think that the dock workers will strike?" the sister asked. "It would be rather hard on the whole city, I'd imagine."

"I don't know. There's been rumblings at the mill as well."

"Does your father work at the mill?"

Sorcha said, "No, my brother is the one that works at the mill. My da is a supervisor at the docks. The strikes could affect them both, unfortunately."

"Why aren't you married?" the old nun asked, completely changing the subject.

Sorcha shrugged one shoulder. "Same as you, I suspect. Demands of the job and all that. Surely, Sister Barnabas, of all people you can understand this."

She pointed a crooked finger at her. "Let me tell you what I understand. My job requires me to give up men. It's a struggle every day. Even at my age, although it got easier with time. If I could have been a bride of Christ and had a man to warm my bed, I'd have done it. I'd have had a couple of children as well. But my life doesn't allow that luxury. You, on the other hand, can have it all. Besides, the word around the hospital is that you've got a fine-looking copper driving up here from Dublin to win your affections."

Sorcha was stunned. "How on earth did you come by that information? And may I remind you, good sister, that gossiping is a sin?" The nun winked, unaffected by the attempt to guilt her and lazily taking a sip of her tea.

A voice came from behind Sorcha. "I hope all my training isn't going to go to waste. I wholeheartedly refuse to let you marry some knuckle-dragging Neanderthal and move down south."

Sorcha smiled. "Dr. Childs. It's been over a week. It's about time you came for a visit. We retained Mrs. O'Cleary. She was so busy worrying where her next fag was coming from, she missed the fact that she was dilated two centimeters. The baby is in the breech position. I'm just headed to try turning the little rascal. Would you care to join me?"

"Yes, I will. No doubt Stirling is sharpening that spinal needle hoping for a shot at her," he said with a grin. He actually respected the Yank doctor.

Sorcha said, "She's a good candidate. Although, we just caught her smoking again."

"Daft cow," he murmured.

Sorcha was in no position to argue that point. She was a daft cow. "Too right. Now, let's go have a look in on her."

Sorcha hated walking alone late at night. She was no coward, but she also wasn't stupid. Her brother was pulling a double shift at the mill for extra money, padding his coffers in case the strike happened. She hated it—he should be off at uni or still living with their parents. port.

Jesus, this city would be the death of her. Strikes threatened both at the mill and at the dock. Her mind wandered for the hundredth time to a different coastline. One where the sun set over the sea instead of rising. She'd sworn to herself that she'd stop thinking about that beautiful little village by the sea. About the cliffs and the clean country lanes. The farms and the smiling faces that all knew each other. And she was absolutely not going to think about that damned tower. Her body flushed, remembering. The sounds and smells, the feel of him. The sight of Sean O'Brien on his knees. "Dammit!" she cursed to herself.

"Easy, pet. Don't let your fancy doctors hear you talking like that." She knew the voice. She'd been listening to the little weasel make comments as she walked by since she was in pigtails. *Damn, damn, damn.* Denny O'Rourke came off the step of a worn-down building. "Why don't you like me, Sorcha?" He fell in step beside her.

"I like ye fine, Denny, but I'm busy. I've been at work all day. You should try it."

He ignored the jibe. "Aye, I hear. Crossing the lines to work at Queen's Hospital. I have to say, I thought you were a good girl. A nationalist. Imagine my surprise when I hear you've left the Mater to go work at the Jubilee."

She stopped, stunned. Had he been checking up on her? "So, the IRA is gathering intel on midwives? I'd have thought you had better things to do, Den."

"It's not right. You shouldn't be mixing with those types. The women on this side of the wall aren't good enough for you?" She smelled the whiskey on his breath.

"You ignorant jackass. I'm doing it for them! I'm in a good training program, Den. Then I'll be back at the Mater. If you knew anything about putting in an honest day's work, you'd understand. Besides, what I do is none of your business! You have no right to be checking up on me or questioning my loyalties. Or are you forgetting what was done to me?" She felt the searing pain of that knife on her arm, like it was happening now and not a few years ago. "Now piss off, before you make more of an ass of yourself than you already have!"

"You've always thought you were better than us. You're going to learn one of these days. That mouth of yours is going to get you in trouble." He had a grin that made the skin up her spine crawl.

A police car came around the bend just as he leaned in. "Stay close to home, pet." And at that moment, it didn't seem like a threat. She heard concern in his voice. Sorcha made a hasty exit as

Den O'Rourke slipped back into the shadows. He was up to something. She knew it in her bones.

"You need to tell the hospital that you can't work late if I'm not around." Her brother was furious. She was an idiot for telling him, but she didn't like the way Den looked at her. He'd always had a thing for her, and now there was a tinge of adult, male anger to the interaction that made her nervous. Someone needed to know in case he tried something else.

"I can't do that, John. I'm sorry. This is the job. I work long days and have home visitations. I won't let the likes of Den O'Rourke keep me from doing my best."

Her brother sat down next to her, taking her hand. "He's in love with you."

"Den O'Rourke wouldn't know love if it bit him in his lazy ass."

"Not Den," he said with a little laugh. "Sean. He's in love with you."

"He hasn't known me long enough to fall in love with me. How did we start talking about my love life?" Sorcha said, looking down at their joined hands.

He ignored the second question, responding to the first part: "Sometimes it works like that. Sometimes you grow into it, but sometimes it's like a lightning strike." John sounded older than his words.

"You sound like Mam. She said it was like that with Da." Sorcha stood, clearing the dishes from the table. "Last time we talked, I made a cock-up of things. He'd had a hard night at work. An awful night, really. He needed someone to be there for him. I tried, but I ended up hurting his feelings, I think."

"Well then, love, that phone works two ways. Ring him and make it right. Just don't talk too long. I'm not working double shifts to fix your love life." She punched his arm as he went toward the shower. "Call him, sister. Don't be stubborn about it."

. . .

He wasn't home. She knew that he and William worked swing shifts, so it wasn't a surprise. She put the phone back on the receiver and went to her room, knowing that she still had a few days left with long shifts before she'd be back in Dublin. She'd agreed to work back-to-back in order to get some spare days off for Katie and William's wedding. She had three patients near their due dates, but not so close that she couldn't leave for three days.

On Wednesday, she would take the last bus to Dublin. Sean would pick her up after midnight, and she'd stay with Katie for two nights until they left for County Clare. On Saturday evening, they'd have a small family wedding and dinner, then go back to Dublin. Katie was going to live with William and Sean until he could get transferred back to the coast. She thought about that and suddenly felt sorry for Sean. Everything was going to change. He'd have to find a roommate. He'd live away from all his family. He wouldn't be eligible to transfer for another year. William had been a special case because he was getting married, and he'd agreed to become a motorbike officer.

Sorcha shuddered, hating the idea of William riding a motor-cycle on duty instead of being on foot or in a patrol car. Katie didn't like it either. She'd called Sorcha last night, just to catch up. She was so happy, and Sorcha was glad for it. They both deserved the happiness that had come to them in such an unexpected way.

She brushed her teeth, put on her night clothes, and climbed into bed, settling in with a good book and trying to forget about that conversation with Sean. She listened to the sounds of sirens going through the city and suddenly wished she was sitting at the base of that lighthouse with him. His intelligent, kind, blue eyes. His broad shoulders and trim waist. The way he smelled when he was close. His first kiss, so tender. It had been more devastating because of his gentleness. The other kisses, not as gentle, blazed with passion. She refused to let herself cry, or she'd never get out of bed. A two-hour drive may as well have been a world away.

TWELVE

Sorcha arrived at the hospital bright and early. Her unruly patient was fully dilated after a long night of labor. The problem, however, was that they hadn't managed to turn the baby. Every time they made headway, the child would mock them by turning his bum back to the birth canal. He was as contrary as his mother. And it was a boy. She'd been lucky enough to get her hands on the ultrasound machine. Mrs. O'Cleary hadn't wanted to know the gender, but the tech who had been in the room with her confirmed Mrs. O'Cleary would have a boy. He was small, which was most likely due to the smoking she'd done off and on throughout the pregnancy. Probably about six pounds. Given the size of the thigh bone and the parents, he should have been an eight pounder at least. She just hoped the boy was healthy. They were starting to learn more about birth defects and the harms of smoking while the baby was in utero, but it was a coin toss. The most common one was a harelip or cleft palate. She hoped for the family's sake that he was okay.

The Caesarean birth was scheduled in two hours. Just enough time to do her rounds and scrub in. Midwives didn't do surgery, but Dr. Stirling had insisted she be allowed to observe the spinal tap and surgery, so as to better understand the procedure when advising her patients. Some women just couldn't give birth the old-fashioned way. Sorcha knew a few of her patients that would have died in childbirth, along with the babe, if they'd been living a hundred years ago. Surgical birth was no picnic. It wasn't some easy way out. It was a difficult recovery for a woman who needed every ounce of strength to care for her newborn. And after working with Dr. Stirling and Dr. Childs, she knew that both doctors used the procedure only when other options were gone.

The morning went quickly, and before Sorcha knew it, she was walking toward the operating room where she'd find her patient waiting. "Good morning, Mrs. O'Cleary. Are we ready to get this baby out?" She noticed the woman was shaking. "Are you cold? I could probably get you a blanket until right beforehand."

"I'm not cold. I just..." Her face curled in on itself. "I don't like needles. I hate them. What if that Yank doctor paralyzes me? It's going into my spine!"

"Oh, my dear. I'm so sorry. I know this wasn't expected. I assure you, Mrs. O'Cleary, if I thought for even a moment that Dr. Stirling didn't know what he was doing, I'd step in and insist on general anesthesia. As it turns out, you are very lucky to have that Yank doctor here. He's at the top of his field. Given your history of smoking, I think this is safer than putting you under. Safer for you, and you'll be able to stay awake and see the baby when it comes out."

"I don't want to see them cut me open!"

Sorcha smiled, smoothing the woman's hair back. "Don't you worry. There will be a cloth shield, almost like a sheet. You won't see the baby until he or she is totally out."

"My husband hopes it's a he. He won't say as much, but I can tell. He's dreaming of weekend rugby matches and buying him his first pint."

"Well, we'll just have to see, won't we? And you'll know before he will. You'll be awake and able to tell him." That seemed to cheer her up. Then the surgical nurses were there, ready to shave her and prep her for surgery.

. . .

Sorcha watched in awe as Dr. Stirling worked his trade. Dr. Childs and his top anesthesiologist had come from across town to assist, wanting to observe the spinal tap and the delivery. A wave of relief washed over Sorcha as the small but complete little boy was brought out of the uterus and into the world. Sorcha assisted the nurse as they cleaned and swaddled the child, delivering him to a weeping and overjoyed Mrs. O'Cleary. Sorcha smiled, watching the mother kiss his tiny, bald head. "He looks a bit like Churchill."

Dr. Stirling barked out a laugh. "Yes, before all that liquor fattened him up. I see the resemblance."

Sorcha gave the doctor a murderous look. She said, "Not at all. He's a handsome lad. He's perfect. Now, let's get you closed and into recovery. Then we'll see if this little boy wants to take to the breast."

It took an hour to get them both settled, and the mother was in terrible pain, but Sorcha knew from experience that sooner was better with latching. It took another hour and a lot of patience, but finally both the mother and baby got the hang of it. "Now, Mam. We need to talk about the smoking."

"Is that why he's so small?" The woman looked down, tearing up at the sight of the child who'd weighed in at five pounds fifteen ounces.

"I'm not going to lie to you, it is the most likely cause. He's full term, so I'd have expected him to be at least a pound larger. He's okay. He's just going to need a lot of feedings. He needs you to stay the course, otherwise you will pass the nicotine to him through your breast milk. You must continue to watch your diet, and no drinking or smoking. You will likely need to supplement with formula if the baby doesn't gain enough weight. I need a commitment from you now. If you don't think you can give it up, then we will start bottle training him today."

"I'll try. I'll try harder than I ever have. I don't think I fully understood. You told me, but I didn't get it until I saw him. I'm so sorry I didn't try harder." Her tears were falling continuously.

"That's all you can do. I'll check on you twice a week. If you do smoke, you can't let shame or fear keep you from being honest. You have to communicate with me and your husband. The smoking will hinder your healing as well. You've been cut open, Mrs. O'Cleary, and good circulation is crucial to your body healing. Please, you must listen to me."

"I understand. I really do," the woman answered, and Sorcha hoped for her sake that it was true.

Ignorance is the softest pillow on which a man can rest his head...

—Michel de Montaigne

Sorcha left the woman in search of Angelina. When she found her, she asked, "Could you please add Mrs. O'Cleary to your home visits? Just until I return? She's a good person, really. She's just going to be under a lot of stress and I'm afraid she'll relapse on the smoking. Her husband works a lot and her mother smokes like a bloody chimney."

"Don't worry, Sorcha. Just enjoy your time away. I have to admit, I'm rather jealous. I'd love a holiday on the west coast. It's so beautiful there. Maybe..." Then she stopped, and Sorcha noticed her cheeks turning pink.

Sorcha pounced. "Oh, you cannot stop there! Maybe what? My love life is in shambles. I need some good news."

She tried to play it cool, but Sorcha knew better. "Maybe if things continue the way they are with Nigel, we'll rent a cottage in that little town you told us about."

Sorcha squealed so loud that everyone in the cafeteria looked up. "You little vixen! Tell me everything. Don't leave anything out!"

They enjoyed a quick lunch, and when they were almost finished, a pair of male doctors came into the cafeteria. The man wasn't even trying to be quiet. "Yes, at the mill as well. Bloody ingrates. They should be lucky to have the jobs. This is what happens when you hire Catholics for cheap labor."

Sorcha tensed. She knew the man by sight, but wasn't acquainted with him. He was some sort of specialist. Pediatric nephrologist, if her memory was correct. Apparently, he was also a complete prat. He didn't leave it there.

"Yes, well, perhaps they should put that old noose to good use instead of letting it gather dust. They can hang all of those trouble-makers taking up space on Crumlin Road and send a message. It's the only thing those types understand."

That did it. Sorcha stood, ready to let the little bastard have it, when that smooth Virginia drawl came from the other direction. "And what type would that be, if you don't mind my intrusion?" Stirling stood, and the asshole with the big mouth cleared his throat. Stirling continued, "Because it seems like you were making some sweeping statements about Catholics."

"You wouldn't understand the politics of this area, being from America." His tone was so condescending, Sorcha wanted to slap him.

Dr. Stirling said, "Oh, I think I can follow along. We have bigots in America as well, and it just so happens that I am a Catholic." Jesus, he really was Wyatt Earp. This was like the show-down at the OK Corral. John loved old westerns, and she'd picked up a thing or two.

People were openly staring now, interested to see how far this was going to go. The doctor he was having lunch with looked like he wanted to shrink under the table. Dr. Childs came to Dr. Stir-ling's table, setting down his tray, and said, "Ah, yes. At it again, are you, Evans? Well, it just so happens that I, too, am a Catholic." Sorcha's mouth almost dropped open. Lie. Total lie. He was Church of Ireland, but right now, they were both her heroes.

Evans, the asshole in question, started sputtering when an unexpected intervention came out of the woodwork. His direct boss, Dr. Henry Patel, was the hospital's first Indian Head of Department. He stepped forward, the mark of his Hindu faith worn prominently on his forehead. "And I am a Catholic."

Then Angelina was on her feet. "And I'm a Catholic!"

Well, hell. Sorcha started tearing up. She stood, facing the idiot with her chin raised. "And I'm a Catholic. And my brother works at that mill. And my neighbors have sons in that gaol. So, if you are going to spew your ignorant views, don't do it in the workplace where the rest of us have to hear it. It's completely unprofessional."

Sorcha was laughing harder than she had in a long time. She sipped her Coke while Dr. Childs and Stirling tackled their pints. Angelina took another drink of sherry and asked Dr. Stirling, "Are you even a Roman Catholic?" She whispered it, not wanting to draw unwanted attention in the pub.

"Nope. I'm a cradle Presbyterian, but that Evans guy was a dickhead."

Childs said, "Cheers to that, mate." They all clinked glasses. "Sorcha, we can surely do better than a Coke?"

"I've got to have my wits. It's a long bus ride and a bit of a walk to my flat. Maybe another time."

"Yes, after your wedding and your hot date with the copper, you can have a night out here and stay at my place. I've got a spare bed!" Sorcha smiled. Angelina was so happy to be out, and she was obviously very satisfied with the showdown in the cafeteria. She just had such an easy, friendly way about her. It was refreshing.

"Maybe. I work a lot—I have this terrible boss, you see." Dr. Childs feigned offense which set Angelina to giggling again.

Dr. Stirling said, "A cop, huh? Well, doesn't that figure? And here I was planning on sweeping you off to America."

Sorcha snorted, "I'd be a terrible doctor's wife. You've narrowly escaped a lifelong disaster."

He winked at her, sipping his beer. He was a handsome devil, but he wasn't Sean. She was ruined for any other man.

Dublin, Ireland

Sorcha stepped off the bus, an overnight bag and her purse on her shoulder. She looked around, her heart sinking. Sean said he'd pick her up, but she didn't see him. She adjusted the strap, walking down the street toward a call box. Then, around the corner, she saw a figure rushing. He saw her and stopped about twenty feet from her. He was so beautiful, it hurt her to look at him. At first his face was unreadable, then he started walking fast. She dropped her bags just as he swept her up. "I'm sorry, Sean." But he was kissing her and everything was better.

"No, it was me. I pushed you."

She cradled his face in her palms, kissing him all over his cheeks and forehead. "Would you shut up?" she ordered. "It's not very often I admit I'm wrong. You need to savor the moment." That had him laughing against her mouth. "I missed you, Sean."

They walked to Katie's flat, Sean carrying her bag. Katie came bursting down the stairs to greet them. "Sorcha!" She embraced Sorcha like a sister and tears misted her eyes. "I'm so happy you're here. Thank you for making this work. We need to talk." She shook herself. "I'm sorry, Sean. I didn't even say hello, did I?" She kissed him.

Sean smiled indulgently at her, and it warmed Sorcha's heart to see how well he treated William's intended. "It's wedding nerves," he said. "But don't worry. Wild horses couldn't keep us away. The day will be sunny, and I think an island wedding will be just the thing. You'll see, deirfiúr." He kissed Katie on the forehead affectionately and took his leave of them.

Sean walked the blocks toward his own flat feeling so warm and cuddly that he cursed himself as a hopeless sap. Their girls were both here, and they were together. He came into the flat, surprised to see William there. Willy said, "I can't stay. I needed a snack, but I didn't want to eat out. Time to start watching my spending—I have a family now." And Sean was sure his brother's back was a little straighter, his chest puffed out a little more. How could Katie have thought for a second that William wouldn't want this? Want her and a child they'd made together?

Sean felt the tightness in his throat as he said, "I'm happy for you, Willy. Lucky for you that it won't be so costly to live back home."

William said, "Listen, Sean, I want to pay the rent for a couple of months. Until you find a roommate. We'd stay a little longer if it wasn't for the baby. I just want to get her settled as soon as I can."

Sean lifted a hand. "Da already offered. It's not going to happen, brother. You'll stay here until the transfer is complete and then don't think about it again. I have time to look for a flatmate—I think Sullivan is interested."

William thought about it. "Aye, he's a good sort. Mature for his age. I like him. He'll be an easy flatmate."

"Yes, he will, and he plays the piano and the accordion. I'll have a new partner to play the pub scene." Sean said it lightly, but William's face fell a bit.

"Everything is going to change, isn't it? We've never been apart." His face was painful to look at. His handsome brother, with his easy smile, was breaking his heart a little.

"It's not so far." Wasn't that his new mantra? He'd said the same thing to Sorcha. "Three hours or so. We'll see each other every time I come home. It's not so far." He repeated the words, trying to swallow the lump in his throat. Then, his brother was across the room, grabbing him in a tight man hug that could only be reserved for a brother and best friend.

William said roughly, "And you'll follow in a year or so. You'll come home, brother. And you'll bring Sorcha with you."

Sean's shoulders sank downward, letting William bear the weight of him. "I'm not sure about that. I think when it comes to a choice, she'll stay where it's familiar. I love her, Willy. I love her so much it's like a missing arm when she goes back up north. She wants me, but I don't think it's the same for her."

William leaned back, looking Sean in the eyes. "She's your mate, brother. That is for life. You won't take another." He leaned in, his face intense. "So, you've got to fight dirty, Sean. You don't stop until she's yours. She loves you. I see it in her eyes when she looks at you. But she's stubborn. Christ, is she stubborn." He shook his head and laughed. "You're going to have to fight for this if you want it. Fight for her. You'll start by showing her that she can do everything she is doing in Belfast right here in this city, and no one's going to throw a wall up and tell her where to live just because she's a Catholic. You have to help her see how good it could be. Not just between you, but for her life as a midwife. She won't be one of those women content to stay home by the hearth."

Sean nodded. He was right. He'd seduced her with his body, but he hadn't considered this angle. He'd start after the wedding. He would start by talking to the dean at Trinity, then he'd visit the maternity hospital and arrange for them to give her a tour. He found himself smiling. "You're a genius, Willy. You're a bloody genius."

"You look pale, Katie. Are you eating and sleeping enough?" Sorcha asked.

"I nap a lot, but I don't sleep well at night. It's stress, I think. I'm eating enough. I haven't been feeling ill, if that's what you're asking. It's odd, because my sisters all felt sick. My mam said she threw up for two months with all of us."

"Well, everyone is different, so I wouldn't worry too much. Have you seen a doctor?"

"I did go in for a blood test, but that's all they did. The doctor told me to take a multivitamin. Is that okay, do you think?"

"Yes. If you were my patient, I would have said the same thing," Sorcha assured her.

"I wish you lived here. I wish I could be your patient," Katie said. "I wanted to talk to you about the wedding."

"Yes? What about it? No cold feet, I hope." But remembering

the persuasion methods and the dazzling good looks of the O'Brien men, she couldn't fathom it.

Katie asked, "Would you be my maid of honor? My sisters will end up fighting over who it should be. I want them there, of course, but it would be better if it was my best friend who did it. And you are, you know. I mean, I've had other friends, but I feel close to you. I know we haven't known each other that long, but..." She was starting to blush and Sorcha cut her off, taking her hand.

"I'd be honored to stand up with you, Katie."

The music traveled through the flat, Katie working on the breakfast dishes and singing along to her Sam Cooke record. Sorcha smiled, thinking about Katie's eclectic album collection. Dylan, Joplin, Aretha Franklin, John Denver, Creedence Clearwater Revival, and some British icons like the Beatles, Stones, and Led Zeppelin. In that, she and William were in sync. He loved Zeppelin. She was currently working on repacking her bag for the trip to County Clare. Then they were going to go to a shop today to try finding a dress for her. The simple frock she'd brought for the wedding wasn't going to do for such a special day now that she was the maid of honor. Katie's flowers would be cream colored and decorated with blue ribbon, so Sorcha wanted to wear Katie's favorite color: the shade of William's eyes. A deep, dusty blue like the sea on an overcast day. Just like his father's eyes and Sean's. Eyes that could haunt a woman's dreams. She shook herself, finishing her task and putting on her shoes and coat.

They started toward the shop, but Katie stopped abruptly for some reason. "I'm okay. It's just a stitch in my side."

"Do you want to sit down for a bit?" Sorcha asked, her brows tipped down in concern.

"Nonsense. Let's keep going. I can't wait until you see the dresses. There are several in the color you want. Just nothing too scant. We'll be on the beach. It's warm all weekend, but it'll likely be a lot colder on the island."

She'd been right to choose this particular shop. The selection was good and the prices were discounted. She chose the blue dress and then smiled as Katie came out, wearing her own simple ivory gown. Katie's beauty was all the adornment it needed. "You're beautiful, Katie. Have you chosen a veil?"

Katie shook her head. "No, we have a family veil, an heirloom that has been passed down. Someday my daughter will wear it. It's three generations that have worn the veil. It's made with the small shells that wash up on our shore."

"I think that will be lovely. You're a lucky woman, Katie. I don't have to tell you that. William is going to make you very happy." Sorcha's heart swelled with love for this union. The two of them were an inspiration, and soon they'd have a child.

Katie paid the balance on her dress, and Sorcha bought hers. Before they left, Katie said, "I've forgotten my gloves in the dressing room. Wait just a minute while I get them." Sorcha took her dress, waiting at the counter, so Katie was out of sight when she heard her cry out in distress. A garbled, awful sound.

She ran to the dressing room. "Katie! Love, have you fallen?"

"No! No, no, no! Oh God!" Katie was deathly white and in agony.

Sorcha went to the doorway and a flood of terror struck her right in the belly. Blood. Katie's hand was bloody and the large stain of blood on her tan trousers was spreading. Katie doubled over and Sorcha caught her before she fell. She screamed to the clerk, "Call an ambulance!"

Sean ran into the police station, almost knocking Sullivan over in the hall. "Where's William?" He shouted the words.

"He's booking a drunk and disorderly," Sullivan said.

"I need you to take his place. Please, we have to hurry!" Sean shouted over his shoulder.

"What's happened, Sean? For feck's sake, calm down."

Sean said, "It's Katie. She's been taken to the hospital."

. . .

Sorcha rode in the ambulance next to Katie. "She's about seven weeks, I think. Her pulse is elevated and erratic."

The paramedic yelled over his shoulder to the driver. "Twenty-year-old female, seven weeks pregnant, hemorrhaging. BP is eighty-eight over fifty-four! She's going into shock!"

Sorcha bent low, whispering to Katie in soft, soothing tones. "It's okay, Katie. Sean will bring William. It's okay, sweetheart."

Katie wept, her eyes soaked and unfocused. "My baby." She croaked the words and Sorcha couldn't find her own voice. Couldn't comfort her. No platitudes were going to help her right now. "I'm sorry, love. Just try to rest. Please, just close your eyes. We'll be there soon."

Sorcha knew she was right to be upset. With the amount of blood she'd lost, there was no way the fetus had survived. She hadn't seen many miscarriages, but she knew for certain that this was indeed a miscarriage.

They arrived at the hospital, and the hospital staff took Katie through to the treatment area. Sorcha was led to a small waiting room. It wasn't until she went to sit down that she realized her arm was smeared with blood. So was her shirt and the leg of her trousers. Jesus, poor Katie. She didn't want William to see her like this, so she went to the nurses' station. "Excuse me, ma'am. I'm afraid I'm not from Dublin. I am visiting. My friend is the woman who came in the ambulance."

The nurse gave her a pitying look. "I'm sorry about your friend. How can I help you?"

"Her fiancé is on his way. He's a Garda officer. I just... I don't want him to see the blood on my clothes. I need to clean up. I'm a nurse midwife in Belfast. At the Royal Jubilee, actually. Would it be possible to clean up a little bit? Before he gets here?"

The nurse looked at her clothing and the blood smears. She gave a nod and said, "I can have one of the nurse's aides take you to the women's locker room. It's just two halls over to the left. We can't give you a uniform, but maybe we can come up with some scrubs?"

"That will be fine. Thank you," Sorcha said with relief.

She worked quickly, bagging up her dirty clothing. They'd left their new dresses at the bridal shop. She would have to go and get them... although... Oh God, she couldn't even think about that right now. All she could think about was Katie and William.

She padded down the hall in her long coat and scrubs, feeling so sad she could barely contain the tears. Then she saw Sean and William. Sean came to her, hugging her tightly. He whispered against her hair, "I'm glad you were there, mo chuisle."

William's head was in his hands. She knelt in front of him. He said, "They won't let me see her. They said she's too weak. And they have to do something. It began with a *d*, I think."

"They may do a D and C. They'll have to examine her first. It's early, so it may not be necessary. William, I'm sorry, I'm so sorry, but she's lost the baby."

He shook as he wept. "I shouldn't have been with her. She said it was okay when we were together, but maybe I hurt her. Maybe I hurt the baby when we were together."

Sorcha pulled his hands away from his head and lifted his chin. "Look at me, William. You did nothing wrong. She was right. Making love would not hurt her or the baby. This is not your fault. It isn't anyone's fault. It just happened. Sometimes it just happens."

"I love her so much. Oh God, Sorcha. I hate that she's alone. Why can't I go in there? If I was her husband, would they let me go to her?"

Most likely, but she wasn't going to say that. He was feeling bad enough. She looked at Sean, and his face almost undid her. It was streaked with tears. "I'll talk to them. I'll see what I can do."

She went to the nurse in charge. "Please, their wedding is in two days. This was his child as well. I really think it would be better for her mental health if he could be there with her. They should be together."

The nurse looked over at William and her face softened. "Fifteen minutes. He has fifteen minutes before I give her the valium."

"Is that necessary? Can't she just get something for the pain?" Sorcha hated the fact that they wanted to drug her.

The nurse whispered, "I'm afraid she's a bit out of her head with grief. Maybe if you calm her down, we won't have to drug her."

Sorcha went in with him, and the sight of Katie pierced her heart. She was so white, her eyes ruined. William sat down next to her and took her hand. "I'm sorry, my love. I'm so sorry."

She looked at him and a tear escaped the corner of her eye. "I guess we don't need to get married now. I'm sorry for it. I really..." She stifled a sob. "I really wanted this baby. I did. But it's okay now. You won't have to marry me."

William's face blanched. "What? Don't say that, Katie. We're getting married. I love you. I wanted this baby, too, but it's not the reason I was marrying you. You're just grieving. You don't know what you're saying."

Katie turned away from him. "I do know. I'll finish my courses, and I'll go home. You don't have to worry about taking care of me anymore. They found something when they checked me with the ultrasound. I didn't totally understand it, but the doctor said I'd have trouble having a baby. You should be with someone who can give you children, William. It's better we found out now before you married me."

"Katie, stop saying that. I don't care about all that. I'm sorry we lost this one. And, if God gives us another chance, then so be it. The only thing I can't live without is you. We'll postpone the wedding until you're feeling better. I don't need a big affair. I just need you." He was crying now, so wounded by the day's events that Katie turning her back on him was like a knife to the heart.

Tears dripped off his nose and Sorcha wanted to scream. Why would a doctor tell her something like that in the throes of a miscarriage? It could have waited. No wonder she was out of her head. She went to Katie's other side. "Katie, once you're feeling better, I'd like to see your chart. I'm not going to talk to you about having another baby right now. Another baby isn't going to replace this one. You have to let yourself grieve. You have to lean on one another. When you're ready, we will talk about the rest." She took her hand, pleading with her silently not to shut William out. She took her hand and drew it across Katie's chest to give it to William. He held both so gently and kissed the tops, but Katie was far away. So far away.

Finally, Sean and Sorcha went back to the flat. William wouldn't leave, but they needed to ring Katie's family and his own. Sean kept it brief, then rang off. He seemed to sink into himself, still palming the receiver on the cradle. "Jesus, her mother is a mess. So is mine. They really were happy for them. Not everyone would have been."

Sorcha said, "Because they're good people. Now, let's go lie down. It's been an awful day. Tomorrow, we'll go pick them up and they can decide what is next."

Sorcha surprised Sean when she came into William's room. She was in her flannel nightgown, looking as pretty as a picture. "Come stay with me, Sean. I need you to hold me. I think maybe you need it, too." So, he did. He stripped off to his boxers and crawled into bed beside her. He reached for her, not out of lust, but out of the need for comfort. For contact. And as they fell asleep with her nestled under his arm with a hand over his heart, it was somehow more intimate than what they'd done in that tower. Two souls seeking succor. Two broken hearts winding around one another.

THIRTEEN

Sorcha stayed with Katie in her friend's flat, but William was sent away. It gutted him, this dismissal. Before he left, he knelt by the bed. "You can have all the time you need, Katie. I'm not going anywhere. We can have a spring wedding, when the blooms are budding. Or a Christmas wedding if you prefer. I'll get some sleep and come back so we can talk. I know you need your rest." His words were nervous. Like someone trying to reassure themselves with mundane chatter. Sorcha gave him an understanding look. Katie was grieving. This would all sort itself out.

But it didn't. By Sunday, William had reached the edge of his patience. "She can't just shut me out. She can't just go home. We love each other, Sorcha. She's my mate. She is it for me. O'Brien men don't walk away from their mates. It's forever. You have to talk to her!"

She didn't understand, but she offered, "I've tried, William. That damn emergency doctor should never have told her that this miscarriage meant she couldn't have children. I'm going to have Katie release her films to my head of department. There's no way that an emergency doctor could make those assumptions based off a simple ultrasound. He's an idiot. That said, I think there's more going on here. I really think Katie felt like you were just marrying her because of the baby. She likely thinks that guilt is the only reason you are persisting."

"Christ, she's stubborn. I won't give up. I know she loves me. I know it. And I love her. I want this marriage, baby or not."

Sorcha looked at Sean, and she saw so many things in that blue gaze. Things that were for her alone. The wanting he felt and such deep affection, she felt sure she was going to weep. She wasn't sure what to do with his feelings and even less sure what to do with her own. But this day was not for them. She turned to William. "Then you have to convince her, William. Do what you O'Brien men do best. Start wooing."

Katie was in better spirits. It was the day after she should have been wed, and she was actually up and about in the flat. She drank a cup of tea and her color was returning. "How is your bleeding, Katie?"

"It's less today, like a heavy period. Is that normal?"

"Yes, and it will lessen every day. Then it'll stop altogether. You should start cycling again after that." She took her pulse, happy to find it back in normal range and that she was showing no signs of infection. She gave Katie a piece of buttered toast. "Eat that before you try the vitamin. It won't hurt your stomach as much."

"Do I really need these?" Katie asked, looking at the large vitamin tablet that the doctor had given her during her checkup.

"Yes, dear. I'd keep taking them for another month. Then go on a regular multivitamin. I don't want you getting anemic. And some orange squash in the morning."

"Yes, Mammy," Katie said wryly. She sat up, hearing something odd. Speaker feedback maybe?

Then a male voice saying, "Test, test."

She asked, "What the bloody hell is that? A street concert?" Sorcha said nothing, hiding her grin behind a cup of tea. Then the electric keyboard started and a guitar. "It's half nine on a Sunday morning. Who would be playing music at this hour?" She got out of her chair and went to the window, then shot back, putting her back to the wall. "That bloody man has lost his mind!"

"What bloody man?" Sorcha asked, playing dumb. She went to the window and there they were: Sean with a guitar, Sullivan on the keyboards, and William holding a microphone. Where on earth had they plugged it all in? She raised the window.

Katie cursed. "Don't encourage him! Tell him to go away!"

"William, dear, Katie wants me to tell you to bugger off." Katie heard some male chuckling.

Sorcha leaned back. "He said he'll stop this instant if you agree to marry him tomorrow evening. He has it all arranged back home. No? Okay, I'll tell him."

That's when the music started. Crooning, sultry and sweet. Katie cursed again. "Damn him. He knows I can't resist Sam Cooke." The music trailed through the air, into the window on the autumn breeze.

It was like a red flag in front of a bull, however. It just made Katie angrier. She hissed down at him from her second story window, "Stop it, William! Go home! You are making a scene!" And he was. A crowd was gathering. Not only due to the spectacle, but the fact that they were all three in uniform. Katie growled. She actually growled at him when he reached out a hand, singing his heart out to her from the sidewalk. There were women watching. No, not watching. Swooning, by God.

Sullivan whispered to Sean, "Do you think it's working? She looks a bit out of sorts."

Sean answered, "If I knew that, I'd have married the other one by now."

William turned to them. "Oh, ye of little faith," he said as he covered the mic. That's when the first china saucer hit him in the shoulder and crashed to the ground. The infernal woman was throwing dishes.

"Go home! I'll call your boss and have you arrested! Get now! Go!" She was as mad as a wet hen, flushed and beautiful. William was so happy to see her temper up. It was a good sign—it meant she was feeling better. It was killing him that she wouldn't see him. He put more feeling into it, closing his eyes like a lovesick sod.

That's when the tea kettle came at him. He ducked and it rolled into the street. That was a close one. Sullivan was shaking his head, convinced that whatever William was trying to accomplish, he was failing.

The crowd was growing, and Sorcha had to give William credit. She peered down and was rewarded with a wink from Sean. "He's not going to give up, Katie. The man is totally in love. And, if you won't marry him, half the women in Dublin will line up to take a crack at him."

"Let them have him!"

"Ye don't mean that, and well ye know it. What else is he going to have to do, Katie? None of this is his fault," Sorcha said patiently.

She put her hands over her face. "I don't deserve him. He could have anyone."

"You are so wrong, dear girl. And, if it takes a lifetime, he'll prove it to you. He doesn't want anyone. He wants you."

The song continued, and Katie was suddenly so tired. The tears misted her eyes.

William was starting to panic. He was almost to the end of the song. Where was she? She'd disappeared back into the flat. The last notes ended, and he dropped his head. His voice was hoarse through the microphone. "Katie, love. Please. I love you, a mhuirnín. Till my death I'll love you."

The women behind him sighed. One of them yelled, "If you won't have him, I'll bloody take him!" Sean turned and shushed her. That's when the outer door to the building opened, and Katie appeared.

William's heart stopped in his chest. "Katie, love." He handed off the microphone and went to her, scooping her into his arms.

Inis Oirr, Aran Islands, Co. Galway, Ireland

The wedding was simple. Katie's immediate family, the O'Briens, and Sorcha. Sorcha had explained the situation to her boss at the hospital, and they'd allowed her a couple more days off. The parish priest from William's village parish married them on the island coast, and then they all went to tea. Sorcha bundled her thick wool shawl around herself, a gift from Katie, who was also wrapped in an identical one, protection from the sea air. She liked the smell of the sea and the feel of the rocks under her feet. The craggy shore had its own charm, and there was something rather pagan and exciting about getting married out in the elements. To be one with nature as you joined with your soulmate.

Katie was pale, but so heartbreakingly beautiful it made her heart squeeze with a deep, sisterly affection. Her hair was long and wavy, with golden highlights that caught the sun. Her veil was unique, something handmade from an old island lineage. Katie's eyes were the rich, golden color of whiskey and when she looked up at William, the love shone out of them. Sorcha hadn't attended many weddings, but she felt sure that this was the most beautiful one she'd ever witnessed.

They all took carriages to Castle O'Brien, wanting to get some photographs before heading back to the mainland. Sorcha was fascinated by the ruins that stood at a high point on the island. A devilish part of her remembered what they'd done in the last ruin, and she looked at Sean as she wove her way through the crumbling structure. His glance was searing, and she knew he was wishing they were alone. She started up a dodgy looking set of stairs, reaching toward the sky because the ruin was missing its roof. "Sorcha, don't. It's not safe," he said. Then he cursed as she continued to climb. It wouldn't help for him to follow her; both their weight on the ancient steps was a bad idea altogether. He hissed, "Get down from there."

She gave him a look that would have withered any other man.

"I'm just looking. Ye can see the whole island from the top, I'll wager."

"Christ, what you must have been like as a lass. Do you ever do as you're told?"

"Never." She flipped around, continuing her ascent. He caught a flash of leg under her blue dress, and it stirred him to distraction. He heard her gasp, and he looked away from her shapely calf. "It's so beautiful, Sean. Oh." She put her hand on her heart and his chest tightened. She was in one of their clan strongholds. It was a primitive, pounding need in him to pull her into a dark corner and take her. Make her his. Claim his birthright and lordly privileges. He was a rotter of the first order, thinking that way, but he was, after all, a thick-blooded O'Brien man.

Then the voice behind him sapped the lust right from his body. Maeve said, "Oh, I want to climb up there, too!"

Sean gave Sorcha a chiding look. His father said, in a deep baritone voice, "You are not goin' up there. Sorcha, love, you're giving poor Aoife a fright."

Sorcha blushed, creeping down the narrow, winding stairs. She wove her arm into Maeve's and distracted her. "Do you come here a lot?"

Maeve said, "Once a year, with the school. Then Dottie Tomblin gets all out of sorts because she's not an O'Brien. She's from peasant stock."

"Maeve, really." Her mother's tone was stern. "That's an awful thing to say."

"Well, she is. She doesn't have any family lore to speak of. Not like us. We've got bloody mayhem, tales of love and betrayal. At least one day a year, I'm the envy of that little shrew and her tosser of a brother."

Sorcha was covering her mouth, trying not to laugh. She walked with Maeve, indulging the girl as she told her the condensed history of the O'Brien clan. It was an altogether beautiful day for a walk. She curled into her beautiful, thoughtfully made shawl Katie had woven into her own clan pattern: the

O'Maolin or Mullen weave. Katie had made her own shawl not of the Donoghue pattern, but of the O'Brien one. And if Sorcha felt a pang of envy, she swiftly buried it.

They were on the boat headed back to Galway, where Sean would begin the drive back to Belfast. William and Katie wouldn't get much of a honeymoon, because they both had to be back in the city. And Katie was still healing—a sobering thought and terribly sad.

Sorcha stared out at the rolling swells of the Atlantic and had to admit to herself that she hated leaving Sean. But it was for the best. She had patients who were coming up on their due dates. Her brother would be worried if she extended for another day. It was time to get back to her life in the north.

She replayed the conversation in her head when she'd asked Maeve about something William had said. *What did he mean when he said Katie was his mate? That it was forever and he couldn't walk away?* That's when she'd finally heard the lore about the O'Brien clan. The legend that had been passed down since chieftains and kings still ruled this ancient land—a tale that Sean hadn't shared with her for some reason.

The O'Brien men only have one true mate. Once fate brings them together, it's forever. The O'Brien man never comes easily to his mate, but once he finds her, he'll love her and only her. And, if he loses her, he's e'er ruined, never to love again. The men in our family, and the women really, they all believe it. When we love, we love forever. It's not like a regular courtship. We fall hard and fast, and it's a love that lasts. Nothing else comes before an O'Brien and his mate.

They made small talk on the long drive to Belfast, but she couldn't put the conversation off anymore. They were almost to the city. "Sean, we need to talk." Sorcha stared out the window, unable to look at him. The feelings the wedding stirred in her were still humming through her mind. The nearness of the man beside her made her blood sing. It scared her. She couldn't get involved with someone who fell that hard. Who loved that deeply. She didn't know how to put everything on hold for love. She couldn't be that for him. She wasn't right for him. Katie deserved someone like William. She'd put him first. Sean needed someone who would drop everything without hesitation. Someone who'd wait for him every night with a hot meal and a warm bed. Not someone who worked long shifts and was called out in the middle of the night to deliver someone else's child. She was too selfish and ambitious, and he needed someone different.

"Famous last words. We need to talk. Jesus, Sorcha. How is it that we always end up here?" He knew. He shook his head, as if trying to clear it. "Are you always so at odds with yourself?"

Funny, that's almost exactly what her brother had said. "Sean, I know about your family legend. Maeve told me. About how you all think you have one fated mate." He was silent and she looked at him. He wouldn't meet her eyes. "I know that this thing between us is... intense." She hated herself right now. "And, if I was a different person with a different life... If I could give you what you needed, then..." She trailed off, not sure what she was trying to say.

"You don't know what I need. You're too busy running away to bother asking. Just stop it, Sorcha. I haven't gotten down on one knee. I just don't want to stop seeing you." His jaw was tight, and he slammed his hand against the steering wheel. "Don't do this. I know you care for me. Forget what Maeve told you. It's not important. This isn't the Middle Ages. People choose who they're with. Just let me come get you next time you have a couple days off work. We'll tour the city some more. Don't make everything so complicated." But it was complicated. They were both getting in deeper with every day that passed. She hesitated and his temper flared. "Fine. How about this? You call me when you miss me. If that doesn't happen, I'll have my answer."

"Sean," she said, and the pitying tone made him mental.

"I mean, don't break a sweat or anything. I understand how things are. You haven't even let me meet your parents. You like me.

You might even want me. But that's it. That's all I'm going to get. And I'm enough of a pathetic sod that I'll take the scraps you offer. So, like I said, you can reach out if you miss me and want to see me. I won't bother you again if you don't."

He pulled up to her building now, not parking. He got out, opened her door so she could leave. He handed her the two bags. "Goodbye, Sorcha. Take care of yourself." He looked up to the window and her brother waved. He got in the car without looking at her again. He hated this loop they were in, but he couldn't look back. If he did, he might fall at her feet and beg. He had his pride. As he drove toward the south, he had a sinking feeling he'd never see her again.

FOURTEEN

I must lose myself in action, lest I wither in despair...

—Alfred Lord Tennyson

Dublin, Ireland

William shook his head as he watched Sean throw himself into the pub brawl. His brother was out of control. Damn that Sorcha Mullen. She'd retreated again. Sean hadn't heard from her in six days, and his temper was worsening by the minute. Right now, he was going head-to-head with a man who was two inches taller at least, and about two stone larger. Not many men could claim that, because Sean was a big lad. He wasn't even using his nightstick. Wasn't trying to subdue. Sean wanted a fight, and this ruddy, dog-faced bastard was just drunk enough to give it to him.

Sullivan came from behind him. "Boss is looking out of sorts. Best rein your brother in or he's going to be writing parking tickets."

William watched as the two men wrestled their way into the back room of the pub, where all the patrons had prudently cleared out. He walked up to the door, handed his nightstick to Sullivan, and said, "If he comes out before me, knock the wee mongrel over the head." Then he walked into the room and toward the two men locked in battle. The first one to come through the door was the drunk who'd started this whole mess, his arms wheeling as he landed at Sullivan's feet. "Stay down or I'll take this stick to your fat head." Then he cuffed him and left him to lie there.

He watched grimly as William shut himself in with his brother. The commotion that came out of the room was a string of growls and juicy curses. Then, something that sounded like a tin rubbish bin being dropped down a flight of concrete stairs. He looked at the other men, but there was no way anyone was going to get between two O'Brien men with their blood up. The next sound was wood splintering. *Shit.* Sullivan briefly considered the need for an ambulance, but decided against it. After some sizable shouts and crashes, silence descended.

The men shifted nervously. Then Sullivan took charge, despite his junior rank. He walked to his fate, thinking about what he'd like to be said at his wake. When he opened the door, he first saw the splintered chair, which had obviously been thrown against the wall. Better that than over William's back. Then he saw them. Both exhausted, breathing heavy, and sitting shoulder to shoulder. Their tree-trunk sized legs were splayed out like two small boys, tired from play. It kind of warmed a man's heart if you ignored Sean's bruised cheek and quickly blackening eye, and William's bleeding lip.

William reached his far hand over and cupped his brother's face, their heads together in deep contentment. "Feel better, brother?"

Sean's mouth turned up on one side. "Aye, a bit."

"Good. I think Sullivan can take this arrest. You and I need to get cleaned up and eat something. Don't think I haven't noticed you've been skipping meals. You can tell, by the way. That right hook of yours was like getting hit with a rotten grapefruit."

Sean chuckled for the first time in a week. "Piss off. That trickle of blood would say otherwise."

"Aye, well, ye better hope I don't tell Katie where it came from. She'll have your hide." He stood then, extended a palm to his big brother.

"Fair enough," Sean said. And they left the pub together.

Belfast, Northern Ireland

Sorcha walked out of the entrance of the hospital, her mood as black as the sky. She caught movement out of the corner of her eye and was surprised to see her brother standing on the corner. He was arguing with someone. They saw her and the other man turned and walked away. *Shifty as always,* she thought, *and on the wrong side of the wall.*

John approached, clearing his face of irritation. He leaned in and kissed her face. "Hello, love. I was hoping I'd catch you." The mill wasn't all that far from the hospital, but something was off.

"Why aren't you at work? And why is Denny O'Rourke on this side of town?"

"We had a walk out. The IRA showed up for reinforcement. I got out of there, because it was starting to get ugly. He followed me. He's thinking to tell me how to manage my sister, among other things."

"Well, he can sod off. I don't need to be managed. Unlike that lazy prat, I have a job."

"Aye, well, he fancies himself a freedom fighter. Meanwhile, the girl he got in trouble is in government housing, not getting a dime from him. He's a nasty bastard, Sorcha. Just steer clear of him."

"With pleasure. I don't like it, John. Things are heating up again."

"He's an asshole, to be sure, but maybe he's right. Maybe you should stay home for a few days."

"Not bloody likely. I have patients, John. And I don't care which neighborhoods they live in. I'm not going to jeopardize the last months of my training because of O'Rourke or any conflicts.

When I'm done, I can transfer back to the Mater. But if I blow this opportunity, they may not want me back."

He walked alongside her as she made her way to her first home visit. Angelina was meeting her there, observing her for her next review. "Sorcha," John said, and she knew that tone. "Have you called your man?"

"He's not my man, John. He's a friend. I mean, he was. It's complicated."

He said, "I guess I can understand that. More than you might think. I liked him, though. He was good for you. He didn't try to tame you, for one."

"As if any mortal man could." She smiled wryly, covering her heartache with humor.

"All I'm saying is that in a few months, you don't have to go back to the Mater. You could go wherever you wanted."

"I know, John. Don't you think I've thought about it? I've thought of little else, but Sean isn't the sort to do anything halfway. He'll want to marry me."

"And what the hell is wrong with that? If he loves you, I'd hope he'd marry you and not just try to get you on your back. Christ, Sorcha, that's what honorable men do."

"I know!" she snapped at him, then stopped. "I'm sorry. This isn't your problem. I shouldn't take it out on you. I'm just... scared. I'm afraid of losing myself. Ireland isn't like Belfast. A lot of women just marry and start having children. He comes from a small village. He's in the city, yes, but deep down he's a traditional sort. He's a force of nature. Not like a bully, that's not it. It's just he's so overwhelming. He's so wonderful. I could see a woman doing almost anything to make him happy."

"He's the sort of man who wouldn't be happy, I think, unless you were. Don't sell him short, Sorcha. A lot of people would love to have what you've found with him. Don't throw it away because you're a coward." Fighting words, and he knew it.

"I'm no coward." Her face was tight with insult.

"Aye, so you keep saying," he said lightly, undaunted by his sister's temper.

Her retort was interrupted by a scream through an open window. She came back to herself. "Don't worry, that's Mrs. Sutherland. Duty calls."

"You've chosen quite a career, sister." He kissed her then, and pulled her into a hug. "Be careful, Sorcha. Trouble is stirring. Warn the other girls. I don't know anything, before you ask. Den doesn't trust me in that regard. I just have a bad feeling. Things have been quiet for too long. I don't trust it. Just be careful. I'm going to come back and escort you home—I've got nothing better to do. At home on the west end, you'll be safe. They stay clear of the midwives, but I don't want you getting stuck in the crossfire somewhere over here. Just stay alert."

Another scream came through the window. "I have to go, John. Just meet me at the hospital, that's the easiest way. My last appointment is north of the hospital by one of the checkpoints. I don't want you wandering around up there."

Sorcha went to the door of the townhome, wondering how on earth Mrs. Sutherland had negotiated a home birth with her doctor at the Jubilee. When she went into the well-appointed row house, she figured it had something to do with influence. They were significantly more well-off than most of her patients. She'd have thought the woman would rather have one of the private birthing suites the wealthier clientele had access to for childbirth.

She heard Angelina arguing with the woman. "No, Mrs. Sutherland, I've told you the conditions for this particular situation. No dogs in the birthing bed, no matter how cute they are."

Sorcha then noticed the pictures all over the wall as a domestic servant led her to the bedroom. Dogs. Specifically Yorkshire Terriers. "How many dogs does she have?"

The housekeeper's face told Sorcha exactly what she thought of the beasts. "Four. She had five, but Prince Albert died this past August. She names them all for royalty. Won't be parted from them for more than a few hours. This is her first child, ye ken." The woman's thick Scots accent was dry and sarcastic. "She had trouble, so the little furry beasts have been a sort of..." Her face actually softened a bit.

"A substitute. I see. Well, that's all well and good, but they've got no place in a birthing room. They'll have to stay out."

She came to the door just as the woman's husband was coming out of the room with, she would find out later, a male dog by the name of Richard the Lionheart. Her favorite, apparently. The couple was younger than she'd expected. The furnishings spoke of old money. Her husband, indulgently looking back at his wife, offered an explanation, even though she hadn't asked for one. "This was my father's home. He and my mother have retired to Bath. It's warmer and has a better social climate. He was a dignitary. Now, I'll leave you ladies to your work. Please, do try to make her comfortable. She's terribly nervous about the birth. It took us so long to get here, you see. I'm away a lot for my work, and she has been incredibly lonely. Hence the, um, preoccupation with pets. I think this child will help in that regard."

"A child is not a dog, Mr. Sutherland. And this is not the fifteenth century. Your wife and your child will need you to make an effort to be home more."

His face was grim. "I understand. Thank you. I'll just be downstairs. Haddie will stand by in case you have need of anything. And please, regardless of what she says, call an ambulance if something is amiss. I'm afraid she's been a bit unreasonable about this whole business."

"You seem so out of sorts, Sorcha. You know you can talk to me? Is it something at home?" Angelina was changing into her regular clothes, the shift over. The birth, fortunately, had been easy and uneventful.

Sorcha sat on the bench in the locker room. It was empty but for them, and she knew she could trust Angelina. "Nothing is wrong at home. My parents are actually on holiday in Gordes. It's their anniversary—twenty-three years of wedded bliss. They make it look effortless."

"Then it's your man. The copper?"

Sorcha had kept it together for too long. The tears welled up in her eyes, and she finally let them fall. Angelina came next to her and sat, putting an arm around her. "You've had quite a big adventure with those three. I thought you'd be the next to marry."

"I think he was hoping so as well. He never said as much, but..." Then she told her about the enduring myth that followed generations of O'Briens.

"That's very romantic. Why does it scare you, Sorcha? I mean, you care for him, right?"

"I think I love him." She shook herself. "Jesus, I've never said it out loud. I love him."

"Were you together?"

"Not fully. He's been holding back because"—she blushed, admitting—"I'm a virgin."

Angelina smiled with approval. "Good for him. Most men wouldn't have. Most men would have considered you a trophy." Sorcha laughed. She was hardly a trophy.

"Sorcha, have you thought about how you are going to avoid getting into the same situation your friend did? I know you're a Catholic. I don't mean to offend, but I've heard you counsel your patients, so I just wondered if you needed some help. You won't have as many options in other places."

"I have, but it hardly matters. I may have already buggered the whole thing. I hurt him."

"He made it your choice. If you want him, Sorcha, you're going to have to make the first move. And you should be ready. I don't think your virginity is going to survive one more visit with him. From what you've told me, I don't know how you've resisted this long. That tower..." She fanned herself. "Let me tell you something from an older, wiser woman. I haven't slept around, but I've been with three men. One was a selfish bastard who didn't worry one shilling about my pleasure. The other was sweet, but he didn't have that hunger that comes from a real man. That appetite for a woman that has just as much to do with pleasing her as himself. Those men are rare."

"And the third man? Would that happen to be our good doctor?" The smile told Sorcha everything. "You're taking the piss! You've been holding out on me—I even told you about the tower!"

"This isn't about me, right now. This is about you. I promise, when you visit me, we will stay up until all hours eating chocolate and talking about men. For now, how are you going to deal with Officer O'Brien? It should start with a phone call. Dublin needs midwives just as badly as Belfast. You need to be ready to woo him, Sorcha. You've made him work very hard and you've wounded his pride. Time to don your best knickers and fix what you broke the old-fashioned way."

Sorcha covered her mouth, stifling an absurdly immature urge to giggle. She wasn't sure she knew how to seduce a man like Sean O'Brien. Did she want to? A small box in her heart, where she kept secret things, opened a crack. Out of it poured every feeling she had suppressed about what life would be like with Sean. Her eyes shut as a fresh wave of tears came. "I love him, Angelina."

"I know you do, my sweet. Your days off are coming up. You'll need a bus ticket. But first you must come in early tomorrow. I won't tell a soul. I think the easiest way to handle this is oral contraceptives. If he's a strict Catholic, it may be better if this is in your hands. Not that I don't think he'd use a condom, but if you don't want to ask him to do that, then you have other options. I have a female doctor who won't ask any questions. When did your last period end?"

"Yesterday."

"That's perfect. Tomorrow is Sunday. You'll be able to start the pack of pills right away."

"I don't know, Angelina."

"Well, what are your feelings about a cervical cap or diaphragm? That would be fairly simple as well. I can fit you for one or the other tomorrow. I just want to help, Sorcha. I want you to be happy, but I also don't want you to fall pregnant if I can aid you in how to prevent it. I just thought pills would be better since this will be your first time."

"You're right, I know you're right. I would have done the same for Katie. I'll meet you here tomorrow morning at seven. My shift starts at eight. I will think about what I want to do."

Sorcha took the bus to work before the sun had completely brought the city into daytime. She'd tried to call Sean last night, needing to hear his voice. Afraid as well. Afraid of the feelings that had surfaced with such permanence and purpose. She loved him, and the thought of him working the streets of Dublin every night and not knowing that simple fact made her feel a gut-wrenching panic. He'd been so loving. So patient. And she wasn't sure where their relationship would take her, but he deserved to know the truth.

Angelina gave her a conspiratorial grin as she walked into the locker room. "Come, before you get dressed. I've secured an exam room. Once we have some privacy, you and I will come up with a solution."

Once she closed the door, she sat on the stool and Sorcha sat on the table. "I have one more option we didn't discuss that I can do without a doctor."

"What is that?"

"The Depo-Provera shot. It's short term. They haven't approved it for long term. I didn't think you'd have it in Ireland, but the UK has been using it since the sixties. It occurred to me that something temporary and non-invasive might be better. I think you'd be more comfortable, when the time came, to discuss what you wanted to do long term with Sean. It occurred to me that this might be a struggle for you both, and I wasn't being sensitive to that. If you are going to have any hope of building a relationship while straddling the southern border, maybe you and Sean need to open up dialogue about this. A Depo-Provera shot will buy you some time, however. It won't involve wearing or inserting anything.

You can let things happen on their own. As long as you're sure Sean doesn't have anything."

"He doesn't. He hasn't been with anyone since his last physical. I trust him."

Angelina nodded. "Okay, then I think we have our answer. If things don't develop into something sexual, then you just carry on like normal. I'm only going to give you a dose that will stop you from ovulating this month. After that, we'll see."

Once you attempt legislation upon religious grounds, you open the way for every kind of intolerance and religious persecution...

—William Butler Yeats

The first part of the day had been busy. Another stormfront had come over the North Atlantic and settled in the North Channel, causing some untimely contractions and a few walk-in deliveries. Sorcha scratched at her arm, walking toward the intersection of Broadway and Falls. Her brother had met her for the last two nights, escorting her all the way home. She had two more visitations before she could call it quits and head back to the hospital to meet him. The city was uncommonly quiet, and it caused the hair to stand up on her neck. Considering the walk-out, she'd have thought there would have been more trouble. Perhaps some small skirmishes or a protest near the mill at the very least. Even the dock workers union was quiet.

"Does your arm hurt?" Angelina's voice brought her out of her thoughts.

"Not really. Just warm and itchy at the injection site. It's normal, I think." Sorcha smiled at her. "Thank you again, Angelina. You are a true friend."

"I am, and so are you. You'd have done the same. Just don't tell those nuns of yours. They'll have me by the ear."

"I won't. I'll take it to the grave. Now, it's half six. Let's grab the bus to Northumberland and Shankill. I don't like walking around that area, and the bus will be quicker."

Angelina took her hand. "I won't let 'em get you, old girl. Just stick with me." Sorcha giggled, taking in the sight of her unlikely friend. Her nurse's cap covered part of her fair hair. She had that Norman look you might see in an English film star. She was such a good person, fair and loyal. Sorcha knew that when Angelina looked at her, she saw a fellow midwife and a friend. She didn't see their differences, or if she did, she celebrated them. Maybe there was hope for this city. They ran to the bus, just as it was leaving, and two older men gave up their seats. Angelina said, "We should grab a bite to eat after work. Bring your brother."

John would never come out with them, she knew this, but it was nice of Angelina to offer. "You don't need us cramping your style. Our Dr. Childs will surely want you all to himself." A saucy retort was on the tip of her tongue when Sorcha felt the first tremble. "Oh, God. Brace yourself, Angelina. I think I just heard an..." The next explosion rocked the city. The bus veered to the left as the storefront blasted debris mere feet from the front of the bus. The front windshield and several other windows blew inward, showering the interior of the bus and the riders with pebbles of glass. Sorcha jumped up, grabbing her friend as the rest of them piled out of the back of the bus. The traffic had stopped behind them. "Are you okay, Angelina?" She got them out of the road and onto the sidewalk.

"Yes, I'm okay. We need to check for wounded!" She ran toward the site of the explosion just as another bomb went off several blocks away. Then Sorcha understood.

All the current events that led up to this attack had been on the news. The detainment and prosecution proceedings for the Shankill Butchers were being reported. That band of merry maniacs had been kidnapping and murdering Catholics in the city. These are most likely the men who had tried to pull her into that van a couple years ago. Those wounds to the Nationalist community hadn't healed, and having the bastards on the news report every day was a fresh reminder for those who fought for the cause.

There had also been an anniversary march last month. The anniversary of the assassination of Máire Drumm, the Vice President of Sinn Fein. She was murdered by loyalists while she lay helpless in the hospital where Sorcha used to work. And, this past January, the human rights court had ruled against the release of the internees.

It had been too quiet the last couple of weeks, and she'd known deep down that this was brewing. "Dammit!" She clutched her medical bag, trying to control a meltdown. This was what the warnings were about from O'Rourke. Comments about her hanging out in the wrong part of town. That bastard had known this was coming, and in his own way, had been trying to look out for her. Now, she was stuck right in the middle of this mess. She ran next to Angelina, toward the wounded.

Sorcha said, "This is going to get ugly, Angelina. I'm afraid this is just starting." And it was. There would be chaos in the streets. Retaliation from the Ulster side. Soldiers would flood the city, shooting first and asking questions later. She hoped to God her brother was safe.

They ran toward the burning pub, hearing the screams of the people around them. The stench of singed flesh mingled with other things. Burned plastic, scorched rubber from the car that had been part of the blast. It was on its side with the tires aflame. Sorcha saw the fuel leak just in time to push Angelina against the building and behind a call box. "Get down!"

They heard a whoomp as the stream of fuel caught fire, then the car exploded from the petrol tank and out, causing more glass and metal to shower the area. Then they were up on their feet and running. The inside of the pub was a black hole. Charred, mangled bodies littered the area, but not everyone had perished, and help had to be coming soon, right? That was her last thought before they started tending to the injured.

Sorcha said, "We need to get them away from the fumes and

flames. This ceiling might not hold." That's when she looked over her shoulder. A few doors down there was a store front. Used clothing, she thought. The door was ajar, like someone had exited fast. She'd imagine no clerk wages were worth sticking around for the next bomb to go off, or to stand by and wait for the riots to begin. She pointed and said, "There! Let's take them into that building!" And so it began...

Dublin, Ireland

Sean woke to William's voice as his door whipped open with a slam against the wall. "Get up, Sean! You have to see the news!"

Sean had worked a double, not getting home until three o'clock and then falling into bed. It was almost seven now. "What is it? Jesus, William, I'm knackered."

William flipped the light on and grabbed him by the shoulder. "It's all over the news, Sean! It's Belfast. Jesus Christ, brother, they've started the bombing again!" The television screen came into view, black and white against the dim lights. William increased the volume as Sean threw on a pair of jeans and went in to listen.

The news reporter said, "Belfast is burning, and experts fear it is only the beginning. The IRA has begun a bombing campaign that has rocked the city."

Sean almost threw up right there. "Jesus Christ, Willy, she might be at work. She might be anywhere in that city. That's between the two hospitals!"

"I'll call Sullivan. He can take my shift tonight," William said.

"I can't ask you to go, William." Sean was pulling on his shirt and a pair of socks as he talked.

"You aren't asking. I'm telling you. There's no fecking way you are driving into that"—he pointed at the screen as he said it—"without your backup! You can just save it, brother, because I am going with you. Give me five minutes."

"You have a wife, now, William. Think! You need to stay here!" Sean yelled.

A feminine voice came from behind him. "Go. Both of you. You're stronger together. Go and get her." Katie covered her mouth and choked down a sob. "Please, dear God, go and get her. We won't survive the loss of her. None of us will. You go now, and I will call Sullivan. You go and get my sister!" Her voice was hysterical as the tears poured down her face.

William grabbed her and held her tight. "We'll bring her home, I swear it, Katie. We won't leave that city without her."

"If I have to crawl through those city streets, I will find her," Sean said, and he meant it. She was his mate. His love. She may have turned her back on him, but he couldn't walk away from her. He'd see her safe or die trying.

FIFTEEN

*A hero is no braver than an ordinary man, but he is brave five
minutes longer...*

—Ralph Waldo Emerson

Belfast, Northern Ireland

The pub had been strategically chosen to target the after-work crowd. The problem was, the surrounding areas were hit almost as hard, as were any passing vehicles. The neighboring delicatessen was now missing its front window, and smoke was pouring into the place due to a shared wall. People were running out of buildings in complete panic. There was also a clothing shop a few doors down, but not connected. It was there in the empty store where they'd decided to drag the wounded. "Where the hell are the ambulances?" Sorcha screamed.

"There are roadblocks. A couple of checkpoints were hit as well. No one is getting anywhere. I called the Mater and spoke with Nigel. They struck in key places between the hospitals and detonated some car bombs."

She gritted her teeth. Her classmates and their kin certainly knew how to blow things up. She looked up just as Dr. Stirling appeared in the doorway. He said, "Nigel called me. They are all tied up at the hospital."

Angelina took in his disheveled appearance. "Did you run the whole way?"

"Bicycle. Jesus, this part of the city is a mess. The city hospital is full of casualties. Four bombs already, that I know of. Tell me what we have here. Have you triaged?"

Sorcha went right into emergency mode, briefing the doctor on the injuries. Angelina was a seasoned midwife, but Sorcha had trained in emergency medicine during her first year of nursing school. "This side can wait. Their injuries are more minor. Abrasions, minor burns, and concussions."

He knelt down beside her, observing that she was compressing a wound under her hands. The dark blood oozed between her gloved fingers and pooled. It was fully dark outside now, and all they had to work by were the emergency floodlights for the building. "Laceration to the right radial artery is most likely. I don't think it's completely severed, or he'd have already bled out. Do you have a surgical kit with you? Anything?"

Dr. Stirling said, "I can do my best until we get him to a hospital. Angelina, I need you here. I want Sorcha on the burn patient."

He looked over his shoulder. There was a mother and child huddled together. "Ma'am, could you do me a favor? Do you see that young man with the bleeding head? I need you to keep him awake. Go talk to him, please?"

The woman dug in her bag, pulling out a paperback. "I can read to him."

"*The Outsiders*. Good choice. I was always partial to the greasers," Stirling said.

She started, "When I stepped out into the bright sunlight..." and her clear, soprano voice was heavenly to the ears in such an ugly environment. Sorcha got the IV equipment ready to treat the man who was burned, and she noticed that he seemed to calm at the sound of the woman's voice. She looked at the doctor.

Dr. Stirling said, "Just keep him comfortable. There's a vial of morphine in the bag if you think his stats are strong enough to take it."

If they aren't, does it really matter if it offers him some final relief? She saw the unspoken message in his eyes. She leaned over the man. His face was burned horribly, his ears charred past saving. His hands and wrists were likewise. She kept the bile down as she noticed that his shirt collar was melted to his neck. He was in so much pain that he just made little mewling noises and trembled with the effort to simply keep on breathing. She looked for a viable spot to run an IV, carefully lifting his sleeve, then she took scissors from her kit and cut up the length of his coat sleeve and managed to find a vein just above his inner elbow. She wiped her face, realizing she was weeping. Such pain. Who was this man? Did he have a family? Once she gave him a dose of morphine, he began to drift off. But she saw emotion in his eyes. Gratitude, mostly, and resolve. He knew he was going to die. She touched his exposed arm, a bit that had been spared from the blast, and she said a prayer for this stranger's soul.

Then she went to the next patient, a handsome young man maybe a few years older than herself. She removed the gauze that he'd been holding against a gash on his head. "I'm afraid I don't have any lidocaine."

He looked at her weakly and said, "It's okay. I've got my own numbing agent." He pulled a flask out of his coat.

"Okay, but not too much. You have a head injury. And I'm going to have to cut a patch of hair, I'm afraid." He just gave a grunt, granting her leave to do so. A pity, because he had nice hair, thick, chestnut waves that curled at his temples. She used her scissors to cut the hair around the wound, giving her a cleaner area to stitch. He tensed when she pierced the flesh. "I'm sorry. You're going to need about three more and it'll be done." He took a sip of whiskey, and then she continued. When she was done, she cleaned the area again and wrapped a fresh bandage around his head.

That's when a car pulled up in front of them. Sorcha tensed, wondering what fresh hell was starting next. The man who ran into the store yelled, "Jenny!"

"Colin!" It was the woman with the child.

He said, "I managed to get around the back roads. They can't get the ambulances through."

Sorcha looked out at his compact car. She asked, "Can you make it to the hospital from here?"

The man took in the horror scene. "I can take two people if my daughter sits on my wife's lap, but I need to leave now."

Sorcha turned to the burn patient, her throat seizing up. She went to him, feeling for a pulse. Her eyes teared up as she closed his eyes. "I'm so sorry, lad. I'm sorry I couldn't save you," she said, her voice husky with emotion. Then she turned off the saline drip, in case they needed the fluids. She said roughly, "Angelina should go. She can take him." She motioned to the patient with the arterial bleed.

"I won't leave you, Sorcha!" Angelina's voice broke with emotion. "No way in hell am I leaving you here."

Dr. Stirling said, "No, my dear. I won't leave her, but you must. One of us needs to ride with him. He's not stable and you need to keep a hand on that wound. Go now. They could use another midwife on the ward. They pulled several of our nurses for the main hospital. They need you there, Angelina. Try to get them to send an ambulance or some more civilian vehicles for transport."

Just as he said it, another explosion went off in the distance. Sorcha said, "That came from the north. Go, Angelina, before you get pinned in!" She stood, hugging the woman. "If you see my brother at the hospital, you need to tell him to go home. Do you hear me? You tell him I'm safe and to try to make it back to the flat. If he can't do that safely, tell him to stay at the hospital. He'll be safe there. And make sure he eats something."

They loaded the man, so pale and weak, into the back of the small car. His head was cradled in Angelina's lap while she held his arm elevated. He'd lost so much blood, but he was hanging on. Another person walked in, carrying a man with a belly wound.

Dr. Stirling said, "Is that what I think it is?"

"It's a gunshot wound," Sorcha said grimly. It was starting. The rioting was starting. "Please, sir. We are only here to help. We won't ask any questions. But if you are armed, you need to leave your friend and go. Do you understand?"

"He's not my friend. I don't even know the lad. He was just left in the lane. And don't worry, I'm not armed. You've got nothing to fear from me."

It made sense as Sorcha looked at him. He was a bit older than the wounded young man, and more polished. "What's your name, sir?"

"The name's Mick. Where do you want him?"

Sean was ready to go mad. The exodus away from the city was significant—people who likely worked inside the city limits, but lived in one of the outer boroughs like Sorcha's parents. The checkpoints had turned into roadblocks, armed men searching cars coming and going. "You need to go back, William. I'm better off on foot."

"I'm not leaving you, Sean. Forget it. We'll park at the bus station half a kilometer back and both go in on foot."

"I really think you should leave, William!" He raised his voice, thinking maybe William would understand him if he said it louder. Not feckin' likely.

As he said it, they opened another lane. Sean pulled up to a pair of guards, and both he and William kept their hands in plain view. "What's your business in the city tonight?" one guard asked.

"I need to get to my fiancé. She's a nurse in the city. I'm a Garda officer in Dublin. We both are, actually. We don't want any trouble. I just want to get her and get the hell back down south."

"That's not a good idea. Which hospital is she working?"

"The Royal Jubilee," Sean answered.

The guards looked at one another. He said, "I'm not sure you'll even be able to get there. They've detonated nine bombs already, and I don't think they're done. Four of them were right in that area."

Sean put his head on the steering wheel. "Jesus. Oh, God. Sorcha." He looked at the man. "Do you have a wife?"

"I do. She's holed up in our flat, scared out of her mind."

Sean shook his head. "I'm sorry, brother. But you understand, then. You want her safe. And that pigheaded woman of mine is likely right in the thick of things! I need to get her out of there. Please, search the car. Do what you need to, but then let me go. I need to find her."

Sorcha gave water to the wounded who were awake and alert enough to take fluids by mouth. Dr. Stirling had packed the gunshot wound, slowing the bleeding, but he didn't dare risk trying to do surgery in these primitive conditions. The equipment he'd brought by bicycle was running low, but they still had clean bandages, the remaining morphine, and other basic supplies. The man, Mick, who'd come in carrying the gunshot patient had stayed to help them, having been a medic in the Army some years ago. He was certainly capable. He appeared to be in his late twenties or early thirties, and he had the polished, handsome features of a military man.

"Dr. Stirling, I called the hospital again. Word has it that they're working on clearing the roadway. They can't tell me when or if they'll send someone this way, however. I'm not sure how long we can wait."

"Sorcha, I think it's past time you called me Robert," Dr. Stirling answered.

Sorcha smiled at that and said, "As you wish, Robert." She looked up and tensed, and he followed her gaze to the door of the storefront.

Soldiers were walking through the door on foot. "Is this where we can find a doctor?"

"I'm a doctor. I'm an obstetrician, actually, but we are

managing until the ambulances can get through. This is Nurse Mullen. Is one of you injured?"

"I'm Captain Wilson. I need you to come with me," the man said plainly.

Sorcha was irrationally terrified of these men. Her experience with British soldiers hadn't been positive. She looked to Dr. Stirling, panic seizing up her vocal cords.

Dr. Stirling said, "I'm sorry, captain, I can't leave these people or my nurse. If you could bring them here, we can treat them alongside the others."

"That is quite impossible. Your nurse is going to have to handle things on her own for a bit. We have several injured men. They drove a car into the barricade where our men were standing guard and detonated an explosive device. Please, we cannot delay. They tried to fly a helicopter in to pick up the wounded, but the bastards shot an RPG across its bow. They turned the chopper around and refused to land. I'm sorry, but I'm not asking. I was ordered to bring a doctor to them, and you fit the bill."

Dr. Stirling looked at Sorcha, ready to fight. She knew it. He'd fight rather than leave her. "Go, Robert. I've got Mick." A long pause happened then, until the soldier cleared his throat.

Stirling turned back to the soldiers. "I'll come with you on one condition." The captain raised a brow at his gall. "Take it or leave it. Tick tock." He pointed at his watch as if to remind the captain they were needed elsewhere.

"What is your condition?" he asked curtly.

"You will send back a jeep or some other vehicle to pick up the most wounded of the group and get them to the hospital. And you'll take Nurse Mullen with you. A truck would be better, but you must send something and get her out of here."

"I'm not leaving all of these people!" Sorcha said sternly.

"Done." The soldier moved toward the door, ignoring Sorcha. "You can leave her some of the supplies, but bring anything you think you'll need. There are burns, shrapnel injuries, and head wounds. There is one man who may need an amputation. His leg is mangled below the knee, and they've been using a tourniquet in timed increments to keep him from bleeding out. I'm sorry, but we can't delay any further."

Stirling started dividing up the items. "Sorcha, when that vehicle comes, you get into it and go back to the hospital, do you hear me? You take the ones who need it the most, but you leave a seat for yourself. I mean it."

Sorcha grabbed his arm. "Be careful, Robert. Don't trust anyone. They'd likely not do anything since you're a Yank, but you must not let your guard down to anyone you come across. Promise me."

He winked at her. "Don't worry about me, Sorcha. I know how to watch my back."

On impulse she hugged him. "Good luck." Sorcha watched him go, choking down the fear. She heard another explosion, farther away, and she wanted to weep. She had so many thoughts going through her head right now, none of which had to do with the patients in front of her. Did her parents hear of this bloody mayhem from their guesthouse in France? She almost hoped not. The more pressing issue sent a spike of fear through her. Where was John? Was he safe? Had he come to the hospital or was he at the flat? The anxiety over her brother was enough to buckle her knees.

The last thought she had as she heard the sirens in the distance and smelled the smoke from the burned-out pub two doors down... She wanted Sean. She wanted him with a crippling sorrow that ached in her belly. She shouldn't have pushed him away. She should have tried harder. She should have been brave enough to tell him how much she loved him. That if he could wait for her, maybe they had a future together. She should have told him that, without a doubt, he was the bravest, smartest, most loving man that she'd ever known, and she would be the luckiest woman alive if they made this work. She saw a potential there that she hadn't dared to let herself want. Not just about being a midwife, but about living this woman's life in the best possible way. Nestled like a happy little hen in that beautiful village by the sea. She stifled a sob as she thought about giving Sean sons and daughters. Growing older and baking cookies for her grandchildren. It was a dream she hadn't thought she'd ever want, but there it was, laid out before her. And if she got the chance with Sean, she was going to get her shit together and grab it with both hands.

As the tears pricked her eyes, she rubbed the brow of the man with the gunshot wound. They'd given him enough morphine to knock him out, but he still twitched with the pain from his belly wound. She didn't know how he got it. She didn't know which side of this conflict he was on, but she suspected. She tucked the crucifix inside his shirt, because no one else needed to know he was a Catholic. Was he like her, just crossing over the separation lines to work? Had he done violent deeds tonight, or had he just been the victim of a stray bullet? She realized that right now, it didn't really matter. All she knew for sure was he was in terrible pain, and right now he needed her. She met the eyes of the medic who was changing the dressing on a young man's head. "Thank you for staying, Mick."

He looked around at all the wounded people who had made their way to this unlikely clinic, as well as the still figure, shrouded underneath an old coat that had been taken from the rack. The people who were stuck here because every ambulance in the city had been called into service. People who needed a hospital, but had no transport. It was likely going on all over the city, and undoubtedly there would be more. Clashes with the British soldiers. Retaliation attacks from the UVF. All while they sat here like sitting ducks waiting for the tides of fortune to turn their way. Mick cleared his throat and said with a crooked grin, "My kingdom for a horse."

She laughed at that. She remembered it from her history lessons. Some English king had said it. Mick said thoughtfully, "I've seen many troubles ebb and flow in this city, but I'll always be here when she needs me. I won't leave you until it's finished. I swear it, lass."

. . .

Sean ran into the Royal Jubilee intake area, ready to start screaming Sorcha's name. What he hadn't expected was to see John Mullen going nose to nose with another nurse, a pretty, blonde nurse that he'd bet his last pound was Angelina.

"John, be reasonable. You need to stay put. Or maybe I can arrange a ride. The ambulances are starting to transfer out to other hospitals. I can pull some strings and get you close to the flat. Sorcha would want you to go home!"

"If ye don't tell me where you left my sister, then I swear to Christ I'll walk out of this hospital on foot and start going into the worst of it. I'll not wait at home while my sister is out in this mess!"

Sean interrupted, feeling the blood leave his face and rush in a pounding fury to his chest. "Sorcha isn't here? Or at the flat?"

John paused for a moment, surprised to see him. Then he looked at William. "How the hell did you two get into the city? And why are ye so covered in dirt?"

"We have been moving debris for five miles. Now, would you please answer me? Where is your sister?"

"Well, that's the question of the hour, isn't it? It seems Nurse Blondie here left her out in the city somewhere."

Angelina actually shoved him. He didn't budge, as he was quite a bit larger, but Sean had to admire her pluck. "I didn't leave her alone. We had to help the wounded. Sorcha and I just barely missed the second bombing. Dr. Stirling is with her. Once we get an ambulance over there, she'll come back to the hospital."

"Where is this makeshift clinic?" Sean asked. He'd have an answer if she wasn't going to give it to John.

"She wouldn't thank me for it, having you go out into danger. She'll likely have my head," Angelina said, already knowing full well that the power of three was going to win. Three bull-headed men with more balls than sense.

Sean tried to rein in his temper. "Well, Angelina, Sorcha doesn't always know what's good for her. She's bloody-minded and stubborn. She'll stay out there for days if you don't help me. You know she won't leave anyone behind. If you get me a couple of ambulances, we will go ahead and clear the roads for them. The three of us will help those ambulances get where they need to be."

"We don't have any free, I'm sorry, but if you could get your car to her, maybe you could transport a couple of patients yourself."

"How many were there last time you were on the scene?" he asked, sounding more and more like a cop every minute.

"Eight patients, one doctor and Sorcha, after the one man passed away. But, once the word gets around, they'll likely get more."

"I'll never get thirteen people in my car, Angelina. Think about this. Do you have access to another car?"

"No, I don't. A lot of the staff take the bus. Dammit!" she swore, so frustrated with the situation it almost brought her to tears. Then she struck on a thought. She didn't have a car, but across the street... "Although," she said thoughtfully.

The three men ran across the street, coming to the front door of Morgan's Funeral Parlor. They banged on the front door, ringing the bell as well. Nothing, so they tried around the back. Sean jumped as another explosion went off in the distance, from the direction William and he had traveled. They found the side door that had a small placard. *Private Residence of Owen Rhys Morgan. Please ring at the front.*

Sean murmured to himself, "Sorry, Owen, it's a bit of an emergency." He banged a fist on the door face, willing to annoy the man into answering. Finally, they watched through a window as an old, stocky, surly-looking man came to the door. He didn't open it.

"Bugger off! We're closed!" a gruff, masculine voice bellowed.

"I'll stay here all night, Welshman. I need help, and if you don't want me to strip the columns on those two hearses, you best listen to what I have to say." He showed his badge through the window.

Following some very animated curses in what could only be his native tongue, Owen Morgan opened the door. "And ye've got no bloody jurisdiction in the North. You sodding Irishmen are always making trouble, and it's the rest of us who have to deal with it."

William barked out a laugh. "And this coming from a Welshman? The darkest, most disagreeable of all the Celts. Save the speech, my good man."

Owen's eyes swept over them, taking in the trio. He cocked a brow, the corner of his mouth tipping up. "Point taken. Now, explain to me why you are beating down my door in the middle of a riot? You're lucky I didn't shoot you."

"My lass is a nurse. She's stuck in the middle of the city, tending to the wounded. At first, they couldn't get the ambulances through and now they're all tied up. I mean to go get her and the wounded she's been treating."

"And what the bloody hell does that have to do with me? Save my lovely wife, I've got no use for the lot of you." He was a short, stocky man with dark hair and brows streaked with silver.

"She won't leave her patients. They sent one back in a civilian car, but there were so many to tend to that she refused to leave. If you know anything about Irish women, Owen Rhys Morgan, then you know what I'll be dealing with if I show up there in a sedan and try to extract the little hellcat before all of her wounded are transported."

"Oh, I'm well familiar." He pulled his salt and pepper hair back from his forehead, showing a small scar on his brow. "I got this in the first year we were married. I suggested she try making some Welsh dishes instead of all that damn cabbage. She fed me cabbage for six months after that." John chuckled behind him. "And who are these two, might I ask, since you are intent on commandeering my fleet?"

"The stubborn woman in question is my sister. He's the future brother-in-law." He pointed to William who just grinned at the man, putting his hand out.

"Officer William O'Brien. His better half." He pointed to Sean.

"Well, now. Let's get a drink. One thing you Irish do know how to do is make whiskey. I've got a map of the city. I've been watching the news, so we'll mark the bomb sites, and you'll take the lead. If someone's car is going to get blown sky high, I'd rather it be yours."

The soldiers hadn't sent a vehicle back. Sorcha was surprised to realize she'd actually thought they would. She looked at her watch. The night was still, and she'd lost track of how many bombs had gone off within earshot. Six or seven so far, she thought. She was so tired. She ran a thumb along her scar, remembering the night that those men from the Ulster side of the walls had tried to drag her into that van. Wielding a knife and wearing masks, they'd meant to do murder. All the Catholics who had been grabbed, murdered, and dumped had been men. At least that's what she'd been led to believe. She hadn't considered herself at risk for this particular act of hatred. But when it happened, a strength was unleashed in her that she didn't know she possessed. She'd still been a teenager. She'd always been petite and not particularly strong, but she'd fought those four men off like a demon. Like a warrior—even as she'd felt that blade bite into her arm and drag down, more a result of the struggle than a calculated strike. Then John was there, beating the men with anything to hand while he pulled her free.

She loved this city... but there were times, she was ashamed to admit, when she hated it. She loved the roots that tied her to the community. She loved her work, but in the midst of this violence, she felt ancient and weary before her time. She thought about the women and children throughout history who had lived in cities ravaged by war. Families who tried to make a life among the rubble and the countless dead. The destitute widows and mothers who'd lost their husbands and sons too soon. The prisoners' wives who were in a sort of jail with no bars in a community where divorce was a sin, and the wife of a prisoner needed to be an example of loyalty. Even as she raised her children alone and had no man to warm her nights, she could not falter, lest she seem disloyal. This was a hard life, and she was not a prisoner here like some women. She could choose.

Sean's face came to her again. His blue eyes and the dimples that appeared when he smiled. She was suddenly glad he wasn't here. Glad that she wouldn't ever have to worry about burying him too young. Or struggle with raising his children in this city where violence was like mother's milk. No... that wasn't quite right. Not violence. At least, not all the time. It was the threat of it that affected their daily lives. It hung like a fog overhead. The tension and uncertainty of a place where the people were never truly at peace. A city that could never fully rest. The curse of an occupied land.

Right now, Sean was safe in the South. Maybe even having a pint at that pub he favored back home on that beautiful west coast. Gus's? Yes, that was it. Gus's, where he'd sing with his brother and go home for Sunday roast with Maeve and his parents. She tried to be grateful for that, pushing aside any wishes she might have to see him come through that door.

It was funny what things occurred to you when you found yourself cut off from everyone you loved. She looked at Mick and wondered if he'd left a family back in his flat in order to risk the city streets and help those who could be helped. Save who could be saved.

SIXTEEN

Angelina was fit to be tied because they wouldn't let her come. "We can't spare the room. And you've got no business going back out there. We'll likely be stacking them three high to get them all back."

She packed the canvas bags with supplies. Fresh saline bags, IV needles, blankets, sterile bandages, iodine, tape, tweezers, suture kits, and some other random supplies that might be needed. "She may have new wounded. They were coming in slowly. She may need to stabilize someone. Just take it, for God's sake!"

She was testy, but Sean understood. She'd been a good friend to Sorcha, he knew. And she didn't like getting benched any more than they would have. He'd overheard a heated exchange with who could only have been the doctor she was seeing. Dr. Nigel Childs, if he remembered correctly. Sorcha's boss at the Mater. He was calling from the other hospital, and had been giving her an earful, no doubt, about going back out into the city. That was good, because he was already responsible for too many people.

Now they were slow moving, he and William getting out to move debris while Owen, John, and some bloke named Jasper, who normally worked as an orderly, did the driving. They all knew the streets better than he and William did. They took back roads, and Sean heard the sirens, the sounds of loudspeakers with booming voices telling people to get back in their houses. There was a curfew being enforced within the city limits. To hell with that, though. He had to get to Sorcha. That was all he cared about. She'd likely box his ears for bringing John out in this mess, but how would he or William have felt if Maeve was in this situation? They'd have clawed their way through hell to get to her. John wasn't a boy. He was a man. Young, yes, but he had old eyes which were wise and serious. They would not leave him behind to worry over his sister.

The caravan came to a halt as they took in the mess in front of them. A small motorcar was blocking the entire lane with buildings to either side. The intersecting lane was about fifty meters ahead. The problem was, the damn thing was on its side. "I think we can move it. The four of us can get it righted. Owen, you watch the vehicles."

The older man bristled. "I'm not ready for the old folks' home yet, you little bastard. Now, take the middle where the roof is highest. Jasper and I will take the ends."

John was not overly tall, but he was big considering he was related to Sorcha. He fell in next to Sean and William on the other side. "Alright, then. On three. We rock it on one and two."

Rock, rock, push. They growled in unison as they lifted the heavy metal. "Fecking English piece of shite!" Sean bit out as they finally got it to the tipping point. He was sick and tired of moving things out of the road. He needed to get to Sorcha, and it was fraying his good manners. They all caught their breath, then Jasper jumped in, stripping the column like a pro.

He looked at Sean and William as the engine roared to life. Sean could see the flash of panic as he remembered what he and William did for a living. He shrugged and said, "Best not ask too many questions, eh? All's fair in love and war."

. . .

The wounded just kept coming. She and Mick were kept very busy as the night proceeded. More burns, lacerations, and head wounds from flying debris. Then there was an unexpected walk-in: a case of chest pains from an elderly woman. Sorcha searched the bag, hoping to find some sort of answer for an aged woman who was likely having a coronary incident. She smiled. "Noreen, I believe what is going on here is a panic attack." *You are a shameless, sinful liar,* she thought. Likely, the woman knew it, but if she did, she didn't let on. "I'm going to ask you to sit here by this young woman. I'm afraid she's had a terrible bump to the head and some nasty cuts from flying glass. Perhaps you could find some way to keep her awake and alert?"

The old woman scooted next to the girl and said, "I'm Noreen. I've got a granddaughter about your age. Let's sit a while, and I'll sing you the tunes she favors."

She began, and Sorcha had expected some old ballad from the woman's youth. But it was a lullaby, soft and sweet. Hardly the thing to keep her awake, but the girl seemed to melt into the side of the old woman, like a much smaller child.

Sorcha took in the sight of others and saw that a man about twenty-five or so was beginning to tear up. Did he have a babe at home? Did his wife sing to their son or daughter? She'd stitched his scalp a few hours ago, and she knew he likely had a concussion as well. She listened to Noreen and fought her own need for emotional release. She couldn't start crying. If she did, she'd likely never stop.

At first, Sorcha didn't see the green outline of the army vehicle, but then the men came into view. "Nurse Mullen, we were told to report here for a patient pick-up. We can get through to the Mater, but we can only take one."

She stood, hands on hips. "One? Are you mad? You can see how overwhelmed we are! Why didn't you bring something bigger?"

He raised a brow, wondering at the gall of this diminutive

woman. "We were told to bring you as well. Come, madam. We haven't got all night."

She said smoothly, "I'm not leaving these people. I'll give up my seat."

"Those weren't my orders. And I've got a message from a Dr. Robert Stirling," he said, looking less sure of himself, but determined to follow orders.

"What message is that?" *This should be good*, Sorcha thought. Stirling was a consummate smart ass.

His fellow soldier hid a grin, glad he was not the one dealing with this woman. He said, "I believe his exact words were, *tell her to get her ass in the truck and get back to the hospital*. Only with some strange Yank accent I can't quite manage. Now, carry on. Choose the worst of the injured and we'll load him up."

She walked right past him, giving his mate a shove as he tried to block her way. She looked in the small military vehicle. "You can get three in there if someone rides against the tailgate."

"Two, and you can ride against the tailgate because that spare is too big for anyone else." He was losing his temper.

"Three. You can unhook that spare tire and come back for it," she shot back.

Mick and the two men loaded the man with the gunshot wound and the worst of the burn victims. She knelt down next to the old woman and said, "Noreen, you need to go. I think it might be your heart. I didn't want to scare you, but you need to go. I can't treat you here. I don't have what I need."

Noreen patted her face. "This old city has broken my heart so many times." She sighed. "It'll survive another night. Take him. He's fading, my dear. Mick has changed that bandage three times since I've been here."

Sorcha looked at the thirty-something man. His color was terrible. Then she looked at Mick, and he confirmed it. "He won't last if he loses any more blood. She's right." His leg looked like it had been through a meat grinder. Sorcha squeezed Noreen's hand, then nodded to the men to take him. They'd long since given up trying to get her to leave.

"It should be up on the right," John said as the explosion site came into view. When they saw the ruined pub, they hadn't been prepared for the destruction. "St. Michael, defend us." John crossed himself and Sean was out the door in a flash, John tight on his heels.

Sorcha used the last bag of saline for the remaining burn victim, who had a nasty burn across his right side, having been in the blast radius of the pub. She thought she was delirious when she heard her name. It sounded for all the world like Sean O'Brien. Then he was there, standing in the floodlights inside the door of the storefront. Like she'd conjured him from a far-off galaxy. Piling in behind him was William and...

"John!" She shouted her brother's name. He was wrapped around her in an instant, but she couldn't take her eyes off Sean. She leaned toward him, touching his face. "Sean," she said on a whisper, her voice shaking.

He pulled her to him. "Oh, God. Sorcha." He kissed her face, beginning to weep. "I found you. Oh, God. I found you." He pulled her off her feet, not able to get close enough.

Another explosion went off, and it was a big one. It rocked the ground on which they stood. He put her down and said, "We need to get everyone out of here. We brought help."

"How did you find me?" Sorcha asked, still stunned that Sean was standing in front of her.

"It doesn't matter. Let's get everyone loaded. I've got room for nine or ten and then all of us."

"We've only got ten left. They've kept coming in, but the soldiers took three of them." She looked at the dead man, shrouded with a coat. "They'll have to come back for him. The poor soul."

"Where is the doctor who was here with you?" Sean asked.

She said, "The army came and took him. Apparently, a barricaded checkpoint was hit." Sean's face was murderous. "But they left me Mick. He's a trained medic. I was okay, Sean."

"You're not okay! You're a reckless, pigheaded, stubborn pain in the ass! You should've gone back with Angelina!" The color rose in his cheeks, like an angry boy, but she would not be talked down to, even by him.

"You can sweet talk me later, you overbearing, pushy, thick-headed lout! I don't need rescuing! I've got this under control!" She stood up to him, hands on her hips, chin raised in defiance.

A delicate voice chimed in from behind them. Noreen said, "I hate to interrupt such an entertaining lover's spat, but I believe that little girl behind you is having a wee bit of trouble."

Sorcha and Sean both turned to see the silhouette of a young woman with a sizable, protruding belly... just as her waters broke all over the floor. William cursed under his breath. They really couldn't catch a break tonight.

"Okay, everyone stay calm. Let's ease her down on this blanket. Start loading the others into the..." She did a double take at the vehicles. "Hearses?" She shook her head. "This is by far the strangest night of my life. Get them loaded. Every last one. I need to check her and see how far gone she is." The woman was eased down on the blanket by William and Sean. Sorcha took her hand. "Hello, my dear. I'm a midwife and a nurse, so you are safe now. What is your name?"

The woman's face was tight with pain and anxiety. "It's Siobhan. The pains started around teatime. I was waiting for my husband to get home. Then the bombing started, and I was scared to leave. He didn't come home from work." The panic started to rise in her face again. "It just got so far along that I went out into the street. Some people said there was help here, so I walked the couple of blocks. They're close. The contractions are really close together!"

"Easy, love. Let's just have a look." She put clean gloves on and discreetly looked under her skirt. "I'm going to check your cervix. I'm sorry to be so direct, but I need to know how far along you are to see if we have time to get you to a hospital." The woman's business end was facing away from the others, so Sorcha quickly checked her as the men turned their backs to them, offering some privacy. The news was not good. She was fully dilated, and the child had descended into the birth canal. She could feel the child's head at the cervix. "Is this your first child, Siobhan?"

"My second. The other child is with my mam across town. What's the matter?"

"Nothing, my dear. This is just moving a bit quickly." She looked at her brother. "John, how long did it take you to get here from the hospital?"

"Over an hour. There is a lot of debris, and we don't know where that last one hit." He knew what she was thinking. "Jasper and Owen can drive the rest of them. I'll stay with you and help."

She shook her head. "You three should go as well. They need all three cars. Mick can stay with me. He lives nearby."

Sean shook his head. "We are not leaving you. Don't ask again, because it will happen over my dead body," he said with complete calm.

"And mine," John said, arms crossing his chest.

"And mine," William added.

She let out a growl that sounded like a female cat. "She's going to have this baby in minutes, not hours. I can't cram her in a hearse with four other patients. This baby is coming!" As if to weigh in on the matter, the woman groaned as another contraction overtook her.

Sean stood. "Owen, take the worst of the wounded. If you drive the same route we came, I think you'll be okay. Jasper, you follow him with the other four. We'll have to leave two behind with us until this woman delivers."

John and William looked at him. They both understood there wasn't going to be enough room for everyone in Sean's little car. There'd been sixteen before this woman had come in, but add a woman and a newborn and there was no way.

"That math doesn't add up," Sorcha said plainly.

"Can we get more in the hearses?" William asked.

"No. They are all wounded. Burns, impact injuries, bleeding. It's going to be tough enough with three across and one in the front. We can't stack them like bales of hay."

One of the men stood and spoke up, the man who'd teared up during the lullaby and had a bandage around his head. "I'll stay back." He swayed and Owen caught him.

"That's a good lad. Let's just get you back down on this cot you've made," Owen said kindly.

"I'll stay, too." Noreen was small and fragile, but she had fearsome eyes.

"No, Noreen, I'm sorry. I know you want to help, but let's not tempt fate a second time. You're going to go with Owen. You can sit in the front." She looked at the old man she'd seen clipping his tiny lawn in front of the funeral parlor every week. A familiar face that somehow soothed her, even though they'd never met. "She's having chest pains, Owen. She must be in the first group."

Another man spoke up, raising a hand. "I'll stay. I'm going to need another shot of morphine, but I'll do. Just get the rest to the hospital."

The woman in front of her groaned. "It's settled. Mr. Price and Mr. Kerr will stay here, the rest will go. Mick, give Mr. Kerr the last of the morphine."

Sorcha tuned everything out after that, focused on the woman in front of her. She said, "I'd like to move you, if you think you can stand. There's a small sitting area by the changing rooms. It will give us better lighting and some privacy."

She helped the woman to her feet, and she doubled over, her fingers biting into Sorcha's arm. Then Sean was next to her. "There, now. It's just a few more feet," he said.

William took Sorcha's place. She looked back to see John helping Jasper load the people into the vehicles. Then he came to Sean. "If it goes easier on the way back, Jasper and Owen will come back for the rest."

Sorcha checked the young woman's cervix again, tuning out

the conversation. She met William's eyes. He was at the woman's head, holding her hand. It suddenly occurred to her this was probably torture for him. *Oh, Katie.* But Siobhan started to weep, and her focus returned to her patient. The woman said, "My husband wanted to be here. I know some doctors and nurses don't like that, but we practiced. Breathing exercises and the like. He missed the first one being born. He wanted to be here. What if he's...?" She let out another wail, both from fear and pain.

William said softly, "The city is a mess, Siobhan. He'd be here if he could. He's likely locked down somewhere, and he's calling home as we speak. Don't worry, love. He wouldn't want you to cry. Just concentrate on that breathing you practiced. Can you show me how it's done?"

Sorcha mouthed the words, "Thank you."

Sean watched as the poor woman raised up and gritted her teeth, bearing down for the first push. He'd never seen a woman in active labor actually start pushing. He'd called an ambulance and waited with the one woman, but this was something different altogether. It was truly horrifying. But his Sorcha was as calm as a summer lough. She said, "That was a good one, Siobhan. A few more like that and we'll have this little girl out in no time."

"How do you know it's a girl?" She looked so hopeful. "I have a little boy, but I'd like a daughter. How can you be sure?"

"A midwife's intuition. I'm never wrong. Some of those old wives' tales are true. You're carrying high and close to your heart. I'll wager she liked to kick you in your ribs." The woman laughed, confirming Sorcha's words. "If you're lucky, she'll have that beautiful, fair hair of yours." Her heart broke as William started to breathe with her, stepping in as a birthing partner to offer her comfort. She looked at Sean and he was just as ruined by the whole affair. She felt the next one come as the woman's abdomen tightened like a drum. "That's it, almost ready."

A few more breaths and Sorcha said, "Push, my dear. Let's see that little girl."

There were two more like that, and then the final one. "The head is almost out, Siobhan. Scream your head off if you need to."

She did. She let out a war cry that was as long as it was shrill. The child slid into Sorcha's waiting palms, as ripe as a berry. "She's perfect, Mam. Gorgeous and healthy. What's her name to be?"

"Is it really a girl?" She sobbed as William squeezed her hand. "I have a girl!"

He said, "Aye, you did it. You've brought a healthy daughter into the world." William's tears were unshed, which made them all the more devastating.

Over the baby's caterwauling, the mother said, "I'll name her Brigid. I've always liked that name."

Sorcha smiled at that. "It's my favorite as well. The patron saint of Ireland. I think Brigid is just perfect."

Sean knelt down for a better look as Sorcha put the baby in her mammy's arms. "We'll need to cut the cord and then deliver the placenta. Could one of you make sure she keeps a hold on the child?" But just as she said it, the woman cramped. "Actually, this can be rather uncomfortable. Sean, could you take the baby? There should be a swaddling blanket in my bag. William, you stay right there and keep being her coach."

She knew instinctively he was better off with the mother than holding the child. He hadn't been there when Katie lost their baby. It had been a great source of guilt for him, and holding a newborn would be too painful for him right now. Sean, on the other hand, took one of the swaddling cloths from her kit and wrapped the baby like a pro. Then he held the child in the crook of his arm and stood, rocking her as she cried. He crooned, "Every girl I've ever known named Brigid has been a handful. But you are a beauty, aren't you? Yes, I think that's the perfect name for you."

Sorcha felt her ovaries explode in her belly. Listening to Sean O'Brien croon to a newborn baby was the best aphrodisiac known to woman.

. . .

In the end, it wasn't Owen and Jasper who returned, but a battle-weary Virginia doctor riding shotgun in a military truck. Sorcha called the hospital, making sure that the two men knew not to come back.

Sean watched as the cocksure doctor put his arms around Sorcha. "As if the whole field hospital wasn't enough, you went and delivered a baby in your spare time." He laughed as he cupped her head in his palm.

"I'm glad you're okay, Robert," she said, pulling away.

As if he felt the heat of Sean's stare at his back, Dr. Stirling turned. "Well, well, you must be the cop," he said, his drawl thick from fatigue.

"You must be that Yank doctor who left her here alone," Sean said curtly.

Mick protested behind them. "What am I? Chopped liver?"

Dr. Stirling said, "Take her home with you. That's an order. I want her out of this damn city before sun-up." He cut off Sorcha's protests. "If I see you back in that hospital in the next week, I will put you on bedpan duty for the remainder of your internship. Dr. Childs is with me on this, so don't try any of your tricks, missy."

Sean was starting to like this guy. A lot.

The uniformed driver said, "It's time to go. We're headed to the Mater. They can't take any more at the Royal Jubilee."

John spoke up behind them. "Can I get a lift to the hospital?"

"John, you're coming with us. I'm not leaving you." Panic started creeping into Sorcha's voice. The thought of her little brother out in the city was horrifying.

He went to his sister then, taking her into the corner where they could talk privately. He brushed her hair off her face, because she'd lost her cap in all the chaos. "I'm not a boy anymore, love. I can take care of myself. Once they lift the curfew in a couple of hours, I'll head home and call Mam and Da. They need to stay put until this is over. I'll have one of my mates drive me to their house out of the city if it gets too bad, but I can't watch my own back if I have to chase after you. Go, now." He talked over her protests: "Listen to me, Sorcha. It's time for you to go."

The hot tears welled and spilled down her face. "How can I leave? I'm needed here."

"The troubles of this city are not yours to bear alone. You are needed elsewhere. Surely you know he won't leave without you? And William won't leave without him. It's time to start thinking about what you really want and quit worrying about everyone else. What you want is him. Stop fighting it so hard and let yourself be happy." He hugged her fiercely. He felt it in her body, a loosening of muscles. Her letting go—at least for now.

She wiped her tears and turned to Mick who was helping Siobhan into the truck. He rubbed the woman's hair away from her face so gently, it caused Sorcha's eyes to prick with fresh tears. Then he looked at the baby. "My wife is pregnant with our first. I know it's a boy. She says it's wishful thinking, but I know. We'll name him after my father. I always wanted a son. And daughters, of course. She's a fine-looking little darlin'. Your husband will be so proud of you."

As they drove away, he turned his attention to Sorcha. She said, "I don't know what I would have done without you. You are a real hero, Mick. You should think about medical school. You could've been a doctor."

He smiled sadly. "I could have been so many things. I'm just glad I was able to aid you. I take care of my city." She had such an odd feeling, like he was so much older than his handsome face suggested. For the first time, she looked at his clothes. Conservative and handsomely tailored, he cut a dashing figure. She hugged him tightly. "Goodbye for now. I hope to see you again."

That sad smile came again, but he didn't reply.

The drive to Dublin was the longest of her life. It took them two hours to get out of the city, and they'd barely made it to the petrol station. Finally, she drifted off, wrapped in Sean's coat. She hurt all over. Between lifting patients, doing procedures on the floor, and the bus crash that had started this nightmare, she felt like she'd been dropped off a building and onto the street. Sean and William drove in shifts as she lost herself in a deep and fitful sleep.

Sean was so relieved to see the door to their building, he almost wept. "Just carry her in. The poor lass is knackered." William's voice was soft and brotherly. "I'll park. Then we're headed home. We were supposed to hunt for a house this afternoon."

Sean had totally forgotten. "I'm sorry, Willy."

"Katie can drive, it's okay. And Mam has likely been baking all night. You know how she gets when she's worried."

Sean was torn between going with them and staying. He decided to stay. Sorcha needed to decompress before he took her around anyone else. She'd been through hell. She was bruised and battered, half-starved and dehydrated. Her nurse's frock was covered in other people's blood. He slipped his arms under her and she barely stirred. That told him everything.

As he carried her to the door, Katie swung it open, frantic for news. Sean said, "She's okay. She'll need a change of clothes."

Katie worked efficiently alongside him as William quickly packed a bag to drive west. "Maybe we should stay? We can house hunt next week," Katie said, worry furrowing her brow.

Sorcha's voice broke through the fog. "Go, sister. I'm afraid I'm not very good company." Katie helped her slide a nightgown on and Sean picked up her feet and put her under the covers. He kissed her forehead and left her to rest.

Beware the fury of a patient man...

—John Dryden

Sorcha woke with a jolt. It was daylight, dimming to evening. She could tell by the sun that came through the drapery. It had been a couple of hours before sunrise when she'd left Belfast. How long had she slept? She got up, feeling so much better. But she desperately needed a shower. She opened the door, seeing Sean asleep on the easy chair. He'd moved it forward and faced it toward the bedroom door, like a guardian angel keeping watch as she slept. He was so beautiful, it stopped her heart.

She rifled through his drawer, finding a big Garda T-shirt he'd likely worn during training. For God's sake, she didn't even have clean panties. She smelled the shirt, and it was fresh and clean from laundering. His pillow had been a little slice of heaven, however. At some point during her slumber, she remembered rolling into the scent of him. Being surrounded by his sheets and pillow were like Sean holding her.

She took the shirt and headed for the bath. If she had her way, she wasn't going to need the panties.

Sean woke when he heard her turn on the shower. He stood, pacing back and forth from the kitchen. Then he righted the chair, facing it back toward the TV. More pacing. Damn, that woman could make him crazy. He really didn't know how he was going to handle it if she came out of that bathroom with her second wind and tried to take a bus back to Belfast. He needed to busy himself, so he put the kettle on. By the time it was whistling he heard the shower turn off. Just the thought of her getting out of that shower all wet and rosy made his cock stir. He waited, hearing her rustling around. He sat at the kitchen table. Then he stood, leaning. Yeah. Leaning was better.

When she came out of the shower, he took one look at her and sat back down with a thud. Her hair was damp, her face scrubbed to a rosy hue, and she was dressed in nothing but his old Garda T-shirt. "There's tea in the pot." That's all he could come up with, because all the blood in his body had rushed to one spot.

She seemed unsure of herself, which was ridiculous. "I'll get it. Would you like a cup?"

"No, love, I'll get it." He stood and busied himself, preparing two cups while she sat at the table. She looked so small like that, with his giant shirt reaching her knees. He sat across from her, sliding a cup toward her on the table. He said, "I'm sorry, Sorcha. I'm so sorry you got stuck in the middle of that."

She smiled sadly. "A lot of people did. I was lucky. Another five hundred meters and my bus would have taken the blast full force." She saw his face blanch. "I'm sorry. I shouldn't tell you things like that. It doesn't help. It just causes stress when there's nothing to do for it. The important thing is I'm okay. So is my family. That's a lot." He just nodded. Then she said, "I'm sorry how I left things. It was wrong of me to do that to you at the end of such a beautiful day." She stood then, approaching him as he sat in the kitchen chair, looking over her body with such longing. She reached a hand to his hair, running her fingers through it. She moved closer and he seized her wrist. "Don't, Sorcha. I'm too raw right now. I can't..." He swallowed hard, his eyes shut tight. "I'm not strong enough to hold back. Seeing you there in that rubble and all those wounded. I'm not strong enough. We can't start this right now."

She didn't move away. "Why not? You want me, Sean, and I want you."

His face hardened. "Of course I want you! And I know you want me. I know you're curious and this is some sort of sexual awakening for you, but I can't be that for you! Christ, Sorcha. Do ye think I can make love to you and have you leave me again? Do you think I could bear it? I love you! You're the breath and blood of my body. And you don't love me! I'm asking you to at least give me your mercy if you can't give me your love. We can't do this because if we do, it will gut me when you leave."

He'd expected any number of retorts or emotions from her but the one he got. Anger. Red-hot anger. She smacked both palms on his chest. "You're an eejit! You don't know what the hell you are talking about!" She screamed the words and he caught her wrists when she tried to pull away from him.

"I'm not an eejit! Do you think I like admitting it? Do you think I liked that week when you never rang me? What did I say, Sorcha?

I said, *if you miss me, then ring me. If you don't call, I'll have my answer.*"

"Stop it! You're so stupid! You don't know anything!" She was crying now. He let her go and she backed up from him. *Here it comes*, he thought. She would run scared and ask for a ride to the bus station. Her face was flushed with anger. "When I was there in that shop, tending to those people, do you know what I was thinking?" She hiccupped a sob, and he suddenly felt awful. She'd just been through hell, and he was making this about himself.

"I'm sorry. Jesus, darlin', don't cry." His voice was softer now, which seemed to make her even angrier.

"Shut up and let me finish." She was spitting mad and he could do nothing but offer her the opposite. Offer her his calmness in the face of her storm. He just nodded and stayed silent.

She closed her eyes, her face tight. "All I wished was for you to appear in that doorway. To come to me and take me away from that city. I wanted you there so I wasn't so bloody scared and alone. I wished for you so desperately that it threatened to break me." She put a hand up when he tried to get up. Her face grew fierce. "And I hated myself for it. I hated that I'd let the conflicts drive me away like a coward! I hated that I'd be willing to walk away from my hospital and my patients for even a small chance of what Katie is going to have."

Sean had to glue himself to the seat. It was gut-wrenching to watch Sorcha battle with herself. She wouldn't welcome any attempt to soften her mood, and honestly, he didn't really want to. For it was when her blood was up and her mouth was going that he saw her more clearly. Her truth. The war that raged within her as to which path she should choose. Love warring with independence. The fear he wouldn't be able to give her the life she dreamed of. When other women were reading *Bride* magazine, she was dreaming of catching babies and helping mothers bring life into the world. And he'd never, ever take that dream from her.

She was fully sobbing now, pounding her fist to her chest. "It's my city! My home! Those people are mine to care for, and I just wanted to run like hell and not look back. And it wasn't just because of the fighting. Not just because of the debris in the road and the soldiers boarding the bus on the way to work. It was because I love you, Sean O'Brien. And every time I left you it was like another..." She sobbed, putting her hand over her mouth. "Like another hunk of my heart was being ripped out, until I wouldn't have any heart left at all by the time you were done with me. So, don't you dare say I don't love you, Sean! The best moment of my life was when you came bursting through that door. I didn't need rescuing. It's not about that. It's about letting myself want something else. Letting myself love you enough to walk away from the only home I've ever known!" Then she walked away from him, into the bathroom, and slammed and locked the door.

What the hell just happened? Sean didn't move from the kitchen chair. He was crippled irrevocably. By her words. Her tears. Her love. When she came back out, she'd collected herself. Washed and dried her face. Her back was straight. Her nose was red from crying, however. He was almost afraid to speak, but he had to break this awful silence. "I want to give you everything, Sorcha. I want you to have a life that gives you purpose. A career, a family, all of it. I want you to have it with me, mo chuisle. I need you like I need air in my lungs. This isn't a temporary madness. This is my heart that will be forever tied to you. I can't let you go, my love. Not if we're going to be together. I wouldn't survive it." His voice broke with emotion.

Sorcha watched a tremble go through him, and she needed to touch him. To show him. The time for words was over. She walked between his open legs, and he rested his forehead on her belly. "I love you, Sean." Then she lifted his face. A tear fell down her cheek and onto his. He closed his eyes for her final words, feeling his own tears prick his eyes. "And I will never leave you again."

He moved like a flash of lightning, pulling her forward until she straddled his hips. His mouth was hot, demanding, his one hand in her hair, just behind her ear. He rolled his hips, stroking her heat. When he slid a hand up her hip and over one ass cheek, he broke the kiss. "Holy Jesus. You are missing your knickers, woman. What are you doing to me?" He groaned the words as he pressed his hips up.

"I thought it was obvious. I'm trying to seduce you, Sean O'Brien, and you've made a cock-up of the whole thing."

Both his hands cupped her ass as he kissed her, his fingers sliding between and under, seeking. She whimpered. Then he was up, and she clung to his massive shoulders as he carried her off to bed.

SEVENTEEN

Sean moved above her, not wanting to break contact for a moment, even to undress. Her kisses were like a drug, deep and sweet. She slid her hands up his shirt, sliding over his stomach and up to his chest. The feel of her hands on his body was cranking him up. She broke the kiss. "Let me look at you. I want to see you."

He lifted himself, strong and sure as her eyes devoured him. She was so beautiful, it made his soul bleed. He slid his jumper over his head, then he unfastened the button of his pants. She wasn't the only one with no underwear. When William had woken him for that news report, he'd been lucky to have put pants and shoes on before he was out the door. He unzipped his denims, freeing himself. It was so arousing, having her eyes on his body.

"You are beautiful, Sean." He heard the tears threatening in her voice. He hovered over her, taking her mouth with a sweet caress of his lips.

Against her mouth he said, "As smashing as you look in my shirt, I'm going to have to insist you part with it. At least for now." He smiled devilishly as he slowly slid it up, revealing her body. She was so creamy white, so delicate. Her breasts were round and high, her hips smooth and supple for one so small. The swells and lush valleys made her uniquely feminine. He slid the shirt over her head, then stopped just at the elbow. He took a ripe nipple in his mouth as she arched, pushing on her restraints. Then he kissed her again. He teased her, not letting her touch him. Wanting her to feel everything completely as he explored her.

"Sean, please. I need you. Stop teasing me." She was getting testy and he nipped her neck.

"Patience, hen. You're the one who kept runnin' off to Belfast when things got too hot and heavy."

She wiggled under him, like a kitten that wanted to fight with the lion. When she thought to retort, he kissed her again and she melted into the mattress. "Open for me, love." He lifted himself, and she accepted him into the cradle of her hips. He looked down at her, poised on his big arms. "You are so lovely, it almost hurts to look at you. I love you, mo chuisle."

He slid the ridge of his hard length between them, feeling her slick, inviting heat. He freed her arms, feeling her grip his shoulders. Feeling her nails bite into him at the cap of flesh that joined his arm to his shoulder. His hips jerked at the sensation. Her little punishments, stinging and sweet. His words were rough, his jaw tight. "Sorcha, it's your last chance. If we do this, it can't be undone. I won't be able to part with you. Do you understand?"

She touched his face, running her finger over his bottom lip. "It's already too late, Sean. I couldn't part with you even now. Don't you know that?"

He cupped her neck, pulling her face to meet his. Her green eyes were like the valued marble that grew in their native hills. Her auburn waves splayed across the pillow. Her rosy mouth opened just a bit as small sighs escaped her. He went so slowly, knowing he was hurting her. Letting her adjust to him. He saw so many things in her face. Pain, pleasure, lust, and he saw love. Finally, she'd taken the barriers down between them, and the love shone from her eyes.

Their hips fused and he was seated deep inside her. That's when a moment of clarity came to him. "Sorcha, I don't have any condoms. I didn't plan this."

She smoothed her hand over his back, taking in the feel of his straining muscles. She could sense that he was struggling with the urge to cut loose. His body was tight with the effort of his restraint. She said, "Then it's lucky for you that I did plan this. It's taken care of. I'll explain later, but for now, for the month, it's taken care of."

He smiled and moved inside her. "For a virgin, ye've got the mind of a vixen." Then his face grew more serious. "I don't like hurting you. Is this okay?"

She hissed a little as she pulled his hips back to her. "I'm okay. The pain will ease. Don't you dare stop, Sean." Chuckling low in his throat, he pressed into her, starting a rhythm as he reached between them. She felt her body respond as he skillfully stroked her. She felt it, then. A building tension. That climb she'd heard about from her books and from other women. Like ascending to a peak.

Sean felt it when she began to reach her pleasure. Her short breaths on his face, the daze that clouded her eyes, and the tension in her body. She was so tight. It was murder trying to hold back, but he would have this from her. Her release and surrender. "That's it, my girl. Let go." She didn't need the command, however. She was on the edge, ready and willing to plunge into oblivion. She cried out as she exploded around him. She convulsed as her body came in crashing waves.

Sorcha couldn't control the powerful climax that tackled her body. It was so much more intense with Sean inside her. She hadn't thought it possible for him to take her higher than he had in that damn tower, but she'd been an ignorant fool. She felt herself contracting around him, caught in the maelstrom of pleasure.

Sean put his hands on either side of her face. His voice was strained, almost harsh. "I'm going to come inside you, Sorcha." She whimpered, her voice strained and weak. He intensified his pace, thrusting deep into her releasing body. His eyes bore into her. "Now you're mine." His deep, husky cry mixed with hers as he let himself go, and she felt his release deep within her body like the rolling swells of the sea.

. . .

Sorcha was on her back in delirious contentment as Sean tended to her. They'd been like this for an hour, him petting her and kissing her. Nibbling her skin. He'd brought her a warm cloth, easing the soreness between her thighs. But as he thumbed her nipple and teased it to a stiff peak, she felt the need stir between them again. It was cut off by a phone ringing, and he sprang off the bed to answer it. He leaned in, covering the phone. "It's John. I'll run out and get some dinner and give you some privacy."

She slid his shirt back over her head, feeling like a stranger in her own body. She shook off the drowsiness. "Hello, John. Where are you?"

He was home. Not at the flat, but at her parents' home outside the city. Thank God for it. But as the conversation progressed, her heart sank. When she finished and said goodbye, she called the hospital. Everyone was safe and accounted for. Many of the staff were sleeping in the empty beds of the maternity hospital, taking round-the-clock shifts until the worst of it was over. And it wasn't over. The steady, punishing attack by the IRA continued to hit key points in Northern Ireland. She suddenly felt very tired. She also felt guilty, because there were doctors and nurses working around the clock and she was here. The good news was that all her patients had survived, other than the man who had died earlier in the evening. She'd known that his burns would be fatal without immediate care, but she still saw his face so clearly.

She went to the television set, pushing the power button and waiting for the screen to warm up, then she turned the knobs until she found what she was looking for. The news reporter was standing outside the Crumlin Road Gaol, more for dramatic effect, she supposed. The sod. *And the IRA bombing campaign rages on.* Not just in Belfast, which wasn't a surprise. It was happening in Derry, Armagh, Castlederg, Cookstown, and Enniskillen. A coordinated attack that had likely taken months to plan. She knew this was a war. The Irish had been pushed to the breaking point in so many ways. But the healer in her could not have stood by and not aided the wounded. She couldn't base decisions on which side of the walls the wounded lived. She was, first and foremost, a nurse. She felt irrevocably torn by this conflict after witnessing the carnage from the opposite side.

She curled onto her side, watched the news reports, and wept. She wept for the innocent people who were always injured or killed during wars. She cried for her brother, who would stubbornly go back into the city and resume working at the mill. She cried for Siobhan, who gave birth in a clothing shop while her husband was stuck somewhere in the city. And she cried for Mick. A handsome, dedicated man who'd lifted a Catholic boy with a gunshot wound to his belly, and carried him to safety. Who'd stayed with her and tended to the wounded instead of hiding in his flat.

Sean came through the door and was surprised not to see Sorcha. But the TV was on and the news report on the screen was grim. Then he saw her, curled up on the sofa sleeping. He put the fish and chips on the table and went to her. She looked so small, it pulled at his heart. She had been crying, and he could see the wetness drying on her face. She stirred, and even in her sleep a tear escaped the corner of her eye. "Oh, darlin', I'm so sorry," he said softly. Then he pulled her into his lap and let her cry.

He imagined that she was torn by the events which had transpired, and continued still. She was a nationalist, believing in a free Irish state. She was also a Catholic. And she'd seen her people ill-used by the reigning power in that city for her entire life. But she was also a nurse. She'd been on the other side when the bombing happened, and she wasn't the sort to let an injured person go untreated. The truth of it was that not all Protestants were as fanatical as the UVF bastards who had brutalized and carried out their own bombings. Some of the Protestants, likely many of them, wanted peace. Angelina and Dr. Childs, for example. There were, in fact, Protestant nationalists, mostly Church of Ireland. It wasn't a clear-cut division in every case.

He shook his head, wishing that he could make the world a brighter place for her. That he could singlehandedly bring peace to her broken and divided city. It was her birthplace, after all. No less precious to her than Doolin was to him. All he could do was hold her and offer her a safe place to land.

The fish and chips were so heavenly. Airy, crispy, and perfectly battered with a firm, fleshy cod fillet that tasted like the sea. The chips were good, too. The salt and the tang from the vinegar made her stomach roar to life. "How long has it been since you've eaten? I'm an ass. I should have kept my hands off you until you'd been properly fed."

"As if you could resist me." She wiggled her brows as she took another bite. "Remember, I'm a vixen in training. If you read romance novels, you would know that no man can resist a vixen."

The look he gave her could have refried the fish and chips. "Careful, hen. I'm three times your size. If you want to finish your lunch, you best behave."

Sorcha warmed inside, because she really did love the teasing they did. She rather liked being a seductress. She'd never in her life felt so powerful or desirable. He did, however, have a point. She was starved, and he'd get this fish and chips out of her cold, dead hand.

"You make little noises when you're enjoying your food." Sean smiled, watching her.

"I do not."

"Ye do. It's adorable. It's similar to the noises you make when... ow!" She smacked him, then got up to throw her newsprint away. When she went into the bathroom to wash her hands, Sean knew exactly when she made the discovery.

"Sean." There was a warning in her tone. "Where are the pair of knickers I had drying on the rack? They're my only pair."

He appeared in the doorway. "I don't know what you're on about." But he couldn't keep the grin from creeping up on his face.

"Where are they?" she said more forcefully, as she closed the distance between them.

He backed out of the doorway, putting his arms out and spinning slowly. "I guess you're just going to have to look for them. Who knows what nook or cranny I may have put them in?"

"Don't make me search you, Officer O'Brien. You may not like the tables turned." Then she was on him, checking his pockets and patting his chest. She pulled his shirt off, and the determination on her face had less to do with seduction and more to do with not letting him get the best of her. "Give me my knickers, you big lout!" The fact that he was laughing was making it so much better... and worse. "You don't think I'll look, but I will." That's when she went for his zipper.

"Sorcha, if you wanted more loving, all you had to do was ask. OUCH! You pinched me, you little she-devil."

"I only have one pair of underwear, and I washed them out in the sink so I could wear them. Hand them over!" She yanked his jeans down around his knees and pushed his big body onto the bed. She stripped him, and she didn't even seem to notice that his cock was at full salute. It was downright delighted by this strip search. She frantically checked the legs of his trousers, convinced they'd appear. The minute it occurred to her, he grabbed her and pinned her under him.

"I never said they were on me. You assumed. They're in the top drawer of the bureau." She writhed under him, accusing him of all sorts of evil deeds. Then she bit him on the chest. "Now you listen to me, Sorcha Mullen." He slid his hands under her bum and palmed her ass. "If I have my way, I will keep you bare-assed and on your back for the next week."

"You shouldn't tease me," she said, with no real heat behind it.

"I'll never quit teasing you. You're gorgeous altogether when your temper is up." He kissed her then, soft and undemanding. He pulled away, looking down at her. He said, "Since you've seduced me into bed, you know you'll have to marry me." It wasn't phrased as a question, which made Sorcha laugh. He spread her thighs, poised at her entrance. "I'm serious," he said as he slid into her. She arched and gasped.

"Are you, now?" She tried to sound flippant, but her body betrayed her as she made those little noises he loved so much.

His eyes bore into hers as he cocked his leg, pushing further into her, and started to pump his hips. He raised her knee, driving. His kiss branded her, his body invaded her, his eyes worshipped her. "Say it," he said, his breathing labored. "Say you're mine."

She dug her nails into his ass and said defiantly, "You're mine." His harsh laugh echoed through the room.

Sorcha listened to the beat of Sean's heart with lazy contentment. It was so peaceful just now. As if by being close to him, hidden in his bed with nothing between them, they could make their own world. They could be sheltered from the ugliness of the previous day. She thought he was asleep, but then he spoke.

"I'm sorry I lost my temper the night I came to find you. I was scared for you. That's the only excuse I can offer. But I want to tell you that ye made me that proud as well. To see what you'd done in that shop. Watching you tend to the wounded without a care for your own safety." He exhaled, needing to collect himself. "You're a rare woman, Sorcha Mullen. You've the heart of a lion. Some men I know who wear a badge and carry weapons wouldn't have shown such courage. You saved those people, a mhuirnín." He kissed her head, rubbing a warm palm along her back. "And, if I act like a boorish brute, it's only because I love you, and I take care of what is mine. You may not always welcome it, but it's how the good Lord made me."

She said, "I'm sorry, too. As you've noticed, the good Lord made me into a stubborn pain in the ass." His laughter rumbled against her ear, but he wisely kept his own counsel. She said, "Sean, can I ask you something?" She lifted her head, getting eye contact.

"What is it?" he asked.

She was almost embarrassed to ask. She knew he'd found pleasure with her, but the clinical part of her brain had called up everything from her human sexuality studies. And nothing she'd researched had prepared her for the power that surged between them. She just wanted to know if he'd felt that power as she had. Like the world had shifted on its axis. How did she ask without seeming like she was fishing for compliments? She said dumbly, "Did you enjoy it? I mean, I know men aren't that complicated, but I'm still just wondering if..."

The look on his face was puzzled. "Sorcha, I didn't just enjoy it. Whatever I'd imagined paled in comparison to having you for real. You are mind-blowing. You're as fierce a lover as you are at everything else you do. And I am officially the luckiest man alive."

Perfect answer.

They woke later, the hunger upon them both. She felt him at her back and arched like a cat. He rolled her onto her belly as he raised one of her knees, exposing right where he wanted to be. "Open for me, Sorcha. Tilt your hips up." He cursed. "Yes, that's it. Jesus, woman, you're killing me."

Sorcha moaned his name as he slid a hand between her body and the mattress, finding her wet, silky flesh. Then he slipped inside her from behind. He covered her with his whole body, his chest to her back, stretching her arms above her head as he pumped into her. His body broke out in a sheen of sweat, his knee parting her so he could get deeper. His broad back and shoulders, and his muscled ass and legs, flexed as he found his rhythm, his hips tight to her ass as he invaded the deepest part of her. She felt every inch, every ridge. Her body took over, gripping him. She heard his groans, felt his teeth close on the muscle between her neck and shoulder. She spasmed under him, helpless as she came so hard that she felt herself milking his sex.

His voice was guttural against her ear. "I'm going to come inside you, Sorcha. Don't stop." As if she could? The spasms racked her body as he continued to fill her with that hard length of his, contracting around him as he went nice and deep. Then he was climaxing. He arched and cried out, a low, growling sound as she felt his release fill her up. Her orgasm whipped around and crested again, and she lost all sense of time and place as she felt her hips tilt further, demanding more. Taking everything. He screamed her name, and it thundered through her body as his hips jerked tight against her.

Sean held Sorcha as she shook in his arms. He was still behind her, a palm between her and the mattress, feeling her heart pound as hard as his. He could understand what she was feeling. The need between them was a force. He'd never felt this sort of connection. Each time he took her, it only made him want her more. He tasted her skin as her back was pressed tight against his chest. They were still joined, neither wanting it to end. He cupped her chin, turning her mouth to his. "I love you, Sorcha. I love you so much, I can scarcely bear it."

Doolin, Co. Clare, Ireland

Two days passed while Sorcha slept late into the mornings, finally letting the stress of the experience slip away. She'd inevitably break down and call her brother, the hospital, and Angelina by dinnertime. The bombings lasted four days in all. Over fifty bombs were detonated all over Northern Ireland, but it finally ended. The city was a mess. They'd brought in more British reinforcements, and there was a curfew in the city. Anyone caught out on the streets after hours was arrested. Essential persons like first responders and medical professionals were given leave, but were often stopped and questioned if soldiers came upon them after hours. The whole thing was going to make getting across the checkpoints that much harder when she had to get to work. They would ease up eventually, no doubt, but tensions were high.

After work, Sean would come to her. Greedy for her body, wanting to possess her soul. He feasted on her, a glorious, gluttonous banquet of flesh as he had her over and over again. He learned her body and he gave everything to her in return. Gave his heart and soul to her through their lovemaking. A swirling fog of pleasure keeping the world at bay. She never knew it could be like this. The wanting, the need, and the surrender.

Now Sean had a couple days off, and they were driving down Fisher Street in Doolin toward his favorite pub. Gus O'Connor's had a lively Sunday roast, and Sean's family would be there to celebrate William and Katie renting a house in Kilmoon, just north of Doolin, a small place between her parents' winter home in Galway and the O'Briens'.

Even as the brilliance of autumn was giving way to winter, County Clare was green and beautiful. They'd taken their time, driving through the rolling countryside. Sean parked in front of the pub and Sorcha somehow felt more nervous this time than before. Last time, she'd been here to support Katie. This was altogether different. After this, they'd likely go to meet her parents. They were coming back from France tomorrow and it was far past time she brought Sean to meet them.

She took in the front of the old pub, with its dark wood and stone, and absorbed the quaintness of the whole picture. It was such a lovely, coastal village. Everyone cheered as they walked inside. She took in the warm, inviting space. A stone hearth as you came in the doorway. A long, wooden bar filled with smiling patrons. Beer taps and bottles of whiskey reflecting light from the glass and amber liquid. It was like a maze, the pub being larger than it appeared from the outside. There wasn't an inch of space wasted. It had different rooms with exposed beams and decorated walls. The O'Briens were gathered around several tables that had been pushed together. Maeve jumped up to hug her, and Katie wasn't far behind. Sean pulled out a chair and seated her next to his mother, Aoife.

The lovely woman put a hand on her back, warm and reassuring. "It's good to have you with us. I'd love to sit and talk, when you've got a quiet moment. We were very worried about you."

Sorcha said, "I'm okay. It was difficult, but I'm fine."

"You're strong. And likely too brave for your own good. Now, let's talk of more pleasant things and get you fed. The lamb roast is very good, as is the chicken. But save room, because the sticky toffee pudding will make the angels weep."

Sorcha took comfort in Aoife's calm, undemanding presence, and she smiled as she caught Sean exchanging glances with his father, a masculine sort of understanding between them. The contentment of knowing they'd found their mates.

After the meal, Sorcha was settled at the O'Brien house. She took the room with Maeve again, of course, although Sean didn't relish a night of separation. She was speaking to Maeve as she unpacked a few toiletries they'd bought on the way out of Dublin. She and Maeve were chatting about the trip back to her parents' home, when Sean appeared in the doorway. His face was hard.

Sean hadn't meant to eavesdrop, but it was a small house. No sooner had he settled Sorcha in her room, than he heard her making plans to go back up north. Sorcha's face was bright, until she took in his shift in mood. She actually looked puzzled, which baffled him. He said, "Maeve, could we have a minute? Thanks."

Sorcha said jokingly, "You should see your face. Who's put a bee in your bonnet?"

He closed the door behind him. "What the hell are you doing making plans to go back up north? I told you before we were together, this is forever. Will you go back on it now?" And Sorcha was surprised to see a bit of doubt in his face. "You'd spend these last few days with me and then just leave me again?"

"Of course not, but I still have to finish my internship, Sean." He froze, his face going blank. Then he went for the door. "Sean!" She scurried from around the bed and followed him, stopping his retreat. He was staring at the half-open door, hands on his hips.

"I thought you understood, Sorcha. I thought you loved me."

"Of course I love you. Are you mad? How can you even doubt it?" He shook his head, saying nothing. "Would you turn around and look at me!"

He slowly turned, his face grim. She softened. "I love you. And I do want to be with you. But Sean, I am in the middle of an internship. I'm on the final lap. If I want to be a certified midwife, I need to finish this. I can't just leave the hospital short-staffed. I have patients due next month. Please try to understand. I can't just stay here. Move in. Elope. I would no more do that to my hospital than you would the Garda. They depend on me. My internship is almost done. It won't be forever. Just a few more months. If you love me, then you will understand this. I will come to you then, but you have to trust me."

"Trust you? And what exactly have you done to earn it? Every time we get close, you push away from me. You leave. Now you tell me you want to go back? How the hell am I supposed to let you go back to that city when you are lucky to be alive?" He swore, running his hands through his hair. "Jesus, woman. I don't know whether to turn you over my knee and tan your hide or throw you in that bed and roger you until you're too weak to argue!"

She shouted back, "Well then, ye best drop your britches, Sean O'Brien, because if you think to take a hand to me, I'll smother you in your sleep!" Her words were thick, her Belfast inflection accentuated.

Sean's retort was on his tongue when a soft knock came from behind him. Sorcha's face flushed in horror at the realization of where they were. She'd let her temper get the better of her, and Sean's mother stood calmly in the doorway. Proof that everyone in the house had heard them. She was going to die right here where she stood.

"Forgive me, Aoife." She walked by Sean's mother, red-faced and eyes averted, Sean following behind her. Then she saw everyone frozen in the living room. It started with William. A stifled giggle that earned him a jab from Katie. Then Maeve started. It was contagious until everyone but Sean and Sorcha were containing fits of laughter.

Sean's father David winked at her. "I'm afraid we've all got a weakness for spirited women." Which earned him a smack on the shoulder from Aoife.

Sean's mouth turned up, trying not to smile lest Sorcha throttle him. "Come on, love. Let's take a walk."

They walked the property, Sorcha taking in the remnants of a hearty kitchen garden. "Sean, you are an infuriating man. Did you really think I was just going to stay here from this day forward? Abandon my brother and job and survive on one pair of knickers? You aren't being rational. I wanted to go to my parents' home and introduce you. I need to make arrangements to move. I need to finish at the hospital and get letters of recommendation."

He was quiet, looking out over the broad landscape. He finally said, "I know." His head dropped to his shoulders in defeat. "In my head, I know. I just hate the idea. You have to understand, Sorcha. Look around you. I know I live in a big city, but this is where I grew up. You can't understand what it was like to drive through that chaos to find you. What it was like to see you with blood on your dress and all those people who were hurt." He choked back the emotion, continuing, "It goes against every protective instinct I have to take you back there."

She rubbed a hand up his back to his shoulder blade, an intimate, reassuring touch. "I understand, Sean. I grew up in Belfast, and I was still terrified to let John out of my sight. I'm sorry, my love, I know this is difficult. I will be careful, and I won't take any unnecessary risks. I will come back to you. I vow it." She took his hands in hers and forced him to meet her eyes. "Can you trust me to do that? Will you wait for me?"

He rested his head on hers and sighed. "Okay, you win. I will wait. But I'm going to need regular conjugal visits." And finally her laughter came, all the anger seeping out of them both.

Sorcha sat at the kitchen table, feeling the absence of the crowd in this peaceful, quiet home. Maeve was at school, William and Katie had gone back to Dublin, and Sean and David were helping the neighbor whose cows had escaped through a broken fence.

Aoife sat after pouring tea and laying out a platter of scones and biscuits. "I'm glad we finally got some peace and quiet. I wanted to see how you were doing. It was quite an ordeal, given what I've seen on the news. Sean didn't say much, and I think that's because he wanted to give you the opportunity to tell your own story. After all, he wasn't there for a lot of it. I know your parents are in France..." She put a hand over hers and finished, "And sometimes women need to talk."

Sorcha found such comfort in the presence of this woman, and kinship that seemed to defy logic. After all, they barely knew each other. It had been the same with Katie, though, hadn't it? She sipped her tea, and it was perfect. The art of tea-making was a dying one as people found new ways to do it faster and easier. The tea seemed to seep into her bones, loosening something. And suddenly she found that she did want to talk. So, she did.

She started with why she'd been in the area, instead of working at the Mater closer to home. She continued, telling her of the first bomb she'd felt shake the earth under the bus, a preamble to the pub bomb exploding the windows of her bus with a second blast. About Angelina's bravery, Dr. Stirling riding a bike to get to them, and about Mick and Noreen. Two wandering souls, offering assistance to scared and wounded people.

By the time Sorcha finished with the story of Sean and William helping her deliver Siobhan's daughter, Aoife was in tears. "I'm sorry, I didn't mean to make you cry," Sorcha said as she blotted a tear from her own face.

Aoife said, "Tears aren't always a bad thing, I find. They are a woman's defense against the world, which can turn a heart cold if you let it." She smiled warmly. "Your heart runs warmer than most, Sorcha Mullen." She stood and went to Sorcha, opening her arms to pull her into a motherly embrace. Sorcha soaked in the contact, missing her own mother. "You've had a hard time of it, sweet girl, but you are courageous and smart. Your mother would be proud."

She kissed the top of her head, letting her go to pour Sorcha another cup of tea. She heard the men coming up the path from the neighbor's house. "I hope those days will be behind you, Sorcha. My Seany loves you." No sooner had she said his name, than he came through the door.

She helped Aoife and Maeve make a grand family dinner. Maeve made the colcannon while Sorcha diced parsnips for roasting. The entire house smelled of the pork shanks which Aoife had been braising since before teatime. Now, she was working on an apricot tart. Sorcha asked, "Aoife, where did you learn to cook so well? I sense a French flare to your recipes."

"David and I went to France on our honeymoon." She smiled at Sorcha's face. "We weren't rich, by far. We stayed outside Paris in the country where the room tariffs were cheap and the village markets were plentiful."

"My parents have just come back from Gordes. Do you know it?"

"Oh yes, in the Luberon Valley, near the Senanque Abbey. They should go back when the lavender is in full bloom."

"Yes, it was kind of spontaneous. I guess it's like that when you don't have small children anymore. You can just pick up, spur of the moment, and whisk your sweetheart away for a few days."

"Your parents sound like they have the right idea." She leaned over to yell to David. "Darling, when is the last time you whisked your sweetheart away, spur of the moment?"

Without missing a beat, he said, "Last week when you were at your mother's. How did you know about that?" No sooner had he said it than an apricot shot across the room and hit him square in the back of the head.

"Nice shot, Mam!" Maeve said proudly. David ran to Aoife and swung her around. Then he kissed her on the mouth, to all the children's protests. But Sorcha shared a secret smile with Sean. One that spoke of growing older together. Of a lifetime full of teasing and kisses.

After dinner and to Sorcha's delight, the family decided to

have a bit of a traditional music session in the living room. Maeve brought out her violin and handed it to Sorcha. "Do you know the old tunes?" Sean asked.

"Some of them. The English didn't manage to beat our music out of us," she said wryly. She watched as Aoife sat at the piano and David and Sean began tuning their guitars. That left Maeve with her whistle, as Sorcha had her fiddle.

They played some reels, and then some folk songs where the men harmonized so beautifully it made her heart thunder. Sean had a fine voice. A rich, pure baritone she felt to her toes. Maeve and Aoife did a duet, then, a song she didn't know, so Maeve relieved her of the fiddle, singing the harmony to her mother's rich melody. They were a striking family. Blue eyes and different degrees of light hair. The men were tall and broad-shouldered and altogether beautifully made.

Maeve said, "Sorcha's turn! What will it be, sister?" She warmed at the endearment. Then she looked at Sean. His eyes were hungry for this, she saw that now. A longing for her to sing for him. It made her blush. Aoife chastised Maeve for putting Sorcha on the spot. She spoke the admonishment in Gaelic, but Sorcha could tell by the tone.

"No, no, it's okay. If I'm going to frequent the O'Brien house, I'll have to learn to sing along." When she named the song, she saw a ripple of emotion go through Sean and she nearly lost her nerve. They started to play, knowing the tune by memory. It wasn't that old of a song, really. A rare modern ballad by Michael MacConnell that captured what it meant to live in a divided land.

The song had no piano, only guitar and whistle. She felt the intensity of David's eyes on her. She couldn't even look at Aoife. Instead, she looked at Sean. And she was steadied by his face. By his strength and his love. Her light at the end of a long and dark journey.

Sean watched his beloved Sorcha sing the heartbreaking tune and had to fight back the tears with every ounce of strength he possessed. It was a sixties folk song that was a favorite in the pubs.

Always sung from the safety of the west coast. But the lyrics and the melancholy melody had never really touched his heart until now. Until the love of his life, so small and yet so mighty, sang the troubles of her heart. He'd seen it firsthand, now. The devastation, the walls that separated fellow citizens due to their religion. The violence and the poverty. But her chin was up and her eyes never wavered from his, so he had to be brave for her. To show her equal strength. To be her sanctuary.

Later, they took a nighttime drive. The night was clear and soft for November. He took her along the coastal path to a secluded beach on the rim of the Burren. They sat there on a blanket, the stars a brilliant landscape over the dark sea. "I've never seen the stars so bright," Sorcha said dreamily. "Do you come here a lot?"

"I did when I lived here. Whenever the night was fine, I'd come here to think," he said softly. "When you sang tonight, I thought I was ready for it. I knew you had a lovely voice. I just..." He shook his head. "There's singing and then there's *singing*. When someone is able to transport you into the deepest corners of their heart, where you can feel their pain."

"It's an old pain, Sean. It's a bit fresh just now, like a picked wound. I'm sorry if I brought the mood down."

"Not at all. Quite the contrary. It was a gift you gave to us tonight. A rare glimpse that I suspect you don't give to many." He leaned in and brushed his mouth on her neck. "Tá grá agam duit, mo chroí."

"Would you teach me, Sean?"

He ran a hand up her thigh, "I thought that's what I've been doing."

She swatted him. "I meant Gaelic."

He smiled against her mouth. "I will. It'll be useful. I tend to use it a lot when I'm angry, and other times." Then he eased her onto her back on the blanket and showed her.

Glengormley, Antrim Co., Northern Ireland

Sean liked Sorcha's parents. Her father Michael wasn't as large as his own, but he was strong and fit. He saw where John came by his sharp wit and handsome face. Edith was a fair beauty, petite and the type of woman to put others at ease. They seemed to know without words that he was here for good. He and Michael watched the daily news with intensity, seeing Belfast in the aftermath, the British government and the monarchy speaking out against the attacks that had rocked Northern Ireland. Finally, Michael turned it off, disgusted with the whole thing. Sorcha and Edith had gone into the back room and Michael was able to speak freely.

"I can't tell you what it was like to be out of the country when this happened. To have both my children loose in the city, knowing Sorcha would likely be on foot and working late." His voice caught. His gaze was direct. "Only a man in love would have driven into that hell to get her."

Sean returned that sharp gaze. "Yes, you're right. She's the pulse of my heart. I want to marry her, Michael."

He seemed to ease a bit. "And take her south, no doubt."

"It's not so far," he offered.

"It's far enough," he said. His eyes were fierce as he finished, "So that I know she's safe."

Edith handed Sorcha a small package, wrapped in tissue paper. "That one is for your wedding trousseau. For your new home."

Sorcha cocked her head, because she hadn't said anything about getting married. Her mother smiled. "You think I can't tell what it is between you? He's in there making honey in his heart over you, and willing to stand up to your father's scrutiny."

"I wasn't sure I'd ever marry, to be honest." Sorcha played with the tissue paper.

"That was because you hadn't met the right man. You have now, I think?"

Sorcha warmed at the thought. "I have."

Her mother said, "Well, then. It's past time you added to that hope chest I've been filling." Sorcha knew, of course. It was filled with her grandmother's tea set, a family quilt, her own christening gown, and now this.

She opened it and gasped. A tablecloth made in the French fashion, oil cloth dyed with the vibrant colors of Provence, covered with poppies and lavender and sprigs of herbs. "It's gorgeous, Mam. Truly."

Edith handed her another. "And this is for you to give Sean on your wedding day." Sorcha took the small gift, finding that warm tears were welling up in her eyes and spilling onto her cheeks. "I bought that from the monks at Abbaye Notre-Dame de Sénanque. The sisters of a nearby cloister do the embroidery."

Sorcha ran a hand over the soft linen handkerchief, embroidered with a lavender sprig. "It's beautiful, Mam." She leaned into her mother's arms. Suddenly the thought of moving away took on a new tinge of sorrow. "I'll miss not having you near me."

"You won't be that far away, my dear. Just a couple hours' drive. Nothing could keep me from my girl. You're my greatest love. Someday you'll have a daughter and you'll know what it means to love so deeply."

"Mam, can I ask you something? It's personal, so you don't have to answer."

"I'm an open book, my dear girl, you know that. Ask away," Edith said.

"It's about children, or rather the getting of them. You and Da only had two. Did you do anything to... um...?"

"Prevent them?" Her mother was smiling now. "No need to blush, my dear. You're a woman now and a midwife. To answer your question, I suppose we did. We were in that small flat for so long. And once we had you and John, we were happy. I mean, if it had happened, then we would have welcomed another child, but we did take precautions."

"Some sort of birth control?" Sorcha had never thought her mother was that modern.

"No, nothing like that, although I know women who did and still do. It's frowned upon by the church, but it's available more so here than where you'll be living."

"So then the rhythm method?" She couldn't believe she was talking about her mother and father having sex.

"Yes, and during the more risky times, the other." Now, it was her mother's turn to blush.

Sorcha grinned. "You mean coitus interruptus?"

Edith gave her a crooked grin. "I believe your father refers to it as pull and pray."

Sorcha clapped her hand over her mouth, and they both broke out into riotous giggles. Sorcha's father appeared in the doorway. "What are you two hens cackling about in here?"

"Sorcha was just talking shop." She winked at her daughter, who was trying hard not to look at her father.

Michael said, "Sean's got to push off. He's on the early shift tomorrow. Come now, and let the lad get home to bed."

EIGHTEEN

Some are born great, some achieve greatness, and some have greatness thrust upon them...

—William Shakespeare

Belfast, Northern Ireland

Sorcha was walking into the hospital and toward the locker room when she stopped short. She said, "Hello, Mother Superior. I wasn't expecting to see you so far from the school. Is there a meeting I am supposed to attend?" She hadn't seen her old headmistress since she'd been transferred to the Royal Jubilee.

"Not at all. I just thought I'd meet you here to see how you've been. You had quite an ordeal." They began walking, the old sister suppressing a small smile. When they went through the doors of the main ward, there were doctors and nurses lined up in the hallway. She saw Dr. Stirling and Angelina at the end of the long hall, along with Dr. Childs and the hospital chief. Then, someone started clapping. She walked slowly down the hallway as everyone greeted her with smiles and applause. She wanted to cry. She wanted to run like hell in the other direction. Her face had to be scarlet, the unfortunate side effect of redhead genes. After she'd run the gauntlet, people began swirling around her. That's when Dr. Stirling came to her rescue.

"Alright, we've sufficiently embarrassed Nurse Mullen. Everyone back to work." He wasn't in charge, really, but he was just one of those men who knew how to command a crowd, so they all dispersed.

Angelina looked delighted. "Sorry, love. We all had to endure it. You're just late to the party and the stories have become legend. The little Irish midwife who set up a medical clinic in a second-hand clothing shop."

"It wasn't just me. You were there, Angelina. So was Dr. Stirling." Sorcha didn't like the praise. It made her feel uneasy. She was just doing her job.

Dr. Stirling said, "Yes, but you were the first one in and the last one out. That matters. The Parliament wants to hand out awards to the three of us, and to Mick if we can find him."

"I don't want an award." They all walked into an expansive meeting room so they could sit and talk before her shift started. "I don't need it, and I don't want it."

"Why not?" Angelina asked.

Mother Superior spoke then, "Is it because you're a Catholic and a nationalist?"

Sorcha said nothing. Dr. Childs asked, "Surely you're not ashamed you helped those people? Sorcha, politics has no business in medicine. You know that, and you acted as any nurse should have. You have nothing to be ashamed of."

"I'm not ashamed. I regret nothing I did that day. But I have to walk back across that gate tonight. My brother has to live here. I will not have my face and name plastered all over the news. I didn't do what I did for recognition. You must trust me on this. I do, however, feel that you should go ahead. It would seem like a snub from the hospital if you didn't. And I'd like to go back and try to find Mick. He deserves this. I just don't want credit for it. This is how I want it to be. Please respect that."

Mother Superior spoke then, taking Sorcha's hand and showing her support. "Matthew 6, verse 3: *But when you give to the needy, do not let your left hand know what your right hand is doing, so that your giving may be in secret. And your Father who sees in secret will reward you.*"

Sorcha's back was killing her. The woman before her had been in labor for eighteen hours. Had been on hour ten when Sorcha's shift had started. She'd been pushing for almost three hours. She was exhausted, but this baby was stubbornly determined to stay put. "Mrs. Donovan, I'm going to allow you to push for another thirty minutes, but then we are going to have to consider a Caesarean. Any longer and it is too much stress on you and the baby. I want to try a new position." She'd called for reinforcements and was surprised to see Dr. Stirling come in with Angelina. "We are going to do this the old-fashioned way, like they did in the birthing chairs. I want to see if gravity will help this along. Mrs. Donovan, you are going to squat on the balls of your feet and hold on to each of these kind assistants."

"I don't bloody care if I have to swing from the rafters. Just get the wee fiend out of me!" she bellowed. They helped her first into a seated position, then up on her feet just as the contraction overtook her. The look of determination on the woman's face was impressive. She gnashed her teeth and screamed as she pushed.

Sorcha felt inside the birth canal and her face shifted. "It's working! He's descending."

Another push and the baby started crowning. She screamed, "I'm going to kill that man of mine. I'm going to pinch off his wee bollocks! I hate him!" Sorcha was used to this sort of talk. Long labors brought the worst out in everyone. Dr. Stirling winced on behalf of the father-to-be.

"All right, give us another big one. Push! That's it!"

The woman was purple, straining and screaming until it was possible they heard her in London. The head of the child was impressively large, and Sorcha knew the woman must feel like she was being split in two. But women were made for this. Her body stretched until the child's face appeared, then the shoulders. The woman shuddered in relief as the rest of the body slid free. "That's it, he's out! Well done! Now let's let her lie back down."

The woman started crying then. "Is he okay? I want to see him." So, Sorcha placed him on her breast as she tended to the cord. The placenta followed after as Angelina tended to the child. He was caterwauling as loudly as his mother had been, not liking the cool air or lights, or being fussed with as she cleaned him. It was such a beautiful sound. The strong lungs of a healthy newborn baby.

Angelina picked up the swaddled, squalling bundle and handed him back to the mother. "He's a strong, healthy boy. Full marks, Mum." She smiled at Sorcha. "And you as well. It was brilliant, putting her in that position. You have a gift, Nurse Mullen. Wherever you go, they'll be the better for it."

Sorcha followed Dr. Stirling and Angelina into the cafeteria for some tea. "You're going to leave us, aren't you? I should have known when I saw that gorgeous copper that he'd take you from me." Angelina's tone was pouty, but Sorcha could tell it wasn't sincere.

Nigel came up behind them, nudging Angelina. "What is this I hear? Gorgeous, was he?"

Stirling rolled his eyes. "Ah yes. The allure of the uniform. I must admit I exploited it myself in my Army days."

Sorcha warmed as she watched the loving glance exchanged between Angelina and Nigel. "Well, I won't be leaving just yet. My training isn't done."

Dr. Childs sighed. "I lose my best nurses to marriage. Are you engaged, then?"

"Not officially, but he's made his intentions clear." She wasn't sure how to explain Sean to other people. He was a force of nature.

Dr. Stirling said, "Well, I can tell you he was ready to rip my head off. That boy is in love. Anyone who would drive into Belfast on purpose last week has to be either insane or in love."

"It was rather romantic, wasn't it?" Angelina said dreamily. "And he will marry you. Men like that don't do anything halfway."

"Is that right?" Nigel whispered the words against her hair, but Sorcha gave Stirling a secret smile. It wouldn't be long before those two were walking down the aisle themselves. They sat around a square table, and a sense of sadness came over Sorcha. She'd miss these people. Not just because of her changing circumstances, of course. Dr. Childs worked at the Mater. He was here one day a week to train, and then he'd be gone. Dr. Stirling would go back to America. This was a short time they had, where their paths merged. They'd likely not merge again.

Dr. Stirling spoke, bringing her out of her thoughts. "I'm going to go out with you this afternoon. To your visitations, I mean."

Sorcha gave him a dry look. "To observe or to guard? I don't need a child minder, Robert."

He said, "I realize that, Sorcha. Although, your beau did shame me for leaving you the night of the bombings. No, this has to do with Mick. I'd like to try and find him so he can receive his award."

She lit up. "That's wonderful. I have a patient a few streets over, and then we can go try to find him. All I have is the name of the housing complex, and his first and last name."

"Well, that's better than nothing. Finish the tea, woman. Let's get started while we still have the light."

Sorcha had to keep her smiles to herself as she watched the available and unavailable women find excuses to come to her patient's flat. They had varied excuses, but the Virginia doctor was obviously the motive. He was a handsome devil. And that accent was, she now knew, pure southern gentry. "Well, I thank you ladies for your diligence. I'm glad to see Mrs. Kelly has such good neighbors, to be checking on her and the baby." They brought biscuits, pieces of lemon pie, and apple cake. "If I eat anything else, Nurse Mullen will have to roll me back to the hospital."

They also doted on Sorcha, although they didn't quite muster the twinkle in their eyes that they did for Robert. "We all heard about it. What you did for her. She said you saved the baby's life."

Sorcha smiled graciously. "Well, I didn't do it alone. Oliver helped, didn't you?" The young boy's chest puffed up, proud of the part he'd played. "And Dr. Stirling did the surgery. Now, it's awfully nice of everyone to stop by, but we need a bit of privacy. Once she's done, you can all come back and visit with the baby while she gets her tea and this delicious lemon pie."

He is not here; but far away
The noise of life begins again...

—Alfred Lord Tennyson, *In Memoriam*

"Her incision looks good," Sorcha said absently, more to fill the silence as they walked in the lane.

"I should have been a seamstress," he said, which made her laugh. "You have a way with people. It's no-nonsense, but still kind and respectful. And you maneuvered a nap and two empty hands for eating. Not bad, Nurse Mullen."

"Aye, well, her husband travels a lot. You'd think the bloody sod would take a break and help while she recovers."

"We have the same issue in America. People don't give sick leave to new fathers. Even after a Caesarean birth. It's wrong, but it's how things are. They don't seem like the sort of household that can do without pay for two or three weeks."

"Something needs to change. The world needs to catch up— some of these women also work. Having children shouldn't be so complicated. At least they're starting to let men in the delivery room. A lot of doctors and midwives still don't agree. It's completely ridiculous. How do you feel on the matter?"

Dr. Stirling said, "I think that in a healthy relationship, the baby's father can be an asset in the delivery room. Natural childbirth and Lamaze technique is more common now. Including the partner is more common as well. And you are right about the aftercare—something needs to change. That partnership needs to continue outside of the delivery room. Women are sent home with no one to monitor their health or help them through the baby blues, the sleep deprivation, all of the other things that happen in those first few weeks..." He shook his head. "I had a patient in Virginia who shook her baby. It had colic and she was suffering from postpartum depression and completely sleep-deprived. She didn't mean it. She tried so hard for weeks. But one moment, one bad day, and she snapped. Just long enough to ruin everything and leave the child on life support. It was the worst day of my life, and I wasn't even the father. You are right, Sorcha. We have to do better. They haven't even managed to publish the DSM-III for postpartum depression yet. Until they do, there won't be a definitive treatment. Maybe, if they'd recognized and diagnosed her, that baby would be happy and healthy instead of in a vegetative state."

Sorcha was horrified, but she'd heard of this. It's why she believed so completely in follow-up home visits. "I'm sorry, Robert. I don't know what else to say."

"Just keep doing this." He motioned to the street where they walked. "Wherever you end up in practice, just keep doing what you are doing. It matters."

She smiled, looking up. A subject change was in order. "This is it. This is the building where Mick said he lived. Let's see what we can find out, shall we?"

They went to the front door, looking at the names on the intercom system. "What did he say his last name was again? Reilly?"

"No, I think it was Ryan. Mick or Michael, most likely. Here it is. M. Ryan, flat 22B."

A voice came from behind them. "Can I help you with something?"

They turned to see an old man. "Yes, we are looking for Mick Ryan."

Something strange passed over the man's face. "Mick, you say. Well, there's no Mick here. Hasn't been for some time."

"Well, who is M. Ryan then?" Sorcha said. "Perhaps it's a family member?"

"Perhaps. What's your business?" he said suspiciously.

"Our business is between us and Mr. Ryan. He isn't in any trouble. We are here on happy business. Who exactly are you?" Stirling asked respectfully.

"I'm the building manager." He seemed to take their measure, then nodded to himself. "The M. Ryan is Matthew, but he might be able to help you. Follow me."

They climbed the flight of stairs and went to the door of Matthew Ryan. The building manager waited for someone to answer before he left. Sorcha was surprised to see a girl in her teenage years. Mick hadn't looked old enough to have a daughter her age. "Hello, dear. I'm sorry to bother you, but we were looking for Mick Ryan."

The girl crinkled her forehead. "There's no Mick here, ma'am. That was my grandfather's name, but he's long gone."

"I'm sorry to hear it. Perhaps you might have another Mick in the family. Someone who lives here in this building? I'm sure this is where he said he lived. He'd be about thirty?" A man's voice came from behind the girl.

"Da, it's someone looking for Grandda."

Dr. Stirling said, "Oh, no. I'm sorry. It wouldn't be your grandfather. He'd be much younger."

Which caused the girl to bellow, "And one of them's a Yank!" Sorcha suppressed a smile at that.

The man came into the living room and Sorcha was struck by the resemblance. It wasn't Mick. He was at least ten years older, but there was a striking family resemblance. He put out his hand. "Matthew Ryan. What's this about?" His tone wasn't unfriendly.

Sorcha explained as best she could. "And, you see, he said he lived in this building. He must be kin, because you favor him. He'd been an Army medic. He stayed with me all night and helped me tend to the wounded. The city would like to give him an award."

The man's face had gone starkly white. "I'm sorry. You are sure that he told you his name was Mick Ryan. And he was an Army medic?"

"Yes. I'm sorry, have I said something to upset you?" The man exchanged glances with his daughter. She gave an imperceptible nod.

"No. Sorry. Could you... I think you should come in and sit down. Anne, could you make us some tea?"

Sorcha hastened to reassure him. "No need, really. We've had our tea. But we will come in if it's all right. It's rather important that we find him. I just don't know what I would have done without him. At the very least, I owe him my thanks."

The man saw them seated on the sofa, then he went to pour himself a drink. His hands were shaking. "I'm sorry. I find I need this right now. It's not a habit, but given the circumstances, you may want to join me."

Sorcha declined and accepted a lemon squash from the daughter, Anne. Dr. Stirling took the offered whiskey. "I'm done for the day. Thank you. A man shouldn't have to drink alone, and you look like you've had a shock."

Anne mumbled something along the lines of, "Not as big as the one you're going to get."

Matthew Ryan sat then, meeting their eyes for the first time in several minutes. "Now then, why don't you start from the beginning and tell me in detail how you came across Mick Ryan?"

It took a few minutes, Stirling starting, and then Sorcha continuing after the time the Army soldiers had taken Dr. Stirling away and left her and Mick to fend for themselves. All the way until they had gone their separate ways and said goodbye.

"And you say that he looked like me, and he was in his late twenties?" Matthew asked.

"Yes. I'm sorry, but I'm a bit confused. Why do I think you are trying to get up your nerve to break some horrible news to me?" Sorcha was actually getting frightened that something had happened to Mick during the following three days of the bombing.

"I don't mean to be mysterious, it's just... well, perhaps Anne could tell you her own story. About the bombings that happened a few years ago."

Anne cleared her throat. "It was during another bombing campaign. Not quite so big, but a couple had gone off very nearby. I was home alone. I was very afraid. But then, all of a sudden, a man was here at the door. He told me he'd always watched over me and Da. That I wasn't to be afraid. And I wasn't. I don't know why I wasn't. He just made me feel safe, and he looked a lot like Da and I just... trusted him. He said his name was Mick and that he'd been in the Army. He showed me how to get in the tub, you know. Like they did during the air raids in the war. He stayed with me for hours. I finally fell asleep. When Da came home from work, he woke me. When I told him what happened, he thought I'd dreamed it. Then I told him what the man's name was and that he looked just like him. That's when he showed me the photographs."

Sorcha didn't understand, but the hair stood up on her arms. "What photographs?"

Matthew got up and pulled a photo album off the shelf. "These are photos from when my mother was pregnant with me. They're from 1941."

He sat between Sorcha and Dr. Stirling. When he opened the first page, Sorcha gasped and Stirling took a huge swig of whiskey. Sorcha crossed herself. She could barely speak. "Oh my God. It's Mick."

He was so handsome in his Army uniform. Dashing and well-groomed with a proud smile. A young man with kind, intelligent eyes. Matthew turned the page. Mick was posing with a woman. She was pregnant and he was behind her, hands on her belly. They looked so happy. Sorcha's tears welled in her eyes and fell onto her cheeks. She wiped at them, not wanting to dampen the photos.

"He died in the blitz. Not the London one everyone talks

about. The Belfast blitz. He sent my mother away. She was close to her time, and he sent her to her mother's in the country. Away from the rioting so she could have me in a hospital that wasn't going to get bombed. But he stayed. He was a soldier and a medic. He told her he couldn't leave his city."

Sorcha covered her mouth, stifling a sob. He'd been wearing the same clothes when she'd seen him as he was in the photo with his wife. "He died in a burning building, trying to pull out survivors. They said it was quick. The building came down on him." He cleared his throat, pushing down the knot. "My mother said he came to her now and again. I thought it was dreams. But a love like that never really dies, I don't think. It goes on even beyond the grave."

Stirling put an arm around Sorcha as she tried to take it all in. Tried to rein in her tears. Mick's son had taken to pacing the floor, too emotional to sit still. "Oh, Mick." She looked at the man who was his son. The man who'd never known his father. "He was a wonderful man. He told me—" Her voice caught with emotion. "He told me that he'd always be here as long as his city needed him. There was something sad about him when he said it. And when he said goodbye, I saw it again. Sadness. Like it was our last words."

Anne was weeping too, and Matthew Ryan took his daughter's hand. "I know he was a good man. The best of men. My mother kept the flat. She never remarried. Once she was gone, Anne and I moved in. We lost Anne's mother five years ago. It's just us now."

Sorcha said, "I'm sorry you've lost so much. Both of you." She squeezed the young girl's hand, her heart breaking at the thought of losing a mother so early in life. Her mother was everything to her.

Matthew smiled sadly. "I'm glad you came. It's like knowing I haven't lost him completely. That his sacrifice wasn't for nothing. I like the idea of him still roaming these streets. Still young and strong and brave. Thank you, both. I can't explain any of this. All I can do is pray that someday this city finds peace, and my father can finally be at rest."

As they crossed the threshold to leave, Sorcha remembered something. "Matthew. Named after your grandfather."

He cocked his head. "How did you know that?"

"One of our little emergencies was a woman in labor. When they took her and the baby away to the hospital, Mick told her his wife was pregnant with their first. He was convinced it was a boy. He was overjoyed to have a son." The man's throat convulsed and he stuttered on a sob. He pulled Sorcha to him.

"Thank you," was all he could manage.

Dublin, Ireland

Sean sat on the easy chair, holding Sorcha. He was still absorbing what she'd told him. Something that seemed impossible. He'd seen Mick in the flesh. He hadn't been a specter. Not a wraith or eerie apparition. He'd treated patients. He'd lifted people. Sean had shaken his hand. But still, there had been something of the auld ones in his eyes. Something almost ancient.

"I can't explain it. I just wanted you to know. I feel like he touched us all for a reason."

"I understand. I'm glad you told me, and I'm glad you're here. I missed you. My heart ached from it." He smiled against her hair. "My heart and my balls, to be truthful."

She felt him harden under her. She was in his lap on the easy chair. He had a thing about chairs.

They made short work of the clothing. When he started to rise and take her to his bed, she put a palm on his chest. Then she crept up his body. He cursed under his breath. "Yes, love. Come to me. Take me right here." He palmed her sex as she straddled him and she cried out from the feel of it. "Like honey." His voice was harsh and breathy. "I need to be inside you, Sorcha. Deep and hard and fast." She slid onto his cock and he grabbed her hips, hissing at the sensation. She was so beautiful. She was still getting comfortable with the lovemaking. Learning her body. Learning his, too. What made them both hum with delicious lust and need. She put an arm out to steady herself on the back of the chair, her head falling back to cause a cascade of auburn down her back. Her hair brushed his hands as he explored her. Smooth hands over her straining hips as she rode him and took her pleasure. He sucked a pink nipple into his mouth and she quickened her pace, pulling his head tight as he suckled her.

Sorcha felt the nerve pathways connect somehow. A bolt of energy from her nipple that fed Sean in greedy pulls all the way to her sex. A pulsating need that tied the sucking with his thick, long penetration between her legs. She couldn't quite believe it was her own voice she heard. Moaning, demanding, and then a scream from the depths of her belly as she came. She felt the flood of moisture from her own body as she orgasmed around him, their bodies' fluids mingling as she felt his orgasm deep within her.

They sat entangled, breathing hard, like a mangled pile of flesh and sweat and other things, as if somehow their skeletons had been removed. They were wrecked by the joining. It had made him wild. Sean's voice was weak, like a dying man. "I am never getting rid of this chair."

It's strange that words are so inadequate. Yet, like the asthmatic struggling for breath, so the lover must struggle for words...

—T. S. Eliot

They prepared their dinner together, and Sean was still negotiating. "Just think about it. I think they'd agree to it, Sorcha. Both schools. You've got barely any time left. Hell, after that night of the bombings, they should graduate you early. Ye delivered a baby right in the middle of a battlefield."

Sorcha had thought about it, actually. Arranging a transfer to Trinity and finishing here. "Sean, I can't just move in with you. My parents would have a coronary."

He turned her then, lifting her up onto the countertop. "I know." He kissed her, deeply and with all the love he could put into it. He pulled away just enough to ask her, "Do you love me, Sorcha?"

"You know I do."

"And is it the same for you as it is for me? Is it the kind of love that lasts for a lifetime and beyond? I knew the moment I laid eyes on you, my love."

She took his face in her hands, remembering Matthew Ryan's words about love never really dying. "To the grave and beyond, my Sean. I'll love you always."

He took something out of his pocket and slid it on her finger. "It was my grandmother's ring. Now it's yours. I love you, a chuisle. You're my mate and that's forever. There will be no other for me."

She kissed him then, her tears rubbing onto his face. She thought about Mick dying in that city. Never seeing his child born. Not growing old with his wife. "I love you, Sean. I love you so much." The words seemed inadequate, and her throat ached with the emotion that spilled out of her. He cupped her chin, tilting her face to get more deeply into her mouth. He moaned as he pulled her close.

Finally, she broke the kiss and said, "I'll meet with the dean at the midwifery school at Trinity."

"Are we to be wed? Put me out of my misery, ye wee she-devil." He kissed down her neck, nibbling as he went.

She laughed. "Yes, Sean. I'll marry you. The sooner the better."

Then he set his mind to his task. Turning the stove off, he dropped to his knees right in the kitchen, pulling her to his mouth. He showed her how it would be between them. How their life would be in the years to come. The love, the passion, and the pleasure. He'd always want her. And he was going to make damn sure she wouldn't even consider changing her mind.

NINETEEN

Belfast, Northern Ireland

The wedding was planned in a month's time, and the date was set for a few days before Christmas. Sorcha walked down the hospital hallway with a dress slung on her back. Angelina scurried over. "Is that it? You are killing me, Sorcha. I need to see that dress!"

The other nurses gathered around as she pulled down the zipper of the plastic covering. "Is that a Gunne Sax? Jesus, they must be paying interns better than I thought," one of them said.

Angelina said, "I remember this dress! It was at the shop where we made the field clinic. That was a secondhand shop, but this looks brand new!"

Sorcha grinned. "It is. Runaway bride. The parents sold it to the shop for a song, and their loss was my gain. Isn't it gorgeous altogether?"

Angelina squealed. "One more week! I can't wait to see you walk down that aisle! What about a veil?"

"I thought a ring of flowers might go nice with this. Not daisies. I can't stand the smell."

"Yes, they do rather smell like a bedpan. Perhaps some greenery and little red flowers. It'll be festive for your Christmas wedding." Angelina was almost as excited about this wedding as Sorcha.

"I'm glad you and Nigel are able to come." She hugged her dear friend tightly, squashing the dress between them.

Dr. Stirling caught the end of the conversation. "I'll be there as well. You're going to have to come up with a date for me. Someone single and age appropriate," he said, to ward off a couple of starry-eyed nurses who were way too young for him.

"I'll see what I can do. It'll be a simple affair, a country church wedding and a simple supper. We will have live music. You can't get more than two people together on the west coast without a trad session breaking out."

"How positively wonderful!" Angelina said with exuberance. "I'll wear my dancing shoes."

"Today is my last day," Sorcha said. The mood sobered a bit. "I'll miss you all."

"It's not very far to Dublin. Will you stay there, do you think?" Angelina asked.

"For now. We'll stay until Sean has enough time on the force to transfer west. I'll get some good experience in the meantime. We don't want to raise a family in the city, though. We'll give it two or three years, then we'll move closer to the O'Briens. It really is a wonderful place. I can see myself settling there forever, to be honest. I find the city life doesn't suit me like it once did. It was all I knew, really. Now things are different. I'm different."

"Spoken like a woman in love. Sean O'Brien is a lucky man," Dr. Stirling said. "Now, everyone, get back to work. Those babies aren't going to deliver themselves."

TWENTY

Sean rubbed his palms on his trousers for the hundredth time.

"Relax, brother. You're making Mam nervous. She's over there wondering if Sorcha's going to stand you up."

Sullivan laughed into his fist, covering it with a cough. Sean said, "That's not helpful, ye tosser. Is it time yet?"

As if on cue, the piano started and the doors to the church opened. There was Maeve, looking as pretty as a rose. His throat clenched up. His beautiful little sister was a woman now, headed for adulthood too quickly. Then Katie came in behind her and he heard William mumble to himself, "They are lovely, aren't they?"

Then there she was and suddenly he couldn't breathe. She was otherworldly, wearing a gauzy, long dress that might have been a decorative shift in the Middle Ages, lovely and timeless. Her hair was down and flowing in glossy, red waves around her shoulders. Sprigs of greenery and red flowers crowned her head. He felt tears prick his eyes. The sight of her overwhelmed him. *Mine,* he thought. *She's all mine. Forever and always.*

They went through the wedding vows in a sort of haze, like they were floating above everyone. It wasn't until the priest finally cleared his throat that Sorcha nudged him. "Ye can kiss me now, love. All you like." The crowd rumbled with laughter.

"With pleasure, mo bhean chéile." *My wife.* Sorcha's Gaelic was slow but improving. He'd called her his wife.

The party at the cottage hall was in full swing. The musicians rotated throughout the evening. The drinks and the homemade food were consumed steadily. John Mullen watched the buzz of a well-planned party, silent and reflective. His mother Edith came up beside him. "Sorcha is marrying well. They are good people, aren't they?"

"They are. It's good to see. I'll miss her, but she'll be safer and happier with Sean. It was meant to be, I think. A chance meeting that wasn't chance at all."

"You're turning into quite the romantic, John." Edith put her arm around his shoulders and went on her toes to kiss his cheek.

"Not at all. I see what I see."

"And what do you see for yourself?" Her eyes were questioning.

He said, "I see work. That is all. I doubt I'll ever marry." His mother stiffened, but then there was shouting and gasps of delight from the O'Brien family, and the moment was lost.

Sorcha had been waiting for this moment. Practicing. Angelina leaned in and asked, "What's the O'Brien Set?"

"It's a family dance. You'll have to sit this one out, I'm afraid." But they laughed as Maeve ran up to Robert Stirling and pulled him into the middle of the room. He wasn't old enough to be her father, but pretty close.

"Don't worry yourself, doctor. But if you don't dance with me, one of those village boys will come over here. You've got to save me."

"Well, I'd never leave a lady in distress. You're going to have to teach me. I can dance the cotillion and maybe a waltz, but this I don't know."

"You'll be grand. Just watch William," Maeve said encouragingly.

William was smiling at Katie. They hadn't had a full reception at their wedding, just tea service and immediate family. "Finally, I'll get my dance. Have you and Sorcha been practicing?"

Katie winked at Sorcha. "Oh yes. Get ready to be dazzled."

The plucking sound of an instrument started the dance, slow and deliberate. The set was designed to build, slow moving dancers giving way finally to the intense frolic at its end. It was a lovers' dance. Arms raised, couples skipping down the line. A mating ritual passed down on the O'Brien side. Sorcha looked down at the line of couples, all gazing at each other with such love. Remembering their own weddings, no doubt, and the night was filled with joyous laughter.

EPILOGUE

Of all the animals, the boy is the most unmanageable...

—Plato

University Hospital, Galway, Ireland

Nine Years Later

William tore through the doors of the hospital, his father tight on his heels. Sean stood, hands up. "She's okay, Willy. Sorcha's in there with her. She and the baby are both doing perfectly."

"She didn't have it already, did she?" His voice was panicked.

Sean realized his mistake. "No, sorry. God, no. She's contracting. She's six centimeters. She's progressing nicely. Those were Sorcha's exact words. And they've got a monitor on the baby. The heartbeat is strong and steady."

Sorcha came through the swinging doors, dressed in her bright and clean midwife attire. "William, thank God. Let's get you scrubbed and ready. She's been asking for you."

She turned around to leave and Sean scooped her up into his arms. "Excuse me, love. I haven't seen you since last night." He closed his mouth on hers, giving her a mind-bending kiss. "That's better. Ye get so focused when you're working, woman. You can't ignore your man." Then he leaned down and kissed her still flat stomach. "How's this little lad?"

"It might be a girl, Sean." She smiled as she said it, because they argued this every time she was pregnant. Unlike her patients, she'd never been able to instinctively know the gender of her own children. And taking that as a sign from the Almighty, they'd declined to learn the truth via ultrasound, preferring instead to be surprised.

Sean said, "Not a chance. We make boys in this family. Girls are a rarity. But I'm more than willing to keep trying if you want another girl." He kissed her again, soft and sweet. She, like her mother, had great success those first couple of years with the combination of the rhythm method and coitus interruptus. She and Sean had discussed it together, and it had been a choice they were both comfortable with. But, once that first son had come to them, they'd never looked back. With so much family around, they didn't want for helpers.

She smiled against his mouth, then she heard a screech behind them. Sean turned around quickly. "Jaysus, that daughter of mine. Brigid, stop hitting your brother. It's not nice."

The little girl was not even two, but she was a force of nature. Red hair like her mother, and eyes the color of her father's, like the wild blue sea. Her twin, Michael, was sniffling and approached Sorcha with his arms raised up. She lifted him to her hip and kissed his soft cheek. "There's my lad. Did that sister of yours give you a smack again? She's a wee fiend, isn't she?"

Brigid pulled on her father's legs until he let her climb up and settle in his arms, then he leaned in for another kiss from Sorcha. Michael wiggled between them, giving his father a push away from his mother. Thwarted again.

Sean laughed. "You're forever stealing my girl. You are a mammy's boy, aren't you?"

Aoife spoke from behind him. "As you were." She kissed both

her sons on the forehead as they leaned down in the practiced way of good sons. "You still are. My beautiful boys." Then her face changed as she looked plainly at Sean. "Your son is in the lobby fountain. He's soaked to the gills and your father is having a time getting him to come out." She said it so lightly, unconcerned and more than a little amused.

Sean thrust Brigid into Aoife's hands. "Not again. Aidan! I told ye no swimming while Mammy's working!" Sorcha and Aoife were in hysterics as Sean ran across the room to the large, decorative fountain to fish their eldest child out of the water. Then Sorcha handed her other little boy off to his grandda. "Sorry, David. Nice seeing you, but duty calls." She looked at William. "Let's go have that baby." She waved to Katie's parents as she pushed William through the security doors that led to the maternity ward.

She took him to a sink where he washed thoroughly. When Katie saw William walk into her room, she burst into tears. He said calmly, "It's okay, love. You're both fine. Sorcha and Dr. Childs have both told me so. You have the best team in Ireland."

Angelina breezed in, smiling at that. "Yes, she does. This hospital is lucky to have poached three of Belfast's finest. Now, Mum, chin up. That baby is almost ready to come out. Don't you worry for a moment."

Sorcha took Katie's hand. She knew where this panic was coming from. She remembered that first pregnancy. She'd been the one to hold held her hand as she'd lost their first baby. It had been a long road of disappointment ever since. But they'd done it. With modern medicine and lots of prayers, Katie and William had conceived and carried a baby to term. As Sorcha sat at Katie's side, she knew this was the most important baby she'd ever catch.

The contractions ebbed and flowed, hours passing until Katie was finally dilated enough to start pushing. She was tired and sweating. All modesty was gone as she suffered the pains of the impending birth. "Okay, I think it's time. Are you ready to see him or her?" Then she nodded at William, who went to his portable stereo and pressed play on the cassette deck. Katie was in the middle of a contraction as she choked out a laugh. William was smooth as silk, moving his hips as he walked over to the table, singing along to Led Zeppelin's *Whole Lotta Love*. He'd wanted to start off this particularly difficult part of the labor with a remembrance of why they were here and exactly how he'd gotten Katie into this particular condition. Apparently, he had a thing for Zeppelin when they... um. Dr. Childs laughed as William played the air guitar.

William and Katie hadn't wanted to know the gender. This might be their only child, and they wanted it to be a surprise. It was a boy. Sorcha knew it with an unwavering certainty. She'd dreamed of him. She'd held him in her arms. Golden, amber eyes like his mother. The love Sorcha felt for the boy had caused her to wake with tears pouring down her face. As much love as she felt for the children of her body. This was the child of her heart. Her beautiful nephew. She couldn't wait to meet him.

Katie pushed for a solid hour and both sides of William's mixtape before the baby started crowning. Then it went quickly. The music was stopped and the only sound in the room was Katie's sobbing. "It's happening. It's really going to happen!" She clung to William.

William gave a hysterical laugh and said, "It's got a full head of hair. I can see it! It's golden like yours, Katie!"

Sorcha traded smiles with Dr. Childs and Angelina, because William had one of those contagious spirits that lit up the room. They were so close to their happily ever after. Sorcha said, "Push, Katie, love. One more big push!"

He came then, sliding out of Katie's body like an answered prayer. "It's a boy," Sorcha sobbed. "It's a beautiful boy. Big and strong."

The child let out a screaming wail and Katie cried uncontrollably. So did William. "It's a boy. Oh, God. Sorcha, let me see him." She reached out her hands urgently, needing to know he was alive and real.

As Sorcha leaned down to cradle the child in his mother's

arms, she asked, "What will you call him? You've made me wait long enough." She smiled as she said it. The baby names had been top secret. She knew they'd been afraid of jinxing their happiness.

William smoothed a hand over the baby's head, marveling at the overwhelming joy in his heart. Tears trickled down his handsome face. This was his legacy. His beautiful son. He had so much to teach him. So much love to give him. A lifetime of love. He answered then, his voice thick with emotion, "His name is Tadhg. Tadhg William O'Brien."

A LETTER FROM THE AUTHOR

Dear reader,

Huge thanks for reading *The Irish Midwife*. If you want to join other readers in hearing all about my new releases and bonus content, you can sign up here:

www.stormpublishing.co/stacey-reynolds

If you enjoyed this book and could spare a few moments to leave a review that would be hugely appreciated. Even a short review can make all the difference in encouraging a reader to discover my books for the first time. Thank you so much!

This was by far the most difficult of the novels I've written. Not only due to the time period, but due to the sensitive nature of the political climate. It was never my intention to write a political novel. This is, at its heart, a love story. It's also a story about four brave, intelligent twenty-somethings finding their way in the world. Building careers and finding love. Sean and Sorcha are such a beloved part of the O'Brien Tales, and I wanted to do their love story justice. And it was with a tinge of sadness that during this story, I grew to love their brothers. William and John were both loyal, loving men. I also began to understand Katie in a way I hadn't before. When I met Katie for the first time in *Raven of the Sea*, she was tired, sad, and worn down by grief. It was only by seeing all that she'd had and then lost that I was able to understand the woman she'd become.

I hope you have enjoyed this story as much as I loved writing it. Stay tuned, because we are headed back to the present day for the next chapters of the O'Brien family and their mates.

Stacey Reynolds

www.staceylreynolds.weebly.com

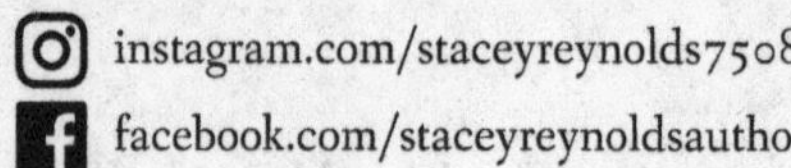

ACKNOWLEDGMENTS

Many thanks to the professionals who aided me in writing this book. The first, Kim Heitt, is an OBGYN nurse and fellow military spouse. She walked me through the field treatment for a prolapsed cord during childbirth. Thanks for the nitty gritty. Secondly, I would like to thank Catherine Tinley, an award-winning historical romance author and native to Northern Ireland. We exchanged several emails regarding the city and the political climate of Belfast in the 1970s. She was very supportive and open to helping me tell Sorcha's story with authenticity. As I had only been to Belfast in 2017 as a tourist, I needed help visualizing the city during those troubled times, and understanding what it would have been like for Sorcha, a Catholic nationalist, to live and work in the city during those years of conflict. Thank you, Catherine, from the bottom of my heart.